OCCUᴩIED

By
Janet Preece

Published by GorgeousMovies Ltd

ISBN: 9798702001388 (paperback)

Disclaimer: This is a work of fiction. Names, characters, businesses, places, events, locales, and incidents are either the products of the author's imagination or used in a fictitious manner. Any resemblance to actual persons, living or dead, or actual events is purely coincidental.

For my children Daniel, Harry & Charlie – don't worry,
I'm not as mad as I pretend to be!
winks

Table of Contents

Prologue   vii

Chapter One   1
Chapter Two   8
Chapter Three   14
Chapter Four   22
Chapter Five   30
Chapter Six   37
Chapter Seven   53
Chapter Eight   60
Chapter Nine   65
Chapter Ten   75
Chapter Eleven   83
Chapter Twelve   88
Chapter Thirteen   99
Chapter Fourteen   115
Chapter Fifteen   126
Chapter Sixteen   146
Chapter Seventeen   154

Chapter Eighteen   159

Chapter Nineteen   166

Chapter Twenty   170

Chapter Twenty-One   178

Chapter Twenty-Two   186

Chapter Twenty-Three   195

Chapter Twenty-Four   206

Chapter Twenty-Five   215

Chapter Twenty-Six   221

Chapter Twenty-Seven   230

Chapter Twenty-Eight   237

Chapter Twenty-Nine   244

Chapter Thirty   250

Chapter Thirty-One   255

Chapter Thirty-Two   260

Chapter Thirty-Three   264

Biography: *Janet Preece*   271

Prologue

She clawed through the dark at the closed door, bashing, screaming, gasping for breath, her lungs threatening to give out before she could make herself heard.

'Open the door! What are you doing? Come back! Open the door! This isn't funny! Open the fucking door!'

Those words, *her* words, were but a distant memory; a recalled hallucination of the moment it had all began; full of confusion. Her pleading voice was now an empty husk, raspy with exhaustion, her body numb to the futility of it all.

Straining to hear above the screaming in her mind, she fell silent. She'd given up asking why in the early days, when the burning agony filled her body, her nails torn from their cuticles. The frantic panic of her first attempts to escape the prison.

That was then.

Now, she prayed in the dark and flinched each time she heard a rustling.

Lifeless, she dropped to the floor.

Starvation had taken its toll, her muscles wasting away, bone protruding through her fleshless legs. As she lay her head down, cheek pressed against the cool stone floor, her eyes flickered closed; the sweet release. In and out of consciousness she drifted, smiling now and then as the warm bodies brushed against her, softly tickling her face.

Her eyelids remained closed. Finally, the end had come. All the suffering became a distant memory as periods of unconsciousness lasted longer and longer – until a new level of pain, one she never thought possible, arrived to take over. More horrifying than all the days before, in total darkness, fresh screams bombarded her ears, agony searing as her remaining flesh was clawed from her body...

Blissfully unaware, Julie slept on peacefully. She heard nothing. She dreamed of returning to her family but couldn't quite reach out to the voices that called for her. Tommy's warm embrace brought her back.

Back to a reality she wasn't ready to face...yet.

Chapter One

It was pitch-black as Julie battled her way through the dark to the bathroom, desperate for the toilet but not wanting to wake the kids. She had successfully managed the witching hour, the prolonged agony of 'I wants', and got them all down to sleep. There was no way she was going to reverse all that hard work.

What's that noise? She froze still, listening. *Nothing, nothing, nothing,* she told herself repeatedly, but even so, she reached for the light switch as she stepped into the bathroom, just in case. *Nobody's there, obviously – it's all in your imagination.* But she couldn't quite shrug off the fear of possibility. What if there was?

Julie Summers was afraid of pretty much everything, and midnight toilet breaks were just one of the many trials that came with being a mother of three. She'd lie in bed willing herself back to sleep on a nightly basis but would eventually have to haul her exhausted body up, make a quick dash across the two steps to the bathroom and turn the light on fast. Anything could be lurking in the dark.

'Hey, Julie, what's all that banging?' Dan called from the bedroom. 'You'll wake the kids! Do you really need the big light on?'

Julie scowled as she washed her hands. 'What about you shouting the house down?' she grumbled back under her breath. Why did her husband try to control her every move? *Save the rules for our kids*, she screamed silently, biting her tongue. *God knows, they need them.*

Even with the light on, she couldn't look up at the mirror; at the horrors that hid behind the glass in the dead of night. Trapped between life and death, hidden faces waited to take revenge on the living. She tried to hurry up, not bothering to dry her hands after a quick token wash, mentally preparing herself for the run back to her bedroom and the darkness after she reached for the light-pulley.

'Dan...? Dan?' she whispered to no response. Why couldn't he speak to her now, when she needed it? He wasn't so quick to get involved when she wanted to hear his voice, his reassurance he was there and had been guarding their safe haven for her return. 'Dan, stop messing about. Where are you?' She climbed into bed and felt for his body, but it wasn't there. 'Oh, God, Dan, please don't! This isn't funny!'

She jumped up again, heart pounding, and turned the light on, trying to locate him while squinting her eyes against the violation to her pupils. Floaters blurred her vision. Dan knew of her anxiety, knew the pain it caused her and the inner struggle she fought on a daily basis, yet he continued to aggravate the situation as if he didn't care, as if he was enjoying her turmoil. He was nowhere to be seen, but she was convinced his voice had come from the bedroom only moments before. Where was he? Why couldn't he act like a normal husband? At the very least, turn over and ignore her? She had accepted his reduced affection over the years as a marital norm, but his actions were slowly becoming tinged with scorn, coaxing her, punishing her – for what reason, she couldn't fathom. She had tried to juggle her role as a good wife and mother, but it was so hard to get it right. If there even was a 'right'.

Great, he's probably gone downstairs, she thought, but why would he do that in the middle of the night? *Did he hear an intruder?* Her pulse raced as she strained her ears to listen, but there was no sound. Maybe he was lying on the floor in a blood bath, hacked to pieces while the killer made his way silently into their kids' bedrooms. She shivered as her imagination went into overdrive: the intruder with the appetite of a vampire, devouring each child one by one, attacking with superhuman strength...before he came for her. She would be left till last to experience the dread, feel the pain, the heart-wrenching loss of her family. A meaningless act carried out purely because it was the middle of the night.

Julie hovered by the door wondering how long she would have to wait for Dan to appear, unwilling to humour the images she told herself repeatedly were the product of an overactive imagination.

There's nobody there, no threat. Breathe through it. In through your nose, out through your mouth... He's just gone for some water, or maybe one of the kids woke up, and he's seeing to them.

Statistically, what would be more likely? But then, there was always the unlucky minority. An image of the local Facebook group came to mind, strangers arguing over night-time burglaries while families slept; vulnerable innocents seeking advice on social media inadvertently alerting their would-be-attackers to weaknesses in their alarm systems and hidden gems within. She tried to shrug off the screaming voices in her head that shouted and argued with each other.

'Pull yourself together, Julie,' she whispered.

Then, a noise from somewhere in the room.

What was that?

It was nothing. Work through it.

Sweating and clammy, she took control, her body going through the motions as she closed the door behind her so she would know if they entered – Dan, or something more sinister.

Climb into bed, leave the light on. Just get in and wait.

Julie pulled the duvet up to her chin, feeling more secure now only her face was visible. She wasn't brave enough to turn off the light, so instead, she watched the clock, concentrated on the ticking, and blocked out everything else in the room with hypnotic focus, willing the night to pass or Dan to return, whichever came first.

As her anxiety grew by the minute, she reached out to grab her Kindle, hoping it might refocus her mind. The novel she was reading was not ideal. For someone scared of pretty much everything, Julie was still drawn to thrillers. They were like self-medication to help desensitise her fears and a break from the daily grind that was her life. She tried to focus on the words, finding herself re-reading the same line over and over, but she took nothing in.

'Julie...'

The tiny warped sound interrupted her thoughts. She sat up and looked around but saw nothing. Had she imagined it?

Then, again: 'Julie...' It came from inside the room.

She leapt out of bed, a chill spreading over her, hairs prickling her body, right up into her scalp. It wasn't Dan.

Now was a time for prayers. Whatever happened next would be down to the God her convent school had insisted was constantly there watching over her. *Strike them down, dear Lord. You, the maker of all things, the provider and the punisher, keep me safe.*

'Julie?' This time, there was a hint of irritation; the voice cleared as if coming into focus, humanising itself. It was definitely a man. Hiding behind the curtains?

She crawled out of bed like a creature of the living dead and reached out a scrawny, ice-cold hand towards the thick paisley velvet. *Just one quick pull and I'll know the answer.* The silent countdown began as she willed her body to move and locate the tormentor. If it was Dan, she would never forgive him, yet she longed for it to be him. How could he do this to her, knowing how anxious she was?

Deep breaths.

She could feel the panic rising to the surface.

Three...

Two...

One...

Julie grabbed and ripped at the material. Nothing there.

Why had she thought it a good idea to fit a decorative curtain in the bedroom? *Feng Shui* would have her believe televisions didn't belong and had a negative effect on life, relationships, even health, but in her opinion, curtains were far worse. She turned around, surveying her environment, her scream uncontrollable, guttural and raw, piercing her own ears as she saw something, a slight movement in the corner of the room. Her skin was clammy as she prepared to face the intruder.

From behind the full-length mirror, Dan came bounding out, laughing like a hyena, but it was short-lived as he knocked it over in his attempt to reach her and hush the siren she emitted.

'Shh, be quiet! Stop it!'

Julie's scream continued as her body purged itself, releasing the built-up pressure and fear within her as she crumpled to the floor.

She didn't stop.

'Shut up, Julie! Shut up!' He became frustrated as she rocked back and forth. 'Stop it. Stop. Shh! It was a joke! You can stop now. Shh. Please, be quiet. Julie? *Julie?*'

She felt him start to shake her, but the sound continued.

He put a hand over her mouth and, eye-to-eye, repeated, 'Stop it now, just stop. Calm down. *Calm.*'

Like an animal caught in a trap, her eyes darting from side to side, she eventually stopped her wailing.

Dan released his hand slowly...bravely...hesitantly, and there was silence again. He pushed her gently to the bed and tucked her unresponsive body under the covers before turning the light off and wrapping himself in the duvet on the other side.

She heard the smile in his voice as he drifted off to sleep.

'Good night, God bless.'

Fuck you too, she thought.

Julie was not smiling. She was barely breathing as she lay there wondering how he could just switch off like nothing had happened. The room was still, silent, but there was a hissing in her ears; she was close to fainting.

Just as she was about to black out, embrace the adrenaline of the fight-or-flight sensation, the bedroom door opened. *Who's getting the last laugh now?* she thought, embracing the intruder she had previously dreaded. *Not so stupid after all.*

Alert once more, she held her breath and welcomed the release death would offer. It was calming to think someone might wipe the smile off the face of her already snoring, oblivious husband. But when she heard panting, breathing and rustling next to her, a chill spread through her bones.

Be brave, Julie. Just one look.

She couldn't bring herself to do it.

Then a familiar smell, breathing close to her face. Closer... closer...

She rolled over and grasped Dan's sleeping body. *Take him first*, she thought. *Don't give him the chance to escape.*

The warm body close to her ear began to climb in next to her. 'Mummy?'

Relief escaped in a sharp rush of breath. Julie turned and pulled Tommy close, never so happy to squeeze the love out of him as she was in that moment.

Chapter Two

As the dawn light filtered through the slats in the supposedly blackout, take-out-a-new-mortgage blinds, Julie tried to fight the realisation an alarm was beeping and it was up to her to turn it off. She lay stagnant in bed, the memory foam doing its job at keeping her dead still.

Maybe if I just lie here and sleep, Dan will get up?

Her snort of laughter nearly woke Tommy, whose feet had somehow ended up in her face. How did children turn one hundred and eighty degrees in their sleep? At least preparing to haul her body out of bed meant the bonus of pushing him into her husband. It wasn't her fault if Dan was accidentally woken in the process.

She wriggled forward and got free.

Remember, always roll onto your side and then push up before you get up, or you'll ruin your back! Julie recalled her Pilates teacher's advice from the long-gone days that allowed for exercise. She smiled as she thought back to the absurdity of the wisdom, which her teacher had repeated over and over, her favourite life hack being: *Remember to always zip up and hollow every time you breathe out, like you're tying your belt really tight while on the toilet to stop the flow of urine.* Yep, life-changing.

Come on, Julie, get up. Don't get lost in your thoughts; get in the moment. You're going to be late, then everyone else will be late because everyone waits for you. Okay, here goes...

She got up appropriately, stood, and then promptly collapsed in a heap on the floor.

A head rush? Got up too quick? Arthritis? A stroke? Julie wondered whether she was due a bit of time off to simply relax in a coma. *A break from life?*

She struggled to move from her heap on the floor, marvelling at the fact her husband and son didn't stir at all. Reaching for her phone to consult Google about her fate, she pulled at the charger but couldn't quite release it with one hand. Frustrated, she yanked it off the cord, knocking all the bedtime essentials off her bedside cabinet: two half-full water bottles, an eye mask, a nail file, some Mr. Men books, a wad of dirty tissues and a bundle of headbands she'd assumed to be lost. All of it came tumbling down on top of her.

Argh. So annoying! Stupid mobile. And she'd broken the charger cable in the process. Why, oh why did these things always happen to her?

Everybody else on Facebook and Instagram seemed to be having a wonderful day already, with full makeup applied by ten a.m.

What? No! It's so late... Must get up. Must hurry. Emails checked, fitness app checked. Nope, still haven't hit the magic eight hours' sleep – ever. Surely there was some other essential she had to check next? *Oh, yes, the weather app!* Julie smiled as she searched London and every holiday destination she could think of.

As much as she wanted a coffee before waking the boys, Julie had her morning routine. *First things first!* She stripped naked in the bathroom, emptied her bladder, (leaning forward to squeeze out any last remnants, as advised by the online diet doctor) and then stepped onto the scales. *Up two pounds since yesterday? Seriously, I just don't get it*, she thought angrily, having fasted the previous day.

She had expected to lose weight after her trauma in the night, all that sweat. So much sweat. The bedding would need to be changed. *Oh great – more washing!* It was a constant cycle, a mountain of clothes, never-ending: wash, dry, fold, put away, let's begin the dance again. Julie needed one of those T-shirts with 'wash, dry, repeat' across the front. *Yep, every mother's motto.* God help them all if the washer or dryer ever broke down; she would walk out on the family. At the thought of a possible out, she took a nice deep breath.

First, Julie made her way to her twelve-year-old's bedroom. She paused, thought twice about waking him, then backtracked down the hall. It was not quite lunchtime after all. She wondered if she could just run away, if anyone would even notice, right as her eldest, William, came out of his room. He slammed the door behind him and ran downstairs, straight out the front door without a word.

'Love you too,' she said. *One down, two to go.* But coffee first.

Downstairs, in the kitchen, she opened the dishwasher. Clean. Grabbing her favourite floral china, thin-rimmed mug, she placed it under the coffee machine with a decaf pod. No point going mental on caffeine until the other children were up to drain her energy. Julie hoped she could squeeze in a few minutes' peace, catch up on TV programmes over breakfast – it was the weekend after all. She briefly wondered where William was off to, but assumed he was en-route to the swimming pool with his friends. She was happy he was being independent and getting some exercise but also knew it would likely consist of ten minutes' water-bombing, followed by a fizzy energy drink and the biggest pack of random sweets the vending machine could provide.

Back to the coffee. Standing around watching the machine do its work was a luxury she had never experienced, and now wasn't the time to start. She quickly emptied the dishes, piled all the dirties into the sink and wiped down the work-tops. *Yep, time for milk now...* Rice milk, of course, from way back when the family had experimented with veganism. That went well. It helped if you ate fruit or vegetables – preferably both – before going on an all-out vegan diet, but they'd tried anyway, followed the craze. After an initial day of success, the children had moaned about their food as usual, nothing new there, then ransacked the freezer for ice-cream, threw out all the new meat-free options and sneakily ordered a McDonald's delivery. The first Julie knew of it was the empty cartons dotted around the kids' bedrooms. They'd cut the delivery man off at the door, having followed him on UberEats so he wouldn't press the doorbell. *Sneaky fuckers.*

Coffee in hand, she listened for the children. Still nothing, so, reaching for the television remote, she decided to flick through Netflix for anything that was adults-only – she'd done her time with Peppa Pig.

While the TV loaded up, Julie took a quick glance at her phone-stalker app to see what William was up to. He might be sixteen years old, but he was still her baby. The phone beeped, unable to locate his phone. *Great, he's used up all his allowance yet again.* She would need to ask Dan to increase the data plan. She dreaded the conversation, knowing how tight he was with his money, cursing once more that she couldn't just sort it out herself with the limited housekeeping allowance he gave her.

The TV was playing up, so she sat listening to the silence of the house and sipped her coffee. The perfect moment: the calm before the storm. *Time to go back on the mobile and work out what to do for the day. Cinema, maybe? Get the other kids out for a bit to end their hibernation.* She crept upstairs and climbed into the shower, knowing this would be the best way to wake the family. Her days of having time for a luxurious soak in the bath were long-gone, but a shower brought the kids out like ants from under a stone, banging on the door for attention.

'Mum? Mum! I'm hungry! I'm starving to death!' came the voice of little Tommy outside, knocking so loud she felt the vibrations reverberating through the shower's pipework. Right on cue.

'Sorry, Tommy, I can't hear you!' Julie responded, so he repeated the phrase four times to no avail. 'I can't hear a thing you're saying,' she lied. 'I'm in the shower. Ask your dad!'

The little feet padded off, and then shouting commenced in the far distance. *Hahaha, good.* But nope, the banging came back.

'Daddy's not getting up. He says he's tired.'

Her shoulders sank. 'Okay, I'm finished,' she called, sulkily turning the shower off and heading out to face the day ahead.

Twenty-one hours and counting until the Monday morning school run, she thought, perking up a bit.

Chapter Three

Julie opened the door, and Tommy and Jack barged past her, fighting for the front seat in the car.

'First of all,' she scolded, 'Tommy, you are not allowed in the front seat, and second, we're walking today. You need some exercise before you get hyped up on sweets.'

Two groans were the only response, along with some whispering.

As they walked up the road to the cinema, Julie marvelled at the beautiful crisp weather. 'Look at the trees, boys! Look at the leaves. They're all red. The last time we came up here, they were green and yellow!'

'Jeez, you are so boring, Mum,' said Jack. 'You're obsessed with trees. Every time we walk anywhere, you go on about them. Yes, they have leaves, and yes, they change colour, blossom, attract bees, cause hay fever, blah, blah, blah. I've seen it all before, I've heard it all before, I don't want to hear it again.'

'Okay...sorry I spoke,' Julie mumbled, feeling despondent and drained of the enthusiasm she'd felt seconds earlier. How could the children not be enthralled by nature and the elements? By the contrail vapour streaks across the bright blue, cloudless autumn sky? The sparkling cobwebs so perfectly formed, each with a green goblin-spider-creature hanging unmoving in its centre – not surprising, after working hard to create its masterpiece (she could empathise).

Why weren't they observing the bright green grass, the changing seasons…? Because they hadn't seen forty years pass as quickly as she had. Julie felt old and exhausted. The winter would be here again soon. Seven years of snow, every year since Tommy was born, and it was only getting colder and colder. She wanted to enjoy the autumn before Tourette's cold set in; the time when every adult conversation was punctuated by swearing. *Fuck, fuck, fuck*, between ice-cold breaths of frozen air. The time when it felt so cold you couldn't function, and all the money in the world would not make up for a day on the sofa with a fleecy blanket and a hot chocolate. Living the dream.

The boys had walked quite far ahead of Julie and were nearing the cinema. She took a moment to watch them. Jack had his arm flung around Tommy's shoulders as they casually walked along, every part the cool kid, with Tommy hanging on his every word. She tried to tune in to their conversation but just couldn't understand what they were talking about. It seemed to consist of an in-depth list of instructions on how to build a wall? Followed by snippets of conversation about acacia, obsidian, iron-ore, cobblestone, lapis lazuli, all strung together with laughter and a lot of nods from Tommy.

They were happy, content together, excited. Maybe she needed to point out what the trees were made of to gain their interest? Which would make the strongest wood? If only she remembered her tree names from the Brownie badge she'd worked through as a kid.

'Mum, can we buy some Pepsi Max for the cinema?' Tommy shouted, breaking the peaceful moment.

She hurried to catch up so as not to shout her business up the street. 'No, Tommy, we're not getting drinks as it's a long movie, and I don't want to be taking you to the toilet in the middle of it.' She had bottled water in her bag and some snacks, and no budget or intention of paying the box office prices.

'What about sweets? You promised!' Jack whined.

'I have them already, in my bag from home.'

'But that's not allowed! You're breaking the law,' Jack said, smug.

'Oh, for goodness sake. It's not breaking the law or even breaking the rules. The cinema allows you to take your own cold snacks, just not hot snacks, and anyway, anyway... Tommy, come back here!' she shouted after him as he made a dash for the movie screen doors. 'We're all going to the toilets together first. Stop running off!' she hollered, a sea of faces turning in her direction, judging her parenting.

Julie hurried forward to show the tickets for the screening and then went up to the ladies' toilets. She didn't want to leave Jack outside on his own, but as he was twelve, she couldn't take him into the ladies with her and Tommy. If only they hadn't locked the disability toilet. She'd gone to the Doctor, explained her extreme anxiety, requested a Radar key, but they'd refused her; it didn't tick their boxes.

'Just wait right there. Sit down right there, next to the usher,' she directed Jack pointing to a spot on the floor, her voice slightly raised despite her immense effort to remain calm. 'Right there! Do not move a muscle.'

She knew how ridiculous it was to be nervous about leaving a boy of his age, for what would be only a couple of minutes, in a public cinema, but still it didn't alleviate her anxiety. She could feel her heart thumping with the knowledge of what was to come. The numerous toilet cubicles within. *Oh, God, please do not forsake me.*

'Mum, stop squeezing my hand like that!' Tommy shouted, but his words fell on deaf ears.

She pushed open the heavy toilet door, a thick wood fire-door designed to keep those within safe – *or trapped*. Suddenly filled with super-human strength, Julie was ready to protect her son from what lay in wait. They entered. Stopped. Listened. Nothing but silence greeted them in response. On first glance, it seemed there was nobody in there, but many of the doors looked closed, displaying the red 'occupied' sign. It was a ruse.

'Just stay back there for a minute, Tommy. Wait by the sinks – it's safe there.'

'Seriously, Mum, I need a wee,' said Tommy.

'Just wait a minute.'

Julie approached the cubicles and crouched down to side-ways-glance under the doors, checking for feet. There were none. Her heart was still pounding, and pressure was mounting in her ears. She could feel herself sweating through her clothes, cold and clammy. Approaching the first cubicle door, with all her might, Julie pushed it sharply back. Nobody was there. Then, she tried the second door, then the third – at which point, Tommy pushed past and went inside. He was so desperate, he forgot to lift the seat and ended up urinating all over the place. Julie didn't notice, her eyes on the final door she hadn't yet checked.

The main door to the toilets opened, and a woman walked past her into the remaining cubicle, locking it behind her. Julie breathed a sigh of relief. Then, as Tommy finished, a voice came from outside the door.

'Come on, Mum, we're going to miss the movie at this rate!'

It was Jack. Julie was relieved to hear his voice and grateful he'd stayed nearby as she had instructed.

'We're on our way!' she said, dragging Tommy for a quick hand-wash and shake across the floor as they made their exit.

Once outside, relief flooded through her. Of all her phobias, public toilets were by far the worst. You never knew what psycho was going to be hiding behind the door waiting for you, wielding a weapon and preying on your vulnerability. Julie had feared public toilets for over twenty years. She wasn't sure where it stemmed from. Perhaps a horror movie might have triggered it? Or that time holidaying in a caravan in the middle of the woods, when her husband donned a mask, ran outside and put his face up against the toilet window? She remembered his laughter, which had gone on for days, and how every time she'd seen the mask since, it had triggered a panic attack. Perhaps masks were the problem, not knowing what could be hiding behind them?

She recalled the horror stories her dad Albert had thought so funny to share with her throughout her childhood. She wanted to blame him too. She recalled one night in particular, the pivotal moment when everything had changed. A long drive through the dark, her parents in the front, her little sister Claire sleeping soundly next to her on the back seat. Her dad had begun his story, delayed the punchline, built the suspense as they drove down the deserted country lane in Somerset. It was pitch-black, no street lights visible, and the cats' eyes seemed to be switched off that night. Then, temporary traffic lights: red, in the middle of nowhere. Her mum Sandra had insisted on stopping, much to her dad's annoyance. She remembered their argument; it wasn't the first that day. Time stood still – such a cliché, but literally, it was like staring into a void. Anything could be hiding out there in the dark. Julie's imagination would be her undoing. Why had her dad insisted on driving through the night to avoid traffic? *Night-time.* She shuddered at the thought.

She remembered her confusion when he'd suddenly climbed out of the car, slammed the door behind him and walked off. 'He's gone to answer a call of nature,' her mum had said – a lame excuse since both of them knew full well he was just being an arse. Julie was twelve and she wasn't oblivious to the problems in her parents' relationship. She closed her eyes, willed sleep to take her away from the upset, the uncertainty, the fear. The dark. Why would he leave them in the middle of nowhere? She sat counting the seconds, then the minutes, wondering at her mother's calm. How long would they sit there?

She heard a noise. *What was that?* Her mother's breath caught with every crackle in the trees around them. And then a feeling of falling, of being dragged from the car; ice-cold hands grabbing at her, pulling her out of the open window while her mother sat motionless, letting it happen. The bushes and the trees had scraped at her flesh, open wounds weeping and oozing and blood trickling down her arms, her legs. The fear, the pain, was so real, still a fresh memory nearly thirty years on. She had opened her eyes and found herself sitting in a warm puddle in the back seat of the car. Her dad's return and the door slamming had woken her up from the nightmare.

Julie had cuddled up closer to her sister, dreading the punishment when her accident was discovered, moving closer guiltily to shift the blame onto *her* – his little rose bud, his favourite. Julie tried to cover Claire's ears, maintain her peaceful innocence, the least she could do and a role she would continue over the years to come.

They didn't see their mum again after that night. Fed up of Albert's constant shouting, she bravely up-and-left, escaped the abuse and reached out for a fresh new start, abandoning the girls to fend for themselves. As a consequence, it seemed Julie inherited much of her mum's anxiety. It was a case of nature rather than nurture, and she felt the stab of pain when she realised that she had chosen Dan, a replacement father figure, with many of the same annoying attributes her mother had run from. She'd never noticed them through their dating years, but now, the connection was clear. All the times she'd had to use her mother's breathing techniques: the dark of a room, the possibility of people hiding, jumping out at you...

The world was a comedy of errors waiting to happen.

Julie and her sister hardly saw each other these days, estranged since their father's death – thanks to Sandra taking that as an invitation to burst back onto the scene. She hadn't thought about the impact it would have on her daughters, selfish as always, only thinking Albert was gone and it was safe for her to re-enter their lives.

Claire had never forgiven their mum for leaving, had no empathy for the difficult life she'd had to endure with Albert. She'd only been little, just five years old, confused and abandoned, looking for someone to blame. Claire had to grow up without a mother and couldn't forgive her for making the choice to leave.

But for Julie things weren't so clear-cut. She understood, no matter how much she wished she didn't, twenty years with Dan had taught her all too well.

How could a parent knowingly walk out on her children? That was Claire's only concern and she wouldn't let it go, even as an adult, refused to consider the other side. Sandra's departure had pushed Claire even closer to her dad who she viewed through rose-tinted glasses – and the feeling was mutual. For Julie she was just the skivvy, taking on her mother's role and trying her best to shield the little rose-bud from Albert's dark side.

Chapter Four

The cinema trip passed uneventfully, much to Julie's relief, but still she wasn't in a hurry to return to the stress of the house, a family trapped together led to bickering and endless mess. Somehow, the world seemed a better place when you weren't cornered within the confines of the same four walls. She wondered what her husband had been up to while they were out – was he still in bed? Probably, and if not, what difference would it make anyway, she thought, picturing the festering washing pile, untouched.

As she put the key in the lock, Julie prayed the house was in some sort of order but didn't hold out much hope. However, she was pleasantly surprised to hear laughter as she walked through the door. William had returned with his friends, by the sound of it. Lots of noise – everyone talking at once, everyone talking over each other. They heard her shout and started to make excuses, a hasty retreat, then quiet. Was she really that intimidating? After the last slam of the door, William asked: 'Can we go out to eat now?'

Err, no. We've just got back home!

Trying to keep her calm and not scream at the entitled teenage, spoilt monster he was becoming, she explained, 'We have lots of food in the fridge so I'll just make us something. What do you fancy?'

She walked towards the huge American fridge-freezer with the double doors. They'd all insisted on getting one to have cold water and ice cubes whenever they wanted, but how often did they actually use it? The huge silver block of a fridge was too big to fit in the gap where the previous fridge-freezer had been, so it sat right there in the middle of the kitchen. Yet they would still rather pollute the ocean with one-off plastic bottles of water, most of which got left to sit half-empty for weeks on end around the house. She was also a guilty offender.

Tommy and Jack had come running like ants at the mention of eating out and were buzzing around her waiting for a decision. *The decision is already made,* she wanted to scream again.

'Look in here, guys. There's chicken, prawns, sausages.... What do you fancy?'

She knew full well the response before it was out of their mouths, but it was Dan who said it. 'Let's have a takeaway if you don't want to go out.'

Great. Now Dan had said it, there would be no backtracking with the kids. Such an imbecile! *It's not that I don't want to go out. That's not the point. It's about using the food in the fridge – the gigantic fridge you always moan has nothing in it when it's full to the brim.*

She couldn't understand why they were all so fussy. Her parenting techniques had started off so well. She'd followed all the books on weaning at six months, and by two years, had them all on a balanced diet, eating everything and open to anything she offered them. Then, suddenly, it all stopped. With William, she'd used a divider plate technique she'd pulled from a parenting book: something he loves, something he likes, and something new. However, as the years progressed, the separate portions had led to him disliking sauces and had given him an aversion to mixing foods. He wouldn't eat stews or stir-fries or any foods that touched. Epic parenting fail. She just hoped he'd grow out of it when he started to do his own cooking.

With Jack, she'd taken the opposite approach. Everything was saucy and everything was messy – cue the move from carpets to laminate floor! This was a help when Tommy was little and eating everything, but he would watch his brothers and pick up on every bad habit going. Yep, her child-weaning story was more like Goldilocks and the Three Bears. By the time she got to baby bear, Julie felt she had well and truly ruined him. Chips, pizza or bread for dinner again – anything beige – and no amount of blending to hide meat or vegetables was going to get past his radar.

She blamed Dan. He had never been a good eater. She thought back to the first time he'd invited her over to his house for a meal, (bad enough that it turned out to be his parent's house and they only had privacy for a couple of hours while they were out bowling). The first time you cook for someone, surely you're trying to impress, even if you're incompetent? That's what she thought but clearly men and women don't think the same way.

She was expecting him to cook something simple, maybe a steak and salad, some oven chips thrown in, and perhaps a ready-made, microwave-heated soup for starters, followed by some bought-in profiteroles? She was ready to place bets on their relationship based on how much effort he made for the meal. Not that she was expecting a miracle or anything – after all, he was a twenty-two-year-old man-child, and likely, his mummy still cooked for him on a regular basis. Julie could tell he was looked-after by his appearance, unless he really did spend more time pressing his shirts than watching his beloved football team, which she doubted very much.

She had been surprised but not disappointed by the spaghetti hoops on toast and a fried egg. He'd looked so proud of his creation, poor baby, and not wanting to appear rude, she'd tucked in, wondering if she was a tad overdressed in her sparkly heels and lace dress. She'd pulled it down a notch, feeling self-conscious. She didn't want to be disappointed, told herself not to be, but she just couldn't help it. Perhaps that was why it tasted so bloody good as she started to tuck in.

From then on, it had been one of their favourite meals, something really special – until the kids arrived, and life demanded they introduce more greens into their diet. *A variety of colours and textures*, she remembered the child nutritionist saying at one of the obligatory prenatal visits. *Tell the kids to eat around their plate, to make sure they have a bit of everything before they get full.*

Julie had been very against the 'finish what's on your plate' mentality she had grown up with. There was no 'if you don't eat your dinner you won't get pudding' bribery. It was simply a case of there not being dessert anyway, with the exception of vegetable juice ice-lollies. Julie recalled with a smile how the kids and their friends would get so excited to have a lolly, without realising it was made up of French bean and blackberry smoothie or whatever she'd grown in her garden that season. It had all gone well until she tried it with leftover vegetable soup – and then never again.

'Julie, are we getting that takeaway? What are you doing, staring at the fridge? Are you okay?'

'Yes, I'm fine, Dan. Let's go out!' No point staying home and sorting all the dishes and the mess that would be left for her. She gave in. 'Where do you want to go?'

'Chinese!'

'Curry!'

'Pizza!'

They began a lengthy argument, with everyone of a different opinion and unable to agree, as usual.

Then, William piped up, 'I'm the oldest, I decide.'

'I think you'll find, that's me!' Dan said smugly.

'Fine then, I'm not going.' William shrugged.

Cue door-slamming, stroppy teen. *Oh, God, why can't they agree for once?*

Julie left Dan arguing with the kids and went upstairs to the bathroom, where she locked the door, turned the shower on and sat on the floor listening to it rain down. She tried to picture the ideal: her kids sitting around the dinner table, smiling, chatting, listening to each other, making polite conversation about their day. Who made up this stuff?

You'll miss it when they're gone, her mother had said when she was over babysitting. She didn't act like the grandmother Julie had expected. Sandra was a stark contrast to how she had been as a mother, probably overcompensating for all those years away. She let Julie's kids run wild. "*Somebody's hungry!*" she would say, giving them a packet of crisps just before dinner, or a chocolate bar at bedtime. "*Oh, just let him stay up a bit longer!*" when it was clear they were over-tired and going to behave like little shits the next day if they didn't get a few more hours' sleep.

Sandra had reappeared in Julie's life when William was born, no apologies for leaving, no explanations, just full-on ready for grandmother duties. It helped that Albert died shortly beforehand, the cycle of life, one in, one out – neither proving to be better than the other so far. She'd always thought Sandra had returned because of the baby, wondered why she hadn't seen through baby-brain fog that in reality, Sandra was just waiting till her husband was out of the way.

She quite liked having her back on the scene, but didn't really talk about what had happened while she was away. That was her business. Julie didn't hold a grudge, just welcomed the extra pair of hands looking after William. She was so chilled, such a natural. It reminded Julie of what an amazing mother she had been to her, and little Claire.

Unfortunately, her re-appearance wasn't such a welcome surprise to little rose-bud who had idolised Albert by the end. And, as she wasn't prepared to contemplate a mother-daughter reunion, it had nurtured a sibling feud ending at loggerheads. Julie needed her mother, valued her and refused to give her up; even at the expense of Claire's complaints. She was acting like a child and Julie had her own to think about now – little innocent ones. She'd rung herself dry for her little sister for too long and if she insisted on cutting their family ties, then so be it. It was Julie's turn to be mothered.

Sandra was so carefree, playing with William, and then Jack and Tommy, so relaxed. Was it because the role of Grandma was a temporary, fleeting part of her week – she didn't have to deal with the consequences? Julie suspected that was the case and made a mental note to try it on her friend's children the next time she looked after them – obviously, only the night before they were due home; she doubted she would hear back about any fallout, but it would amuse her anyway.

On the flipside, having Sandra back on the scene was a little daunting. She was strong, controlled, unquestionable. Not the way Julie remembered her from *before*. Sometimes it felt like she was there to punish her for all the missed opportunities she'd had, not being able to reprimand her for truanting, alcohol abuse and smoking outside the school gates. She knew nothing and yet somehow knew everything.

Julie couldn't help that she'd gone off the rails after her mum left. It was Sandra's fault, but Julie was too exhausted to lay blame. *Just appreciate the help now, she owes you.* It wasn't her fault she'd been caught stealing from her dad's wallet, sneaking out at night, breaking things and ducking his swipes when he tried to discipline her in the traditional sense of the word.

Old-fashioned discipline. Ha! Was that code for a good old beating, or was that just Albert's way? Julie thought of her own boys. They would benefit from some old-fashioned discipline; the naughty step was certainly not cutting it. She remembered the time Jack punched William in the face and then calmly walked to the naughty step and sat himself down for ten minutes. 'It was worth it,' was his calculated response.

Was her mum right to have left them? On her return, she was definitely a changed woman, more confident, satisfied, calm...and fun.

Fun? She swirled the word around in her mouth, trying to remember what it meant. How long had it been since she'd last had any time to herself? *I need a night out*, Julie thought as she began texting the book club she'd joined through school. Not her own children's school – that would be foolish, to let her hair down, lay herself bare in front of people she'd have to see on a daily basis for years to come. No, this book club was something different. It wasn't about the books. It had started out as a group of stressed women, spreading the word like an underground escapist cult, a quest for freedom. She'd overheard a whispered conversation, happened to be passing on an afternoon walk, stood outside too scared to enter.

Then Rachel had appeared, her knight in shining armour.

Scooped her up with a hooked arm and dragged her into the room. 'The Book and Bottle Club', day or night, secretive, exclusive to all those that needed support, why Rachel was there she couldn't fathom but her gratitude was endless. There was talk of books, it wasn't all pretence, not that Julie had time to finish even one since joining, she accepted the forfeit to bring a bottle, and she was more than happy to oblige. If only she wasn't driving every time they had an evening meet, or responsible for mothering the kids during the day...

'Julie, we're going to Pizza Hut! Are you coming?' Dan shouted up the stairs, breaking through her thoughts. At least they had come to an agreement. *Hallelujah!*

'Yes, on my way!' she replied, easier to give in than fight, and there would be no dishes tonight.

Chapter Five

That night, Julie did not want to go to bed. Dan was out at football, and it was already dark. She was expecting him home any minute, but that just added to her anxiety. Should she phone and ask if he was on his way? She decided to text – less the nagging wife if he was with friends.

Julie: *When are you home, darling?*

She waited, phone in hand, watching 'delivered' change to 'read'.

No response. Why did people do that? A text took a second to type. One second for peace of mind. He would know she was anxious, otherwise she wouldn't have asked. It was like he was torturing her on purpose.

After a few minutes, Julie got distracted by email pop-ups and started to surf social media to see what her friends had shared with the world. It was so addictive, like an insight into their diaries, their worlds. She felt like she was reading a series of newspaper headlines about the people she knew; dramatized announcements of happy-happy to create a rose-tinted glimpse into their world. The ideal. What we all aspired to.

She was jealous as she scrolled through the perfectly posed, slim beauties, travelling the world and eating at fancy restaurants, holding up beautiful cocktails that probably cost more than her family's weekly food budget. She threw the phone down, angry at herself for being sucked into the void of pretence. Back in the present, the house was eerily quiet as it approached the midnight hour. How had it got so late? And still, no Dan! Julie didn't want to turn the lights out.

'Please, come home. Please, come home. Please, come home,' she chanted. But nothing.

Julie curled up in a ball on top of the duvet and reached for her blanket, her comforter. He called it the Cloak of Sleep because it worked like magic. The moment she covered herself with it on the sofa, her eyes would close, and she'd drift off into the most relaxed, comfortable sleep – much to Dan's annoyance. Unfortunately, it didn't seem to work upstairs, and tonight was no exception.

Looking around their minimalist bedroom, she could see only the mirror, a picture of the kids and the television. Why couldn't she just relax and watch TV? Because the noise would mask any intruder sneaking up behind her, of course. At least she'd taken the curtain down, much to Dan's annoyance, but in her mind it was safer to brave the wrath of unbalanced karma than feed the alternative – that which could be hidden beyond. It wasn't helping her now. Nothing was. *Dan, where are you?*

Don't panic, just breathe. One, two, three... One, two, three...

She'd thought about taking a sleeping pill, to help her on her way, but the responsibility of being the sole parent in the house took away that option. Some facial yoga stretches, a warm bath, a relaxation podcast, they all helped but not when she was home alone. She couldn't risk switching off – just in case. She tried to focus on her breathing, marvelling at how, despite her brain fighting its best fight, it was becoming shallower, the repetition beautiful in its simplicity. It felt like she would never be able to close her eyes and sleep, but somehow, sweet oblivion claimed her anyway.

When Dan returned home, there was so much banging about, him huffing and muttering to himself along with heavy door slamming that Julie woke immediately, relieved to be brought back from her fitful sleep. He was obviously drunk – she guessed football and a pint or ten go hand-in-hand – but she was happy regardless. He was home. It wasn't the rude awakening she'd expected from *Stranger Danger*. She quickly slipped into her pyjamas, turned the light out and pulled the duvet over her. He would never know of her worry, not this time, and she was glad to be able to keep tonight's panic a secret.

'Wake up, Mummy!' came Tommy's voice from outside the bedroom door. 'We're going to be late for school!'

Julie's eyes burst open. 'Okay, honey, I'm on my way,' she answered in a rush. 'Are your brothers up?' A quick glance at the clock showed she still had plenty of time, no need to panic. 'What would you like for breakfast?' she hollered to no response.

She threw on yesterday's clothes from the heap on the floor, an easier option than turning a light on to find something decent and risk disturbing the no-doubt hungover Dan. Julie rushed downstairs, slipping on the last few steps and banging her arm against the wall.

'Fuck, ow!' she shouted before her head hit the step, and she slipped out of consciousness.

The slamming of a door brought Julie around. *Seriously*, had William just left for school? Did he even notice the crumpled heap on the stairs, or was he an arsehole? Julie knew you weren't supposed to think that of your own kids, but come on!

Choosing to believe he'd sleep-walked his way out of the door, she put on a brave face and made her way to the kitchen, rubbing her head and feeling for blood. There was nothing there, only a bump and a sore bruise. Jack was already in the kitchen getting breakfast for himself and Tommy.

'Thanks, Jack, really appreciate it.'

'No problem, Mum. I thought you needed some help when I saw you asleep on the floor in the hallway! You must have been really tired.'

Julie rolled her eyes. *My kids!*

'Okay, Tommy, eat up. We've got ten minutes until we leave. Bye, Jack!' she called out as the door slammed again.

Two down, one to go, then she would tackle the house – and Dan.

Walking to school in her floor clothes, Julie felt let down. How had life turned out like this? She needed a purpose, to get away from it all. *I must book that night out*, she thought. Tommy was growing up fast. He no longer wanted to hold her hand. *Maybe one more baby?* No way! But how little they were, how loving and innocent and pure... *Another baby to spoil; another child to ruin.* She wasn't cut out for this parenting lark. *It's okay to be shit*, she told herself, *just try not to be really shit. Don't fall apart today. Find the positives.*

They reached the school gate, and she bent to kiss Tommy goodbye. 'Love you, baby,' she whispered into his hair and reached for an air-kiss as he ran off inside.

Finally, she was free for the day to continue with housework, cooking, and the fruitless tidying that was her life.

'Hey Julie, have you seen my jeans?' came Dan's voice from upstairs, the moment the key was in the door.

He was up! She was surprised. Pleased, but uneasy. There was a short window before he had to leave for work.

'I'll get them now,' she replied, making her way slowly up the stairs, already expecting his confrontation.

And there it was.

'You need to sort yourself out,' he criticised. 'You can't keep on at me every time I leave the house. I had a life before you, you know? Jesus, I can't live with you and your crazy head anymore. Go and see someone, or go out, get a job! Do something! You just sit around all day – it's not healthy. And stop nagging at me! We're not supposed to live in each other's pockets. I need a bit of freedom.'

Take a breath, Dan, she thought, rooting herself to the spot until his rant was over. She stared at his back as he walked away, waiting for the front door to slam and his car engine to start up signalling he had left for work. When had their life changed? How could he be so heartless? She sat on the floor and thought about what he'd said. Was she crazy? Was there someone who could take all her problems away? Was he being unreasonable?

Alone in the house at last, Julie listened, still not ready to trust the silence. She methodically checked every room, closing the doors behind her, one by one, a mental and physical signal that all was clear. As she glanced at her watch, she was relieved to note that she'd only wasted half an hour of her precious freedom, the long day stretched ahead, a penance and a reward, isolation and escape.

Opening the drawer under Tommy's bed, she pulled out the duvet covers that sat discarded, from a time when In the Night Garden and Thomas the Tank Engine had been her sweet innocent toddler's favourites. Before they had grown, before they had been damaged. The final cover removed, neatly folded and tucked inside, her collection, her secret, her key to another world.

Walking towards the door, she listened once more, a final check that nobody was going to interrupt her, before emptying pill after pill, painkillers, antibiotics, sleeping tablets, antidepressants; years of horded medication, siphoned off family prescriptions to build up her escape. 'Every bride needs a bottom drawer', she recalled those words from her mother, when she'd played dress up with her jewellery as a little girl. Her earliest memory, or maybe just her only happy childhood memory.

She stood up, her knees creaking as she admired the array of coloured sweeties spread across the floor, wondering how many would pop open easily, like in the movies, letting out an untraceable white powder, the secret to oblivion.

Her watch showed it to be nearly 10 in the morning, she had time.

Could I, a little taste?

Just a little bit would do no harm, just a peaceful dream, an outing into a world where life is repaired, as it should be. Besides, if she took too much, she'd never know anyway, wouldn't have to deal with the consequences herself, then it would be up to Dan.

She awoke to the sound of William and Jack shouting, arguing, banging about, but not asking for her, thankfully as Julie felt her head was going to explode if she didn't vomit first. School must be over and with it, freedom gone. She'd slept on Tommy's bed, grateful that she'd put the extra medication away before-hand while waiting for the drugs to kick-in. She was constantly surprised at how slow sleeping pills were to work their magic and how many she needed to knock her out for a substantial amount of time. She only wished she'd left just one out to take the edge off the hammering migraine that was crushing her skull.

Note to self, 1 less Triazolam next time and maybe an extra Xanax instead?

Through the haze, she heard her phone ping. It was Rachel, from the book club: *All good for this Friday!* Excellent! A night out at last – as long as Dan let her go.

She scooped herself off the bed, smoothed the covers and groggily walked down the stairs and out the door. Didn't tell the boys she was off to pick up Tommy, didn't want to see them, didn't want to hear them, not in her current state. Maybe if she walked she'd be late enough to miss the other nosy judgemental parents, it's not like she could drive anyway with that concoction likely still raging through her system. She leant over the curb and heaved, her head pounding all the more. Life just wasn't fair.

Chapter Six

J **ulie:** *Sorry, can't make it tonight, something's come up xx*

Julie sent the message to the book club group and sat down on her bed to look at the pile of reject clothing on the floor. She had nothing to wear despite a visually full wardrobe. The others would all be gorgeous and glamorous, dressed to impress like ladies do for each other. It had seemed like such a good idea when she made the plan, right up until the moment it was time to leave. Julie looked down as her phone started to ring. *Rachel. She's not taking no for an answer.*

She picked up. 'Hello?'

'There is no way you're staying home, not even if I have to drag your sorry arse down the street in your pyjamas. We haven't seen you in ages!'

'But I'm not feeling well,' Julie started. 'The kids are playing up – I need to help settle them.'

'Nope, no excuses accepted. Let that lazy arse Dan do something for a change. Get your glad rags on, slap on the war paint and out you come. You need it, damn it. You deserve it, girl! I'll see you at eight p.m., and if you're not there, I'm coming to get you!'

The phone went dead as Rachel hung up. Julie sat staring at it. *Well, it would be easier to just get over there than face the alternative.* She didn't want Rachel coming over to confront Dan – she knew how much they hated each other and avoided contact at every opportunity.

With a sigh, she picked up her long black dress with mini polka-dots. *Very Eighties.* It did nothing for her cankles, but it would have to do. She lifted it over her head, arms outstretched and tried to shuffle it down but it wouldn't budge past her shoulders – and there was nobody there she could ask to help without humiliating herself. She tried to take it off but was stuck tight, feeling the warmth rising to her cheeks and the panic threatening to attack any second.

As she angled her body forward to give her tunnel vision through the overhead opening, she felt for the nail scissors and made contact. A few minutes later and she was free, the shredded dress lying deformed on the floor at her feet.

She assessed herself in the mirror. At five foot five, Julie had slim arms and a long upper body, which gave way to stumpy legs and an oversized stomach. She reached for one of the many grey tops in her wardrobe with matching slacks, feeling frumpy and way older than her forty years. They were supposed to hang loosely but everything was skin tight. She looked pale and gaunt, her eyelids drooping down, taunting her with the suggestion that a migraine might be imminent. She wanted to cry but couldn't let Rachel down.

Pinching her cheeks, she remembered how her mum used to

do the same thing to her when she was a little girl, before she left for school. *Always act the part, darling, don't let your front down.*

A simple pinch of colour wasn't going to cut it tonight – not with the book ladies. After applying an overzealous amount of blush, she reached for the lipstick, then thought better of it. It would only end up smeared over her face or on her teeth or would be wiped off before she even got there. Plus, if she was going to kiss the kids goodbye, there would be none of that. They seemed to have a phobia of lipstick – or was it kisses? Who knew? They hadn't always been so lacking in affection.

Growing boys. Growing away; a natural progression. The pull towards independence.

'Have a lovely evening, boys! Enjoy your lads' night!' Julie shouted, reaching for her leather jacket. It made her feel expensive. She'd owned it for years but saved it to wear on special occasions only.

It was a cold night, and the coat wouldn't keep her warm – or dry, if it rained – but it made her feel a bit less mumsy, so it was a necessity for an evening out. Impractical clothing. That was what nights out with the girls were all about. They'd be more appreciative of her outfit than any man could ever be. She wanted them to feel envy, but doubted that was possible.

'Bye, love you!' Dan called from the gaming room.

Wow, she thought, *he's obviously too engrossed in his game to realise what he's saying.*

She could hear the excited giggles around the house and the boys settling in for their big gaming extravaganza, knowing they had ordered in kebabs, which were on their way. Julie felt redundant, worried for nothing that she couldn't go out and leave them when, really, they were absolutely fine. More than fine. They seemed in a party mood.

Slamming the door behind her, she wobbled over to the car, out of practice and walking in her neglected heels and much more akin to her trainers. *Just make the effort tonight,* she told herself, *the other girls will notice.*

Bollocks, she'd forgotten her house key. Julie begrudgingly hobbled back and rang her doorbell, her feet already blistering from her impractical footwear choice. No answer – they all had their headsets on. She rang again and again. *Seriously?* She was already late from all her dilly-dallying.

Finally, Tommy answered the door.

'Tommy, why are you getting the door? Dan! Tommy shouldn't be answering the door!' She scowled as he ran off, back to his game.

'Well, it's a good job he did, or you'd still be standing there ringing. He only got it because he's hungry. Why are you back anyway? Did you change your mind? Too scared to leave the house?'

Julie grabbed the key and slammed the door, not humouring him with a response.

I'm going to have a great time, she thought, revving the car engine and driving off down the street. When she was safely a few roads away, she pulled over and entered the address in her satnav. She didn't want to do it in front of the house – didn't want Dan to know she had no clue where she was going. Part of her wanted to drive off into the dark and keep going.

'Proceed to the route, then, in two hundred yards, turn left,' the American voice instructed.

She turned the radio on: Talk-Sport, of course. Fiddling with the control, Julie tried to access some sort of music, any type, but it just wasn't happening. She turned it off rather than pull over again and risk being even later. She really didn't want Rachel turning up at her house and having a go at Dan. It was a shame the two had never really hit it off, but Julie didn't care if people didn't like him. Hell, half the time, she didn't either!

On arrival at the party, Julie couldn't find a spot to park anywhere near the house, so she had to drive two roads down and squeeze her seven-seater Vauxhall Zafira between a fancy sports car and a Tesla. She hit the curb a few times and heard the hubcaps scrape as she went in too close. *Oh, shit*, she thought, *Dan's going to go crazy!* She would have to worry about that tomorrow though. Everyone had clearly arrived early.

What happened to being fashionably late? When mums were let out, they needed to grab their time with both hands and run before the bedtime routine began – and if they could avoid making dinner too, then freedom!

Ding dong.

Nope, not ding dong. Extravagant church bell chimes played to a classical tune as Julie stood outside the double doors on the Greek pillared porch. *Now, that's a house!* As the doors opened, Julie felt everything move in slow motion. White carpets, women in fancy gowns with champagne glasses and immaculate nails. A buzz of contented chatter came wafting out.

'Come in! You must be Julie! Rachel warned me you were running late, so we're still on canopies and champagne. Would you like one?' Laura, the hostess, greeted with a clearly expensive smile. She was as glamorous as they came: a big-shot lawyer in the city by all accounts, single (on paper) yet never on her own. Laura was the life and soul of the party, with all the etiquette Julie had only ever read about in novels. Gorgeously sassy, with every curve defined in the skin-tight dress that looked like it had been poured on.

Wow, Julie thought, *she's living the dream*. She couldn't even contemplate bridging the gap between their two realities. Nerves buzzed in her stomach as she followed Laura down the hall, where a waiter approached with a tray of champagne glasses.

'Okay, just one, thanks. I'm driving.'

She wanted to down it, take the edge off her humiliation at how inappropriately dressed she was in comparison with what seemed more like The Oscars than a book club.

'Hi, stranger!' came Rachel's voice, interrupting her thoughts as she bounded around the corner. Julie grabbed onto her friend and they squeezed in a proper hug – someone who genuinely wanted to greet her, it was a rarity.

With a sip of her champagne, Julie relaxed a little and willed the glass to last until home time so she wouldn't have idle hands. Why did she feel so self-conscious when she wasn't holding a glass? It wasn't about the alcohol, only the natural break a sip provided during an awkward pause in conversation. Looking around, she felt way too conspicuous in her drab clothing, thought any moment she'd be approached and asked to refill glasses as one of the hired help, God forbid, that would be humiliating.

How did they all get away with wearing glitzy jewellery too, she wondered, when most of them had little children? Maybe they all had nannies handling the day-to-day, safe without fear of a child's hand reaching up with the single warning – 'Pretty!' – before the strangling dance began. With a quick, well-aimed hand or three, most of her own jewellery was destroyed and now sat bead-free, while her precious jewels adorned the redundant toy boxes.

'Let's go and sit down so we can have a proper catch up,' Rachel said. She led the way into what could only be described as the ballroom – way too big for a lounge, but too fancy for a dining room (Julie suspected that was in another wing of the house). An imposing chandelier dropped far too low for safety despite the high ceilings and wood beams. The Art Deco style was like an image from Pinterest: a collage of old and new; an expensive way to make modern decoration look like it had been there for hundreds of years. It seemed to work. The effect was trendy and artistic. If Julie tried to replicate it, she would have to buy a whole shop and still wouldn't get it right.

As they walked in, she couldn't help but think of the potential dangers the room presented. The chandelier, obviously, could fall down, crushing the people beneath it while they danced in the ballroom (or was that a scene from Titanic?). A single shard of glass could fall from one of its many droplets and pierce the heart of an unlucky reveller below. The love dance would be broken forever. The victim's Romeo would find her, remove the offensive object, gather her in his arms and weep for his lost love before uniting himself in death with his Juliet, using the same instrument of her demise for a torturous farewell.

And don't get me started on the wood beams and fire hazards. Where's the fire blanket? Every good house needs a fire blanket! She was mesmerised by the high ceilings, imagining smoke billowing up in clouds and hearing classical music as it swirled around in beautiful waves before devouring the whole house. There were no regulation smoke alarms wired into the main frame. Art had won on this occasion, but would death take its revenge?

'So, what have you been up to, and why haven't we seen you in forever?' Rachel asked, startling Julie from her thoughts.

She smiled at her friend. *Yep, back in the room, girl.* What had she said?

'Julie, what's going on with you? Has Dan chained you to the kitchen sink?'

'Oh, no, erm...everything's fine. It's just he's working a lot, so I'm stuck home with the kids.' In reality, she had simply let her social life slide.

Before, she and Dan frequently went out together – with friends or just the two of them – but now, he was coming home later and later and crashing out on the sofa in front of the television. To be honest, she didn't miss it. On Friday nights, the thought of braving the elements to go out drinking with friends, chat-shouting above the din of a club, surrounded by a load of teenagers wearing the equivalent of underwear, was far from the top of her list. Food was the priority these days. Food and sleep and a glass of wine. Only the one, so she wouldn't be punished at six a.m. when Tommy came in to wake her.

How could she explain to Rachel that it wasn't the fact she didn't want to see her friends, it was just that she couldn't be bothered – not when the alternative was a quick message and a browse of Facebook from underneath her blanket. That would bring her right up to speed and allow her to enjoy the TV in the warm.

Julie realised she was daydreaming, watching her friend talk but not taking in her words. She was a bad friend.

'Sorry,' Julie said. 'I've not been sleeping, and I'm just exhausted all the time. To be honest, I'm a bit fed up with being at home every day.' She knew this would trigger a response and get

Rachel talking more. It was an ongoing battle with her friends to try and reintegrate her into society. She was their pet project. Did Rachel really even like her? What was there to like? What did she really bring to the party? A building regulator's to-do list?

Rachel looked seriously at her friend. 'Come on, Julie, that's not like you! What's getting you down? Is it Dan? Or the kids? Most people get fed up if they spend too much time together, that's why they escape off to work. I don't know how you do it!'

'Have you thought about going back to work? Introduce something in your life that's about you rather than the family. What did you do before you had children?'

Here we go again... Many of the book club girls had met as new mums, desperate for distraction so in those days, they at least shared that in common. Rachel remained childless though, choosing to concentrate on her career, which she loved with a passion. She was a neighbour of one of the mums who'd hosted the first book club, and Julie had hit it off with her almost immediately. Rachel represented escapism; a dream-turned-reality of how Julie's life could be in some alternate dimension.

One by one, all of her other book club mumsy friends had scurried off back to their careers. But not Julie. She had hated her job, hadn't yet discovered her true passion and didn't think juggling a young family and searching for a new career would do either of them justice. No, she and Dan had decided they would rather adapt their lives to live on a reduced budget than have her go back to work.

It used to be wonderful, in the early days. It was still okay for the most part, but she couldn't help feeling... unnecessary? Inconsequential? A wave of annoyance washed over her every time people asked where she worked – followed by their feigned surprise trying to cover disdain.

'Ooh, lucky you! I wish I didn't have to work, but we just couldn't manage without my wages,' was the usual response, she'd heard it all before – over and over and over again.

Yes, clearly, you'd only manage one world cruise a year instead of the five you can afford now. It always made her feel guilty to think that way. Guilty pleasure.

But with Rachel, it was different. She was free by choice; she chose to work and was so enthusiastic. What could Julie say to placate her?

'I've always fancied myself as a bit of a writer,' she threw out there.

'That's brilliant! Although, it's not going to get you out and about meeting people, and I think that's what you need. Have you ever thought of seeing a life coach? They're great! Really worked wonders for Sarah over there.'

Julie glanced in the direction she was pointing. She didn't know Sarah but felt a wave of jealousy at her polished appearance. Julie hated her for it with an unnatural venom, the wealth she exuded. She glanced around the room. When had she turned into such a bitch?

'Sarah, come over here! Let me introduce my friend, Julie,' Rachel shouted over, managing to sound dominant yet welcoming.

Sarah lifted her head casually, flicked her hair in slow motion, mumbled to the ladies in her group and made her way over, perching on the edge of the grand piano stool opposite them. Her stance was non-committal, like she was only humouring Rachel to find out if she was worth joining for the conversation

– leaving her options open to return to the vacuous beauties she was with before.

'Hello. I don't believe we've had the pleasure.' Sarah held out a hand at an angle Julie knew would make for the most pathetic handshake. Still, it beat air-kissing.

'Hi! Rachel said you have a life coach?' Julie blurted, not knowing how to broach the subject. She was out of touch with people – and *life*, it felt in that moment.

Sarah flushed a little but regained her balance and responded. 'Yes, her name is Kate. I think she's going to be here later tonight, if you'd like me to make introductions?'

'Oh, no, thank you!' Julie replied defensively, cursing Rachel for interfering and putting her on the spot.

Sarah raised a single hairless eyebrow, waiting for Julie to elaborate.

'I was just curious to know what she did for you. How does it all work – if you don't mind me asking?'

'Actually, I would prefer not to say. It's a journey of personal discovery. If you're interested, here's her card.' Sarah reached into her purse with perfectly manicured hands and pulled out a plastic card. It was clear, clean, logo-free and simply read 'K' with a number to call.

'Thanks,' Julie said as Sarah floated away, back to her entourage.

'So, what do you think?' Rachel asked. 'Worth giving her a call?'

She nodded, feeling foolish but wanting to please her friend.

Rachel leaned forward and snatched the card from her hand, then started to dial the number. 'No time like the present!' she sang.

Julie's stomach lurched. 'No, seriously, let me think about it for a while!'

Rachel ignored Julie's words, smiling into the phone as she began to speak in her business voice. 'Hello? I'm phoning on behalf of a friend. I'm her PA.' She paused and winked over at Julie before continuing. 'Yes, that would be fabulous. I'd like to book her in for a counselling session…. Oh, yes, coaching session, that's what I meant. Friday at ten? Yes, that sounds perfect. Her name is Julie Summers.' Rachel went on to give Julie's contact details and then hung up with a big grin and a thumbs-up.

'You shouldn't have done that. I had the card and would have arranged something in my own time.' Julie looked around the room, wondering which one was Kate – if she had arrived, or if that was just a lie concocted by Sarah to escape the awkward conversation. Why would she even be at the book club?

'Well, yes, but that's the problem,' Rachel said. 'Nothing will get done in your own time. Nothing for *you*, that is. You think of other people before yourself. That's one of the reasons you need a life coach! Just think of tonight – you even tried to get out of coming here! You need to get over your anxieties, tackle your fears head-on and grab the life you want with both hands.'

Their conversation was interrupted as the room started to fill with other book club beauties, most of whom, Julie noted, did not sit down in their fancy dresses. If she was wearing an outfit like Laura's, she wouldn't be able to bend at the middle either!

'Sorry, Rachel, that's my cue to leave. I didn't get time to read the book.'

'Don't worry about it.' Her friend reached forward and squeezed her hand, preventing Julie from standing up. 'Neither did I! Just relax and enjoy the party – we can blag it. Why don't you have a proper drink for a change? Leave the car and taxi back?'

'I really can't. Sorry. Next time? Dan will be waiting up, worrying.' Julie knew the reality of this was unlikely. It was eleven p.m. and a school night. She expected he would be oblivious to the time and likely still playing computer games with the kids, bedtime not having been factored into his night at all. 'I really have to shoot, but it's been lovely,' Julie said as she started to walk away towards the host. 'Laura, thanks so much for everything. Sorry, I have to go off early.'

Laura smiled and leaned her cheek forward. 'My pleasure,' she purred, then addressed the room. 'So, ladies, shall we start?'

Julie felt she wouldn't be missed.

As she exited the house, she should have been prepared, should have known it would be dark and oh so quiet after leaving the bright lights and sparkle of the party. The door slammed behind her, making her jump, and she stood alone in the street outside. Pitch-black. What had happened to the streetlights in these fancy areas?

Her ears rang through the silence as she started to walk towards her car, the only other sound her heels clicking on the empty pavement. She crouched down quickly to remove them, making a run for it with her heels firmly in her right hand, keys in the left – ready to defend herself against any potential assailant. There would be no Cinderella moment for her; she gripped the shoes so tight, her knuckles cramped around the would-be weapons. She could hear own panting.

Save some energy in reserve, just in case, she told herself. *In case you're being followed.*

Julie looked around in the dark, her eyes struggling to focus as she jogged past each tree on the street. So many huge branches, areas of shadow...places to hide. Why would people choose to live in a place like this? Apart from the isolation, weren't they concerned about tree roots reaching underneath their houses and disturbing their homes, their palaces? The very foundations of their lives?

Just a few more steps. She tried to ready her car keys while juggling her shoes, failing and dropping the lot onto the floor. Fortunately, it just missed the drain. Another horror: Pennywise staring back at her, waiting to pull her into the depths of depravity – down through the drain, into the world that lay beyond the shadows. She crouched quickly, shivering as she scooped up her belongings, willing her body to move in the right direction.

Out of breath and chest wheezing, Julie finally reached her car, unlocked it, jumped in and slammed the lock button down. She was in. *Safe.* Just to be sure, she checked the back seats to see if anyone was hiding there. *Nope, empty.* She breathed a sigh of relief. But what if someone was there, and she had locked them in with her? *Stupid!* She couldn't calm her nerves at the thought of it and dropped her keys down the crack between the chair and the handbrake.

'Seriously?' Julie shouted, rummaging around in the dark since the light had switched itself off.

A tapping noise. She willed herself to look up, expecting nothing but her imagination, a leaf on the windscreen perhaps – but on seeing a figure at the window, she screamed.

Her breath caught in the back of her throat as the person tugged the door handle, but she had already locked it. A face slowly came into focus: *Rachel.* Julie exhaled and tried to steady her nerves as she faffed about with the window button, which wouldn't open as she couldn't locate the key.

Was Rachel smiling? Laughing at her?

'One minute!' she shouted, wedging her hand sideways into the crack and wiggling the keys forward, trying a pincer movement to shift it. Finally, she sighed and put the key in the engine to release the windows.

'You left in such a hurry, you forgot the therapist's card. Don't forget – next Friday, ten a.m.!' Rachel said with a grin. 'Chill out, Julie. You look like you've seen a ghost!'

'Sure, I'll be there,' Julie stammered, agitated, keen to close the window and be on her way.

'Lovely seeing you. Don't be a stranger!' were Rachel's parting words as she skipped off into the dark without a care.

Oh, to be so comfortable, so brave, so free, Julie thought as she drove off in the other direction.

On her return to the house, Dan was asleep. Julie glanced under the kids' doors to see if there was a halo of light emitting from any of them, but they were all in the dark. She snuck into the bathroom, turned the light on and started to remove her makeup. *Why, when I wash my face, does water always spray onto the mirror? Who thought it would be a good idea to put it there as a splashback in the first place?* Julie wished she could just rip it from the wall and get rid – then she wouldn't have to bother cleaning it every time anyone used the sink. More importantly, she wouldn't have to fear reflections from the afterlife peering back at her.

Why was it okay for children to sleep with the light on, yet when you became an adult, everything had to be dark? Adulthood was dark, never mind parenting – that was a total abyss.

She snuck into bed and held her torch light over Dan, checking it was him before she could switch off for the night. She had been surprised, on returning to the house, to find it all silent, him already in bed. She hoped his night had been un-eventful and the kids hadn't driven him crazy. That would re-flect negatively on her chances of having future nights out. She tried to snuggle up close to him, steal some of his heat without disturbing him. She couldn't face the questions.

Dan didn't like her mixing with the book club ladies. She wondered why. Did he think she would be jealous of all their glitz and glamour? Career girls, with families and fancy life-styles, who seemingly had it all and looked fantastic at the same time. Was he angry at her, that she wasn't like them? She thought of Sarah, her taught cheekbones and flawless skin, her pert lips and smoky bedroom-eye makeup. That would never be Julie.

Maybe she was jealous. Just a tad. Sarah was very secretive, reserved and held back in her body language, and she certainly hadn't wanted to share her life-coach experience. How had it helped her? Julie didn't know Sarah, but from first appear-ances she seemed more than satisfied with her perfect life. She promised herself she would attend the appointment Rachel had booked for Friday with the mysterious 'K' – whatever it took to get there.

Chapter Seven

Monday morning came and went. The most relaxing part of a parent's week; the calm after the storm that was the weekend. Julie hoped Friday would hurry up so she could meet up with Kate and get it over with. She was anxious and dreaded the idea of laying herself bare, not knowing what to expect or how much she would have to divulge. She had picked up her phone on Monday morning with the intention of cancelling, her confidence forgotten, only to find a motivational quote forwarded by Rachel with a thumbs-up emoji: *To your new life and all the opportunities ahead! Rachel, kiss kiss.*

She had obviously dictated it to her phone, or had Rachel purposely written 'kiss kiss' instead of putting 'xx?' Julie felt out of touch with her friends and out of touch with society. Everything was changing so quickly, while she sat at home juggling the mundane day-to-day of family life.

There must be more to life than this, she thought as she picked up yet another dirty sock ball from the living room floor. She was stuck in a rut, too much responsibility without the reward, and responsibility for what? Cleaning, cooking, ironing? Just to have it all wrecked within seconds of the family re-entering the house. I will not cry over a sock. *I refuse to cry over a stupid sock,* Julie thought, trying to blink back the tears unsuccessfully. Nobody was home, nobody would see, as Julie gave up the fight, instead wallowing in self-pity, letting her tears stream down her cheeks. The life coaching session was long overdue and couldn't come soon enough.

And then, it was Friday. She hadn't told Dan since she already knew his view on self-help 'nonsense'. Instead, she'd siphoned off money from the week's food allowance to pay for the session and felt relieved nobody had noticed the more frugal menu that week.

Picking out a red top (red meant power, according to Rachel), she tried to squeeze herself inside, thinking back to her pre-children days, power-dressing for her job as a journalist in London. She had wanted to progress up the ranks but never quite made it, getting pregnant each time she was put up for promotion and eventually handing in her notice when the sums didn't add up. Wages, minus childcare, equals debt.

The mirror looked back at her, surely a lie? There was no way she could leave the house dressed like that, the flesh protruding like a risen loaf of bread, white and soft and ready for the oven. *Don't cry. What goes on must come off.* The struggle was real but eventually the top was discarded, the only red she'd be wearing were the scars where the arm holes had attempted to stop her circulation. *Back to the grey of my life.*

It's now or never, Julie, she told herself, reaching for a summer scarf to wrap around the wrinkled lines that decorated her neck in the absence of a functioning necklace. Meeting with Kate was supposed to be a positive enlightening experience, but it felt more like an interview. Even though she knew full well it wasn't a test, Julie felt the need to impress. She wanted to persuade Kate she was capable of achieving greatness, whatever that happened to be.

As she walked timidly into the office, Julie wondered how she should address her teacher/interviewer/doctor. By her first name? Or was it more of a formal environment?

'Come in, sit down,' Kate said, all smiles. Julie would have liked to believe her positive attitude, but suspected it was all part of an act, a persona she had created for the job.

Julie couldn't see anywhere comfortable to sit, only a bright yellow chaise lounge with over-plumped pillows. She glanced up and saw Kate checking the clock – very unprofessional, in her opinion. Perching on the edge of the seat, Julie waited uneasily, letting out a little snort of laughter as she compared herself to Sarah. Had she been nervous at the book club? Maybe Julie had misjudged her?

'So, Julie, welcome. Make yourself at home and relax. This is a very informal setting, and our aim is to explore the life possibilities and choices you would like to make. Really, it's just a chat. Treat me as a sounding board to really think through what you would like to change in your life and how you could get the most satisfaction out of your current situation. So, if you'd like to start by telling me a bit about yourself.'

Julie looked at the floor. She didn't want to make eye contact; she didn't want to share at all. She felt naked, exposed. *Breathe, don't panic.*

'Don't worry, there is no judgement here, Julie, only your own. There are no right or wrong answers. Please, go ahead.'

Julie started timidly. 'Well, I'm married and have three children, all boys – so we have a smelly house!' She did a little fake laugh and looked up to Kate's nod of encouragement. 'I'm a stay-at-home mum, so I don't really do anything, but at the same time, I seem to be doing everything. I never have time for myself, and I'm tired all the time.'

'Well, let's try to work out a way you can set and achieve your goals and fit them into your lifestyle while still keeping up with the family demands. What would you do if you knew you couldn't fail?'

Julie looked down again and shook her head. 'I just don't know. I always wanted to be a writer, but I can't see how I might do that. But if I couldn't fail, that's what I would do.'

'Brilliant! That's a great start and very doable. We'll come back to it in our goal-setting a bit later. I'd like you to also think about a couple of other things. Can you describe your life in six months if you had a magic wand?'

Feeling a bit braver, as she noticed Kate's less-than-perfect foundation lines where her face and neck joined, Julie began again a little more confidently. *This is like telling Tommy a bedtime story,* she thought.

'Okay, so, to start with, I'd have loads of money to play with from my successful career as a writer, and lots of me-time to spare. Dan and I would have more holidays together. Happy, carefree times, where we could switch off all the stress and demands in our lives and just smile. We haven't been getting on great for a while now, and I think it's because we don't spend any time together just being husband and wife.'

Julie looked up at Kate, wondering if she had another question, but was greeted with silent concentration. She wasn't looking at her. She hoped Kate was at least taking mental notes, so she would get her money's worth.

'I'm always the mother, organising, encouraging, disciplining, running here, there and everywhere and trying to be there for the kids when they have a problem. I feel like all my love is already given out, and I'm just not in the right mindset to be a wife. I'm a mother. I can't switch between the two. If I had a magic wand, I'd design that switch. Oh, and while I was at it, I'd make a switch to kill all the electronics, one that would immediately pause the kids' games whenever I spoke, so I wouldn't have to repeat myself or watch my words fall on deaf ears. I think if they knew their games would stop after every word, they'd be more inclined to listen and take it in the first time. It would change the humanity of teenagers. The relief, eliminating so many unnecessary arguments.'

She felt happy, warm and comforted, for a moment believing that alternative reality actually existed; but what was the point in dreaming the impossible?

'And what about for you, Julie? Leaving your family to one side, what would you, personally, like from your magic wand?'

Quick, think of something, anything. Just got to get through these questions. What does she want to hear?

'I'd like more me-time', Julie explained, watching for Kate's response and feeling relieved that she received another nod of encouragement. 'I love watching movies, so maybe I'd go to the cinema more? Exercise and lose weight but without having to stop eating all the bad food I love. I'd spend more time with friends, have a job that made me feel I was worth something more than being a slave to my family.' She paused, wondering how much to share, then continued. 'I'd feel more confident and less anxious all the time. I live in constant fear, and I don't want to pass that on to my boys.'

'Let's discuss some life hacks. You need to make plans so there's clear time set aside for you every day. Maybe start while the kids are at school. That way, there are less distractions vying for your attention. If you want to include exercise, try chatting to some of your friends or speak to the mums after school drop-off, try to incorporate a short walk around the block before you all set off home. You'll avoid the school-run traffic and you'll likely still get home at the same time. I call it "Walk and Talk Therapy."'

Julie smiled politely back at the woman.

'Can you think of any other parents you could approach to do this with? Or any friends that might work shifts who could meet you for a quick stroll? The most important thing is to do it while you're already out. Much easier to be motivated when you're not cosy at home with a million jobs staring back at you! Don't go home and think you'll arrange it once you're back because chances are, you won't. A good friend of mine used to have a great saying: When you're out, you're out! I think it's a great rule to remember in so many situations.'

'Sounds great.' Julie nodded.

'Moving on to your free time... Maybe try and structure your day. List the essential things that have to be done. Lists are great! Enjoy ticking off each thing as you achieve it. I'm assuming every day, you need to tidy or clean the house, buy and prepare dinner and get through a fair bit of washing, so write yourself a timetable for the week. Rome wasn't built in a day, but some of it was. So, a weekly timetable – pencil in walks, meetings with friends, a cinema trip, date night and, of course, household chores if you need to. That would be a great place to start.'

Julie knew all this, but it was nice to hear someone else say it. 'I think the problem isn't that I don't have the time, it's more that my focus has always been on the family. It's family first for everything, but I do think, now they're getting older, maybe I could sneak in a little bit of me-time, then get the chores done when they're home from school. Maybe they might even offer to help if they see me doing them.' Julie felt excited at the thought of her new life. 'Maybe I could start writing film reviews at the cinema?'

'That's a great idea! It's good to hear you setting positive goals and thinking through how you can find ways to incorporate them into your life. Try to apply this to your time with your husband too. It helps to set a date night that's all about you two. You don't necessarily have to go out anywhere if you don't have a budget, just think about what you enjoy doing together and try to plan one night a week you can go back to that.'

The session went on, Kate offering up lots of positive ideas for Julie to try out. After their time was over, she reached forward to shake Kate's hand and slipped her coat on as she walked to the door, thinking about her advice, a lot of maybes. The only thing Julie was struggling with was a way to reconnect with Dan.

We used to listen to music and chat for hours, but I just don't think we've got much to say to each other anymore.

Chapter Eight

I'm going for it. This is the new me! I'm going to put myself out there.

Get on with it. Now. Just do it.

There's nobody home, nobody to tell me what to do.

I'm an adult.

I make the decisions for me.

Be a powerful woman, Julie. Take self-ownership. Put down those dirty dishes and walk away. Hell yeah! Smash them to the floor if you feel like it.

Yes, I will.

You are strong. You are powerful. You are loved.

She'd tried all the self-help mantras, but they weren't soaking in. Sarah doubtless followed one. She seemed the type. She probably looked in the mirror and complimented herself every day like the self-help books recommended. But mirrors told lies. In Julie's case, she would need more than a minute on her 'makeup' if she was going to follow that advice. How did those young girls on social media get it so right? When Julie put eyeliner on, it was a case of either having a gap between her eyelashes and the line, or a jagged edge.

I think the skin on my eyes is just trying to give up and die. Either that, or droopy eyelids, which no amount of holding back whilst applying is going to help. I am definitely not the right candidate for smoky eyes. Even those pretty cat-flicks at the edges ended up looking like crow's feet in the wrong place. The remedy? Apply more black until she looked like she had a bruise, and hope the lights would be dimmed at her destination.

Today's destination was the cinema. Julie had made a plan, found a sparkly pen and written a list of lists. First, to drop Tommy off at school and try to persuade one of the parents to go for a "Walk and Talk". Hopefully, it would tie in nicely with a cinema trip if she could persuade them to walk with her long enough and maybe abandon them when she got there – or would that be wrong? Would they want to go with her to see a movie? That could work.

So, school, walk, cinema, coffee shop to write my film review, then school, home, housework. Power through the washing while checking on the slow cooker to make sure dinner's ready for five p.m. Then, Dan.

It was all doable; it was written in pen.

Dan had laughed when she'd told him she was planning to write film reviews for her new career. 'That's not a job! It's a hobby, if that. Anyway, you'll never make it work – you don't have the commitment, and where are you going to get the money to pay for the cinema tickets? You'll need to get a job to pay for your job!' Of course, he had to bring the conversation back to his job. A *proper* job. And the fact that he didn't give her a *personal* allowance, only one for the housekeeping and kids. Dan had all the control, and didn't he know it.

By trade, Dan was an engineer, but in reality, he sat at a desk all day talking to people who were facing unemployment. Julie felt he wasn't selling himself accurately when he spoke of it. Kate would have pulled him up on it, but Julie didn't have the courage, not yet.

He would come home and rant about how ungrateful people were when they were offered severance pay and that none of them deserved it as they were all idle, unqualified layabouts. He was supposed to be in HR, encouraging them, sympathising, offering advice for the future on how they could move on, but they had picked the wrong person if they thought that was ever going to happen.

He doesn't even listen to me, she thought, *I doubt he's much better there.*

No matter how unqualified he was for the role, Julie hoped daily that he'd keep hold of his job. She couldn't handle him at home with her all day and doubted he'd be snapped up by head-hunters for a new position if a work appraisal showed his achievements – or lack of. How had she not known him better before diving into marriage? Her parents were to blame. Somebody else was always to blame, but this time Julie was going to fight for her place, and if she didn't succeed, she would have no one to blame but herself.

Dilemma number one: How to sort out payment for the movie. Dan was right – she didn't have enough money, especially now she'd already paid out for the first life coaching session...and was looking forward to another. She wondered if he'd notice a direct debit from the joint account. Did he check it? She didn't know where to start but figured it would all be self-explanatory on his laptop. She'd used lots of computers in her previous job, so how hard could it be?

Opening Dan's laptop, she found Santander saved as a shortcut. *Cheers, Dan*. Julie clicked on the image, entered Dan's email into the username box and the cat's name into the password box, followed by his date of birth. He'd never been secretive, and for that, she was grateful.

With a tap, she was in. *Gas, mortgage, council tax, National Rail, boring, boring, boring.* There was a long list of outgoings but still a healthy sum in the account, so why was he so tight? She wished they'd kept individual accounts, but when he'd suggested they set up a joint account back when they married, it seemed so romantic. Seeing their names, *Mr & Mrs Summers.* She'd been carried away in the love-story and was still paying the price years later. She knew in later life having children would affect her career, but hadn't taken into account her loss of independence when that happened – when her income stopped and with it her allowance for all things fun died.

What's Booking.com? She thought, opening a second window on the laptop and quickly searching the web; the URL came up as a hotel bookings site. *Ooh, exciting! Are we going on holiday?* She decided to have a proper look after the cinema – if she got back before the kids finished school.

Julie quickly set up the cinema payment, referenced 'therapy' and logged out. If Dan saw that on the bank statement, he'd be more inclined to let her keep it. He'd probably wind her up about it, the number of times he'd shouted she needed to sort her head out.

'Mum, are you ready? Have the school gates opened? My toothpaste is finished! Where did you put my shoes?'

'Okay, Tommy, I'll be there in two minutes!'

Family time now, me-time later.

Chapter Nine

'Don't slam the door, Tommy! Do you know how much it costs? It's about one thousand pounds to replace that door. You'll be paying it off forever out of your pocket money if you break it!'

'It wasn't me, it was the wind,' he responded with a smirk.

'Where's your book bag? Oh, for goodness' sake!' Julie put the key in the door and reached around for the bag, spotting Tommy's coat at the same time, also forgotten.

'Carry this.'

'No, I don't want to.'

He was so stubborn, and Julie didn't have it in her to start an argument first thing in the morning. It was easier to give in. Bad parenting, but who was judging her? *Sometimes, you've just got to get through the day*, she told herself as they got into the car. She put Tommy's seatbelt on while berating herself for not teaching him, but she was too anxious to trust him when the seatbelt was a matter of life or death.

Julie reversed out of the drive into ongoing traffic. *Be bold,*

Julie. Today is the first day of the rest of your life, but try not to kill yourselves doing it. Arriving at the school, she edged along at a snail's pace, praying to the parking angel a space would be available. And there it was. Great – she could leave the car safe, have a walk and not have to deal with Tommy moaning about walking home after school.

Today's shaping up to be a good day, she thought as she kissed him goodbye and looked around for any straggling parents. How should she approach them? She could feel her breath getting shallow, pounding, pulsing, the panic setting in. The sky was crisp-blue, not a mark on it, with the exception of the moon's faded reflection still showing through from the night before.

In the distance, there was one mother she recognised – Peter's mum. Julie never learned the parents' names. Her legs felt heavy, and her trainers caught on the uneven path as she started to approach, *How do I ask her?* She felt like a teenager with a crush, unable to make the first move despite her gaggle of friends egging her on. Except this time, she didn't have anybody to push her, only her mind and Kate's words.

'Good morning,' she mumbled under her breath. The standard greeting. Would that be enough, or should she jump straight in? What if the mum said yes and actually wanted to walk? What would they talk about? How would they communicate? Would they have anything in common? What if she only said yes because she felt sorry for her? *Right, it's now or never.* She lifted the sides of her mouth in a grimace and went in for the greeting.

'Good—'

'Hi, good morning! How are you? Haven't spoken in ages! Breakfast?'

'Oh, great, yes!' Julie responded enthusiastically, noticing too late that Peter's mum was wearing an earpiece and not directing the conversation at her. Blood flushed to her cheeks in a hot gush of tingles as she quickly walked by, hoping her faux pas would pass unseen.

Rome wasn't built in a day, she reminded herself. *Next step, the cinema.*

As she rushed off, she wondered how long it would take to walk to the cinema. She couldn't gauge the time based on her kids' dawdling pace but guessed half an hour with them meant fifteen minutes on her own. They moaned whenever she suggested going anywhere. All they ever wanted to do was spend time at home, doors shut, PlayStation on.

Cold and numb, repeatedly smacked in the face by the autumn breeze, Julie raised her head slowly, willing herself to look up. *Things are going to get better. Smile. Embrace the future.* She looked around, took in the seasonal changes, delighted at the leaves that fell like soft rain. Her legs felt awkward and sluggish, but she was slowly nearing her destination – they were doing their job. She willed them forward, one little step at a time.

Julie renewed her stride, feeling more positive, smiling at the innocence of a squirrel running down a tree, going from conker to conker on the floor. The outer shell was prickly and confusing, with no promise of the condition of the treasure inside, but the squirrel was content regardless. He was building for his future. She'd always thought they only wanted acorns, but this particular squirrel seemed to be embracing change. The breeze pushed her onwards until she finally reached the huge cinema complex.

'Hi, can I have one ticket to whatever is starting in the next ten minutes, please?' she asked the heavily bearded child behind the counter.

'It's two for one today – do you want a second ticket?'

Julia couldn't help but look from side to side, though she thought better of a full pirouette. 'Nope, it's just me.' *I am brave, I am strong, I am woman*, she repeated in her head, feeling liberated. She bravely approached the counter, instead of opting for the no-need-for-human-contact-or-humiliation self-serve machine.

'Okay, ma'am. Where do you want to sit?' He flipped the screen around and showed her the cinema layout.

Julie stared back irritated, wondering when she had become a ma'am.

'The ones that are grey are already booked, so you can choose any other,' he went on obliviously.

Julie noted a lot of the pre-booked seats were in twos, taking advantage of today's offer. She imagined couples enjoying a sneaky day off work together; that would never be her and Dan. Pointing to the back row, she picked the most central seat for the optimum experience.

The guy held out the card reader, and she scanned her card. Rejected. *How embarrassing.* She couldn't see why the joint account would have bounced, it had money. Perhaps Dan had put a stop on her card, but how could she broach that subject? He was far too sensitive. She rummaged around in her pocket for some cash, hoping that next time, her direct debit would have kicked in, and she could use a pre-paid membership card and not have this worry. If she mentioned the payment issues, Dan might check the bank account and find the new direct debits. It wasn't worth the risk.

The movie ticket read 'Unbroken' and was rated fifteen. She hoped it wouldn't be scary. There was nothing worse than watching a horror on your own.

'Would you like any refreshments with that?' the man-child asked, but she was already walking away, rude but oblivious to her surroundings, preparing herself mentally for a toilet trip.

It was the first time Julie had been to the cinema on her own. She walked through, showing her ticket and headed for the toilets. She put her hand on the door and pushed firmly... just as a woman came through it from the other side. It made her jump, both fumbled their apologies and they began the polite silent dance of left to right, to left, to right... *Oh, forget this*, she thought, then turned around and walked away. She didn't have the patience, *let's see if my bladder can hold it for once,* she thought striding off more confidently than she felt.

Screen five was the furthest down the long corridor. Seeing the lights flickering on each side as she walked reminded Julie of a futuristic movie, the carpet changing into a brightly lit dance floor. *Step on the cracks, and you'll fall into another dimension...*

The cinema door was heavy. There was a bin right outside – not holding it open, only blocking the path for would-be viewers. She squeezed around it and smiled, thankful to see the lights were still on inside and the adverts hadn't yet started. *Note to self: Always come early to the cinema before the lights go down.* There were a few people seated already, chatting and eating popcorn. She wondered what they would think of her, a loner? Friendless? Jobless? Likely all of the above. She could feel their eyes staring and hear their laughter. Were they laughing at her?

Just walk on by. Head up, Julie, back row. Looking down, she noted the letters were going up, and she must have accidentally booked the front row. *Be rebellious, go wild! Break the rules, go for it, walk past your seat and sit wherever you like.* Sitting at the front was just asking for neck ache or eye strain. She wasn't thirty anymore. The voice in her head was tempting – a voice she wasn't used to hearing.

Kate's words came to mind: *It's time to focus on you. Make the choices that will make you most happy. It's your life, and you deserve it.* She didn't think the advice applied to cinema seating, but what the hell?

The lights started to dim as she reached the central seat. From this viewpoint, Julie could take full advantage of the cinema surround sound system and high-definition screens while also having a panoramic view of her surroundings. Nobody would be creeping up behind her, she hoped, although there were plenty of empty seats back there.

Was this a mistake? She felt a bit antsy looking at her watch. *Twenty minutes of adverts! Seriously?* At this rate, she would be finishing too late for school pick-up. She regretted not bringing the car, but her inner voice said, *Exercise, you can run the school run.* Yeah, great. Turn up sweating and shaky – nothing new there.

The movie finally started, and the sound was ear-splitting. *Maybe it's because it's a fifteen?* She didn't remember it being so loud when she took the kids, but then again, she didn't really watch the movies when she went with them. Cinema trips with kids was more about handing out the next snack, anything to fill their noisy mouths when the supply of sweets dried up.

Oh, God. Only thirty minutes in, she uncrossed her legs and crossed them over the other way, hoping it would make her more comfortable and take the pressure off her bladder. *Maybe the trainers should come off too?* She took them off in the dark and lifted her feet onto the headrest in front, realising opting for no socks had been a mistake. She wondered if anybody else was within sniffing range, but wasn't going to look about her and make it obvious she was the perpetrator.

Julie got out her notepad and pen. She hadn't really thought this through – making notes would mean looking away from the screen and potentially missing the 'good bits'. The sound was so loud that every noise made her jump. It was such a dark movie, both in lighting and subject matter. She wished she had researched beforehand so she knew what to expect. *Another reminder-to-self for next time!*

The cinema was silent. It had filled up quite a lot, and there were lots of women in there with her, mostly in pairs, and one man sitting on his own. Another loner like her. She hoped he wouldn't think she was fair game and come sit with her. It was an odd feeling, being on your own in the cinema. It felt wrong yet deliciously right, naughty and self-indulgent. She pulled her coat firmly around her and zipped it up, keeping cosy in her gloves and hat. It was an odd mishmash when partnered with bare feet, but it made her feel comfortable; comforted.

On the big screen, the woman started to strip off and prance about the house. It was night-time, and she put her music on and swayed in the dim candlelight. *No! Why would you? Don't do it! Swigging from a bottle of vodka in the dark, alone in your own house – who does that? Get a glass, dear!* The woman flounced into the bedroom and picked up some tablets from the bedside cabinet, topless now, wearing only a peach thong. *Sleeping pills, perhaps*, Julie wondered, more interested in the dangerous position she was getting herself into than the titillation of the actress being half-naked. She cringed. Those candles were precariously close to the beautiful negligee the woman had so thoughtlessly discarded.

The bedroom was in darkness despite the candles, yet they gave out more than the expected amount of light. *It just isn't realistic*, Julie was glad to report. *In reality, there's a film crew in there with a fuck-off light attached to the top of the video camera.* If it was real life, the room would have been much darker. *Unless she has very fine curtains,* Julie mused, *in which case, she'd likely be waking up at dawn...* Or maybe not, with the combination of drugs and alcohol she'd consumed. Had she opted for Temazepam or Loprazolam or perhaps Nitrazepam, that's what Julie would have chosen, perhaps with a little Lormetazepam thrown in if she could get her hands on it.

Overthinking it, Julie, she told herself as she wriggled in her seat once more, her bladder now straining for release. *It's a movie. Just make a note of the things that don't quite work and include them in your film review.* She started scribbling down in the dark, then jumped as a crash came from behind, the surround sound system making the most of the moment. She looked up to see smashing glass as a hand reached through the front door and turned the doorknob. *Make it easy why don't you! Where's the double lock? The bolt? The latch?*

The cloaked intruder was now in the apartment. He walked slowly towards the bedroom and laughed – a low, deep-throated sound – as he reached the vulnerable sleeping beauty. He started to pull off her remaining clothing and lower himself onto her. *The bedroom scene.* Julie rolled her eyes at the absurdity of it. All Julie could think about was her bladder.

She finally understood the phrase, 'Lost the plot.' She had

no idea what was going on but an overwhelming anger at the stupid woman for making herself so vulnerable. She deserved it. Julie would never put herself in that position. She was prepared, always prepared. Never lower your guard. Maybe the flames would still take hold, engulf them both in the room, put an end to her torture?

Good luck, lady. I hope you're okay when I get back!

She quickly tied her trainers and got up. Nobody sat behind to complain about her blocking the view, though on her way out, she had to apologise to a few people in her row as she crunched popcorn underfoot. She took the stairs two at a time down to the exit, making a fist with both hands in case she needed to retaliate against any attacker. She ran down the corridor and with one brave, strong push, burst into the toilets.

Silence.

It was eerie. So many of the doors read 'occupied' but were slightly ajar. She hated that – and the silence. Needing to be sure there was nobody lurking, she began to push open each door along the row.

One, two, three...

One, two, three...

She pushed each one as fast as possible, holding her breath. They all swung open to reveal an empty cubicle and gave her a fresh burst of relief. Behind the next door and the next, there were no feet, and when she did her usual sideways glance up and down the row, Julie seemed to be alone. She was getting pretty desperate for the toilet. Cursing the ridiculous obsessive habit she'd developed over the years, she pushed open the final door with as much strength as she could muster, adrenaline rushing through her veins.

Then, it happened.

Something barring the door, stopping her from checking, preventing the all clear, something there, hiding in the shadows, waiting to pounce, to devour her.

Oh God help me! Deliver me from this evil, give me the strength to defend myself against the darkness within.

With all her might Julie pounded against the door, willing the evil to stay in confinement, chanting to herself over and over, her mind screaming 'No!'

She would not give in.

Chapter Ten

As she pushed, the door swung backwards like a knock-out punch. There was a loud bump, and as she peered around cautiously, she saw a dark shadow in the back of the cubicle.

Julie banged the door open again, a cry spilling out through gritted teeth, the resulting smash a cracking sound. The figure kept coming, this time covered in blood and moving towards her.

Help me! Is it dead? Must kill it, stop the attack, defend myself. Fight back, come on, be strong, it's not your time to die.

Fight-or-flight, Julie's heart pounded as she continued to smash the door back and forth into the encroaching abomination. She wasn't ready to meet with death. Decades of fear and frustration at her own anxiety flowed out with every bang of her fist against the wood. She imagined bones splintering and cracking, wet blood splattering up the walls, ruining the paintwork. No human sound came out, just that of an animal gurgling blood, and the crunch of snapping sticks.

And then, a whoosh as it fell.

Had she won?

She waited as the seconds passed, then slowly opened the door – her weapon – to peer inside. The bloody monster she'd imagined gave way to an image of unexpected calm. The figure was slumped over the toilet, unmoving. At peace in its serenity. She'd expected blood, lots and lots of it, but surprisingly, there was very little on the body. P*erhaps it was the angle she'd collapsed*, her face covered, hair stuck to her head stemming the blood flow. Julie blinked and tried to make sense of the scene. There were clear splatters across the wall, a substantial amount of blood and… *what was that, skin?* Drip-dripping down the back of the toilet and into the bowl where her head rested.

How convenient. She watched as tiny droplets formed on the walls. Tiny blood blisters, racing each other down but somehow disappearing before they reached the floor. Tiny pockets of joy, relief, escapism, taking Julie back to her childhood.

She smiled, remembering the games she would play in the car with her sister when they were little. *Before.* Her rain stream, her tiny droplet, always seemed to collide with another and then take off on a different path, impossible to follow to the bottom of the window. Claire, oh how she missed her. Where was she now? Staring at liquid droplets drip-drip-dripping too?

They'd parted ways the day her father died, and she hadn't the strength to argue. Julie had tried her best to mother her when their own mother had walked out, but she was just a girl herself, struggling with her own survival. Julie's relationship with Albert had become worse than ever, his anger and verbal abuse transferring onto her in the absence of his wife. Thoughts of ending her own life were forever teasing her, offering relief from the hell she had to put up with. All she could think about was escape, so when Dan came onto the scene, she threw herself towards him and out the door.

That was then, powerless, leaving one hell for another. No control. No confidence. No way out... Julie focused once more on the scene in front of her now, the ringing silence of the moment. *This is freedom.*

She looked at the woman slumped over the toilet seat in front of her, the beautiful serenity. The blood against the white wall was so dark she wanted to touch it, smear it over her cheeks, beat her chest like an Amazonian warrior queen – the victor – in celebration.

I did that. I protected myself. I won. She looked at the carnage she had created and smiled. *Survival of the fittest.*

Julie willed her eyes to take in the full scene, a mental photograph of the exquisite purity. A ritual cleansing, the ease with which a life could be taken away in an instant.

The movie was progressing without her – Julie would need to hurry back. But how to contain the moment, freeze it still inside the cubicle? She pulled out a coin she had been turning over and over in her coat pocket and thought back to the times when her kids locked themselves in cubicles accidentally. Cries of, 'Help, help!' A panicked child; a panicked mother unable to get under or over the door to set the child free.

It would be simple to wedge the coin inside the screw of the lock and twist it halfway. Putting her foot under the door, Julie pulled it closed. No hands, no fingerprints. She still had her gloves on as she fiddled with the coin, changing the sign to occupied.

Simple. Done.

The urge to release her bladder had subsided. Very odd. *Maybe a mental issue rather than a physical need*, she considered blaming the children – their birth, their very existence – for the irritating need to pee.

As she walked down the row, she looked back at the closed door. White, clinical. These things didn't happen.

Was it all a dream?

At the mirror, Julie marvelled at her flushed cheeks. Perhaps she was warm from keeping her hat on indoors to tuck away all that frizzy hair? She would have to book an appointment to sort it out – maybe the straightening treatment Rachel was always banging on about. What was it called again? She couldn't quite remember.

She wondered what the woman was up to in the movie as she walked casually down the strobe lit walkway, back to screen five. The intruder had a knife in his head and was lying on the floor, no sign of the previously sleeping woman. *Was it a trap?* She would have to really focus now to work out what was going on. She took off her trainers and sat back again, crossing her ankles over the seat in front. With a small smile, she thought, *Brazilian blow-dry!*

Julie was totally immersed in the movie and before she knew it, the lights were coming on, and people were getting up, thoughtlessly leaving their rubbish behind. It would be so easy to grab it on the way out knowing there was a bin blocking the exit anyway.

Sixteen, eighteen, twenty...

She lost count. So many people left the screen she hadn't noticed were even there. She was usually so diligent at surveying her surroundings and possible threats. Julie joined the trail and followed them out, taking note most of the women were snaking their way in the direction of the toilets. A few men hung around outside, mobiles in hand.

Nobody had closed off the toilets? Very odd. There was a queue forming outside, and Julie tagged onto the end in curiosity. Had she dozed through the movie and dreamt the whole thing? Putting her hand in her pocket she felt for the coin, it was still there. That doesn't confirm anything really.

The toilets were still very much in action with a one in/one out routine working as per usual, slower perhaps because Julie was feeling impatient. She couldn't understand why she felt no fear or remorse, no panic or anxiety as per her usual day-to-day activities. Her mind told her she should, but her body felt enlightened. Had it not been for the school run threatening her as the seconds ticked by, she would have happily waited more patiently.

A group of ladies stood chatting in front of her, talking at such a rate, so enthused by the movie they were all speaking over each other.

'Yeah, that was so obvious!'

'I don't think she should have gone over.'

'So predictable!'

'The acting was brilliant.'

'Really? I thought it was self-indulgent.'

Blah, blah, blah and more of the same, Julie thought. It wasn't exactly a cinematic masterpiece in her opinion. She should write that down.

'God, how long are these fucking queues?' said a short woman dressed in what could only be described as glitzy party-wear. *Not very Wednesday afternoon*, Julie thought. She hoped the outfit wasn't going to be wasted on a cinema trip with girl-friends and that she'd be going on to somewhere more appro-priate afterwards – at the very least, selling her body outside on the street (she looked the part). She didn't stop moaning, her voice whiny through the din of her group. 'Why do people take so long? I'm literally going to piss myself! I'm going to use the sink in a minute if this lot don't hurry up!'

Julie finally rounded the corner and gave the position of door prop to the woman behind, taking pleasure in moving for-ward and hearing it thump. Her eyes went straight to the end cubicle. The door was shut, the 'occupied' sign shining back at her. She felt excited, waiting for it to open – more excited at the thought it would stay shut. They wouldn't have cleared the body away already and if they had, they would be cleaning up? She pinched her cheeks to check she was still awake, ignoring the frowns from the woman queuing behind.

'Get off your phones, ladies, or I'm going to start kicking those doors in!' Ms. Glitzy stepped out of line towards the cubi-cles and began to pummel her fists on each door, making them shake precariously on their hinges. Julie held her breath as one of the doors flew open. Thankfully, it looked like the occupant was a time-waster and hadn't been caught with her knickers down. *Or her head smashed in, bleeding out into the toilet bowl.*

At Ms. Glitzy's raucous outburst, a number of chains

flushed, and two other women came filtering out, zipping up their bags, angry scowls on their silent mouths as they shared their irritation without the bravery to confront their aggressors. The vacant toilets soon filled, and a fresh gaggle of ladies moved to the front of the queue, quickly forgetting about the end toilet that had not opened.

Relief? The end lock held tight. Disappointment, her dream not yet a confirmed reality. Julie embraced the conflicting emotions flooding through her body, equally frightful and delicious, making her skin prickle and her taste buds tingle. She opened and closed her mouth a few times, swallowing the excess saliva, flicking her tongue to a metallic taste. The lady behind her was staring blindly past, focussing on the closed doors.

Julie's time came, and she walked into a cubicle, calmly sat and urinated. Such a relief – she'd forgotten she hadn't been earlier. Looking at her watch again, she noted the time. There was still half an hour before school pick-up, so she'd have a brisk walk back.

Her pulse flashed up on the Fitbit with sparkles moving around it. 'New low,' it read. She looked forward to going through the app later and seeing how it had fluctuated throughout the day – if at all. Flushing the toilet was a trial, so she just tore off extra toilet paper to cover what she was leaving behind and exited. She thought about apologising to the next person in line, a stranger she would never remember, someone unlikely to feature in her life again. Instead, she spent time trying the soaps, washing her hands and then drying them thoroughly, enjoying watching a little kid cry and make a fuss about the hand dryer. *What doesn't kill them makes them stronger*, she thought, giving them an extra few seconds just for fun.

Exiting the bathroom, Julie took the stairs out of the cinema and breathed in the fresh air. The trees looked beautiful swaying in the breeze, the smell of crisp autumn and the promise of cosy winter nights drawing in. She cuddled herself in her warm coat and gloves and smiled. Her new job had begun.

Julie realised she had not felt anxious using the public restrooms for the first time in as long as she could remember. *Conquer your fears*, she recalled Kate's words – then doubled over and vomited.

Nobody stopped; nobody noticed. She felt cleansed, a renewed power in her step as she walked onwards, head held high.

Chapter Eleven

That day at pick-up, Tommy came out of class timidly, face down and silent. Usually, he'd throw his lunch box in the air as soon as he spotted her, and if she wasn't on guard, it would end up hitting her in the face. But today, nothing. He held on tight, pulling at Julie to move away.

Then, his teacher's voice. 'Mrs. Summers, could you wait behind please so I can talk to you?'

Oh, great. What's he done now, and why is it, no matter what age you are, teachers manage to make you feel like a naughty child? If Tommy had done something wrong, why should Julie get the brunt of it? *Discipline him and move on.*

Usually, she would feel intimidated, but today, Julie couldn't help but stare the teacher up and down. Seriously, what was she wearing? Heels and leggings? She looked young enough be in school herself. When had teachers become so young? Was she trying to assert herself, strutting around like a peacock? Did it make her feel more powerful to wear that amount of makeup? Julie would give it a go. She felt Tommy squirm next to her and wondered what he had done. No child had left with obvious bruises or broken bones, and no other parent had come up shouting the odds, so what could it be? Had he forgotten to write in the cursive, frilly, joined-up, illegible writing they all insisted on? Or perhaps he'd jumped ahead in maths and learned an alternative style of working out his long division?

'Mrs. Summers, thank you for waiting. I'm afraid we had to put Tommy in time-out today.' She looked down at him. 'Tommy, would you like to tell your mother what you were doing in school?'

Tommy looked at the floor, his eyes welling with tears and lip trembling. Surely, she could see he wasn't likely to respond? *Just spit it out so we can all go home*, she thought.

The teacher crouched down to Tommy's eye level and waited for him to lift his face before speaking. 'I'm afraid you were swearing in school, weren't you, Tommy?'

Seriously? Okay, how do I respond to this one? Hmm... Julie took a deep breath and tried not to smile. 'Oh! I'm surprised. He never swears at home! What did he say?'

The teacher slowly stood to face Julie head-on, pausing for effect like some evil nanny in a lame kid's horror movie, then, eye-to-eye, spelled out in a slow, precise manner, 'Penis.'

It took a while for Julie to put the word together because of the length of the teacher's pauses between each letter, but when she did, Julie let a snort of laughter. *Is that really a swear word or is it a body part?* The teacher's face held deadly serious, and Julie felt the required response would be for her to look shocked and offer to reprimand him when she got home. She just couldn't be bothered with all that shit today. *Life's too short! So what if he said fucking bollocks? He's a kid!*

'I believe you're mistaken in thinking that's a swear word. Perhaps a lesson is needed in class to help all the children accurately name their body parts if that was reported by another child as inappropriate language.' With that, she grabbed Tommy's hand and turned to leave, not waiting for a response. She had no doubt he'd been using the word inappropriately, but what the hell? *You only live once.* 'Don't worry, darling, you've done nothing wrong. The teacher made a mistake.'

Tommy's eyes were wide, the teacher dumbstruck, as Julie smiled and led him away.

'Fancy an ice-cream, Tommy?' she asked.

His big smile was reward enough.

I am strong, I am brave, I am powerful, she repeated the mantra in her head as they walked away. A few steps from the school, she bent down to Tommy to give him a hug, wanting him to know, repeating the same to him. 'You are strong, you are brave, you are powerful, and you are loved.' She squeezed him, and he tried to shrug her off.

'Mum, get off me! You're squeezing me to death!'

Oh, seriously, child? Forget it then.

Back at the house, Julie noticed her older boys had beat them home. It had taken her and Tommy a while to finish their ice-creams, and the ridiculous interlude with Tommy's teacher had held them back later than usual. Thankfully they had the car waiting for them round the corner, but she didn't dare eat the ice-creams inside. Dan would be mad if he found out and she couldn't trust Tommy to keep a secret. If it had been Jack, now that's a different matter. He was reliable when it came to deception.

'Hi, guys! Did you have a good day? Jack? William?' Julie

shouted. 'Come down, get some snacks! Who wants what for dinner?' She knew how to get their attention.

The boys came running downstairs, taking advantage of Mum's good mood.

'Snacks? Before dinner? Is this a trick?' asked Jack.

Tommy went running off, stripping his shoes, bag, then coat en route to the goodies cupboard in the kitchen.

'I think we need to be a bit more relaxed after school, chill out a bit. Life is only shit if you make it shit.'

'Why are you swearing?' Jack asked concerned. 'What's going on? Are you and dad getting a divorce?'

Julie hesitated a bit too long, wondering why he'd thought that, why the notion had never entered her head, yet dripped off the tongue of her son as if it was inevitable. For a moment she felt chilled, had Dan said something? Implied it even? He was much closer to the older boys than her, she couldn't help but feel jealous but couldn't do much about it as Tommy took up so much of her time.

She looked at Jack and William, both waiting expectantly.

'Of course not, darling. Why would you think that?'

'You're acting odd,' Jack mumbled, losing interest and following Tommy off to find the crisps.

William seized on the opportunity. 'Did you ask us what *we* want for dinner?' Taking her nod for affirmation, 'In that case, I would like pizza!' He knew the others didn't like it, so that would mean Mum making more than one dinner, which she swore she never would. *I'm making one meal for everyone, and if you don't like it, you can go hungry*. The daily repetition was grating, but tonight was different.

'Yes, of course. What about you, Jack – what would you like?'

They both stared back sceptically.

'Anything I can eat in my bedroom!' he replied.

Rules were made to be broken.

Mum smiled back. 'Go and play on your electronics. I'll shout you when it's ready. Life doesn't have to be a constant argument, you know?' She smiled at their backs as they galloped off upstairs.

Julie walked over to the sofa and slumped down next to Tommy, watching him on the iPad. She relaxed, knowing she would only have to throw some oven food in a bit later, and the kids would be happy to wait since they had free reign until then.

'Look at the world I'm building on Minecraft, Mum.'

'Okay, Tommy, show me.' She smiled back, cuddling up close. Julie was sick of always saying no to the kids. She wanted to enjoy them while they were still little. How had Tommy got to seven so quickly? She leaned over to ruffle his hair and kiss him on the head, remembering him as a baby and how soft that hair had been.

My babies are growing up, and I'm going to embrace every moment, she thought. *And as for Dan? Well, if he doesn't like my new way of life, I'll be happy to oblige with that divorce.*

Chapter Twelve

'Hi Julie, take a seat.' Kate gestured to the sofa, and Julie started plumping the cushions before getting settled.

'So, how are you?'

Julie smiled back, crossed and uncrossed her legs. She looked over at Kate, tried to mirror her body language – so relaxed yet in command, leaning back in her chair. It made her think of super-nanny shows on TV, the techniques for speaking to a child to get them to respond in the right way. It all seemed like a pretence. She thought through Kate's question and what answer she should give. *Pretty fantastic, actually! Proper chilled out, rejuvenated, full of adrenaline and rearing to go! No fucker is going to mess with me, or they'll get their bloody head bashed in!*

Did she say that out loud? She looked over for Kate's response and saw her fixed smile, unflinching body.

'I'm fine. How are you, Kate?'

'Okay, let's think about progress since our last session. We ended with some goal-setting, and I wanted to find out if you ticked off any of those targets. I know it's only been a week, but I want you to set lots of small goals so you can frequently reward yourself. So, have you done anything for yourself this week, no matter how small? It all counts!'

'Well, I've spent more time with my kids, I've spent more time on myself. I've started writing film reviews and uploading them to the internet, and I'm walking back and forth to the cinema for exercise. Sorry, am I talking too fast?'

'Not at all! This is all great stuff. Well done! Please, continue.'

'The fresh air is invigorating, and it gives me a real rush to do things for me for a change. It's surprising how much time I actually have now I've started to plan things in.' *And I'm not feeling anxious or scared of every moving thing.* 'I'm feeling much more confident because I've stopped caring what people think. I mean, what's the worst that could happen?' She thought back to the cinema. *I could start murdering people and feel no remorse? Even find I enjoy it?*

Kate had moved on already. 'Exactly,' she said enthusiastically. 'We all make mistakes – that's just part of being human. You need to keep trying new things and see what you enjoy most.'

Julie was surprised Kate hadn't picked up on her comments. She was still smiling – madness! Her assessment and advice seemed uncanny, as if she could hear Julie's thoughts and was in agreement that the attack was...what, a rite of passage?

Julie looked around the room, not sure what to say next, hoping Kate would fill the silence. There was a huge oak coat stand next to the door – one coat, one umbrella slightly open with raindrops still visible. *Kate's.* What was her life like? There were no family pictures as Julie glanced around the room. It felt stagnant, clinical, impotent. Julie wasn't used to being in an office space and wondered if they were all like this or whether it was purely a reflection of Kate's personality. If it was, how was she qualified to dish out life advice to others? Was she working this job because she was unhappy in her own life? Did the life coach need a life coach?

She stared at the umbrella, willing it to open indoors, wondering if it would bring bad luck to them both or just to Kate. It hadn't rained since about six a.m. that morning – was that when Kate had reached work? Julie wanted to welcome the unlucky omens into the room, ready to try her luck against everything and anything. She wondered how it would smell: damp, stale, like decay? Was that the smell of decomposing flesh? Was that how the cinema would smell now, if she were to revisit the scene of the incident?

Kate's desk was positioned in front of the window, her back towards it as she sat, light gleaming through her blonde hair. It made her look ethereal, ghostly yet not scary, a golden aura surrounding her. She didn't seem concerned about the F*eng Shui* of the room's layout, or the door to the left behind her, which anybody could walk through without her knowledge. She hadn't got it right with the window either. Yay for natural light, but at this angle, it would be streaming itself all over her computer screen – if she ever used one. And if not, why have the desk at all? Did Kate invite clients in here for other purposes? Throw herself across the desk, an offering, as alternative therapy? Julie would love to know what was going on in Kate's world. There were no other chairs in the room, so it was a case of sit at the desk, stand, or try to cosy up on the sofa with her clients. Julie wondered how often that had happened. How many people tried to get out of paying cash by offering payment-in-kind as an alternative? Poor, disturbed suckers.

She looked around at the white walls. They made her feel uncomfortable. Julie started to question whether they were simply white when they could be a host of other colours: "Chantilly Lace", "Snow Day", "Cloud White", "Whisper White", "Vivid White"... the list was endless yet all the same. She wondered if Kate had taken hours to decide on the final colour choice. If she was that kind of person. *Why can't white just be white?* Nothing was clear anymore. Had Kate chosen a colour because of its name, hoping it would inspire her clients to expose their innermost thoughts? Or was she trying to prove something, positioning herself as more observant than the rest of us, able to notice the difference.

Kate looked over at her, probably wondering why they were both sitting in silence. Was she waiting for Julie to speak, open up? She'd have a long wait if she was.

Julie purposely turned and looked to her left, breaking eye contact with Kate. There was a series of three images on the wall, which looked like attempts Julie's children might well have contributed to the décor, although she suspected they were likely worth thousands. She had never understood modern art. It just looked like a swirling pattern; a magic eye drawing you in to a paint-splatter oblivion. *Oh, maybe that's the purpose?* No doubt Kate would be able to explain the significance of each colour and pattern; what made it art.

She stared for ages at the pictures. Maybe they were hypnotic? Was that part of the service, hypnotising clients to get her wicked way? She couldn't' be bothered with pointless chatter now that she was the master of her own destiny, but maybe Kate could still help...

'Kate, are you going to hypnotise me?' Julie blurted out, her brain taking a while to catch up with the words that had left her mouth without consent. *Think, Julie. Process, then speak.*

'Why? Would you like me to?' Kate was serious, her eyes piercing Julie's, already reading deeper into her world than Julie wanted her to see.

Great, a question answered with another question. Argh. That is so aggravating. It's right up there with answering, 'No, no, no, yes!' She hated that too. *Why bother if you're not going to be clear? Work out what you want to say, then say it.* She must have paused too long, either that or Kate was looking for an excuse to change the subject.

'Let's move on,' Kate said, pacing back and forth in the room, but ensuring enough distance to not encroach on Julie's personal space. 'Tell me, do you feel happier now?'

Julie paused, looked at the clock to work out the maths, the value of each second, how much the empty space was costing her. *Therapy.* It was about silence. About thought.

If Kate had fifty pounds and a Honeycomb Latte Macchiato Primo costs two pounds ninety-five, how many drinks could Julie buy with the money?

'Julie? Do you feel you've taken control of your life back and can see a way forward to contentment and personal growth?'

Great, she was still talking.

'I've made a good start,' she responded. 'I'm feeling quite excited for the future, whatever happens. I just feel like this massive stress has been taken away and made me much more relaxed.'

'That's fabulous! I'm so glad our sessions are helping. So, would you say these changes are mainly down to the regular walks and fresh air you've introduced into your life? And your new focus on building your career?'

Perhaps, but more likely the fact my whole life, I've been living in fear, waiting for the worst to happen, and then it did. And I dealt with it. And I survived. Damn it, I won! The buzz of smashing someone's head in! Taking control of life...and death.

She smiled back at Kate and replied, 'Yes, that must be it.'

'It looks like the only area you haven't tackled is your personal relationship with your husband. Are you avoiding it for a reason?'

Julie paused again, listened to the ticking clock. 'I just don't care enough,' she said finally. 'I know I should be organising date nights like you said, but that's about us, and at the moment, I'm enjoying it being about me.'

Kate nodded. 'Maybe that's something you can work on for our next session? Can you think of any progress you've made as a couple with each other, no matter how small? A move in the right direction?'

Julie was silent, wondering how her new freedom was affecting their relationship. Dan had been working a lot of late nights, and with more fresh air and a little exercise, she'd been falling asleep before he came home from work. But there'd been no argument as a result, and his practical jokes weren't upsetting her in the way they used to.

'I'm quite surprised, to be honest, how far you've progressed in just one week! Usually, we don't get a change this extreme unless a major life event happens – a wedding, a divorce, a death in the family.'

She looked up at Kate and smiled. 'No deaths in our family, thankfully.'

Julie wondered if she would ever open up about the cinema incident to the therapist. What were the rules about sharing private information? Was she totally protected, or would Kate go to the police? She recalled the rules of confession and how she didn't trust the priest when she was a child; didn't think he'd keep her words to himself. She'd been a sceptic, not understanding how three Hail Mary's and two Our Fathers would make up for stealing the school Blu Tack or nicking money from her dad's pockets while he was passed out drunk in the other room.

'Well, Julie, you've been working really hard and doing wonderfully. I'm afraid time's up for today, but I'd say you've had a really productive start and should be very proud of yourself. For the next session, I'd like you to focus on one thing in your life you would like to change – the thing most likely to have the biggest impact. Remember, what we think determines how we feel.'

Julie thought of her father, her sister, her mother – relationships gone sour over the years. The ruination, the anxiety, the abusive mental torture from Albert and the release when he had finally died. And now, Dan. History repeating itself. The feeling of abandonment, of worthlessness, of being used as a Cinderella to her now family. She visualised them all, made them into one huge bubble of black smoke obscuring her view, preventing her from reaching her goals. She took a deep breath in through her nose and blew out of her mouth, watched the cloud disperse and with it – her pain, her anxiety, the barriers to her progression lifted. She looked at Kate, grateful to have had the opportunity, for someone to finally listen to her, let her speak her thoughts – some of them, at least – out loud, so she could hear herself think. She knew it was all within herself to change her life for the better, and now, she knew how to make those changes.

'You have successfully started to put things into action, so well done! Keep up the good work!' Kate stepped towards Julie, helped her off the sofa, escorted her to the door. *Pushy.* 'If you could see Elaine at the front desk, she'll book you in for another appointment. I'm afraid I'm away on holiday for a few weeks, so it will be in about a month, if that's okay with you?'

Julie smiled as she left the office, head held high. Getting out her notebook, she wrote down her new mantra for the week: *Think power, feel powerful. Think confidence, feel confident. Think fear, kill fear.*

The wind outside blew fresh into her face as she exited the modern, clinical office. Out in the wild of nature, Julie pulled her snuggly coat around her body and her hood down over her ears, ignoring her mobile phone as it buzzed. Whoever it was could wait for her to make time for them. She was sick of putting other people first. She would be her own first priority from this point on.

Kate had been inspiring, but it was Julie who had made the changes happen. A life coach was there to guide, but all change had to be self-made. Julie thought about Dan. How could they take their relationship back to how it once was? It was all so exciting in the early days – so many giggles, so much laughter. When had they given up on each other?

Suddenly, she thought about the bank statement and Booking.com. She had forgotten to follow up on the surprise holiday her husband was planning. This was the push they both needed. She wrote a quick note in her diary to share at the next coaching session, then crossed it out again. She'd wait and see how things went, then decide if their relationship was worth saving.

As she walked home, Julie wondered about the cinema. She hadn't heard any mention in the news, and it had been five days already. She felt remarkably calm but confused, her lack of remorse conflicting with her preconceived notion of how she should be feeling. Did it make her a psychopath, her lack of empathy? She wondered if the police would come knocking on her door. Was she a murderer? It was self-defence, she told herself – but was it? In the last few days, she'd been thinking more and more about the incident. In the heat of the moment, it had seemed like the victim was anything but – not a woman but a thing, waiting to pounce, waiting to kill. She'd just got there first.

Julie didn't want to admit panic had led her to overreact. *That's what we'll call it, an overreaction that just happened to end someone's life*. The reality was too much to take in. *Murder*. Well, she hadn't planned it. *We'll downgrade it to manslaughter*. She shuddered. Only an autumn shiver. She thought about her situation, wondered what to do next. She was sure it had happened, almost. There was nobody to ask. *Dan, or the police?* Either way, she'd be committed – to prison or a mental asylum. Dan would be happy to get rid of her. He hadn't shown any affection for such a long time... *Oh, but the booking!*

Fumbling for her keys, Julie finally got into the house. Still quiet. The kids were all at school, and Dan at work. She went into Dan's study and booted up his laptop. Still no password protection. *Shouldn't that be a thing?* The hotel website was already open in his browser, so she clicked into 'My Bookings'.

The Woodloch Spa, Cambridge. *Ooh, very nice!* Julie grabbed her diary to check the dates and noted Dan had already blocked that weekend out for a lads' trip. *How exciting! A proper surprise! Well, it would have been if I hadn't gone snooping on his computer*, she thought.

Would the kids be going with them? The booking was a double room for Mr. and Mrs. Summers. She smiled. He'd arranged a babysitter for the weekend too. Perhaps she had been too harsh on him. She would make him spaghetti hoops for dinner – her little secret wink to say she knew, she cared and she was looking forward to finally having some quality time together.

Julie turned off the computer, still smiling on her way downstairs. Only two weeks to go until the surprise trip, and she couldn't wait.

The letter box rattled, and a pile of post landed on the front doormat along with the daily paper. She picked it up and threw it onto the dining room table, the neat pile spewing out across last night's leftover dry dinner stains. She'd cleared the dishes into the kitchen and forgotten to wipe it down. God forbid anybody else had thought about it!

Oh, for God's sake, seriously? She shuffled the post into a neater pile hoping it hadn't picked up too many stains, it wouldn't pay for Dan to come back and find the mess, his beloved paper soiled. The paper needed refolding where the TV guide had bulged out. Julie cursed it as a useless piece of landfill, just trying to make the job of creating a neat pleat even harder. Dan wouldn't be happy if it lost its crease – he hated reading a tainted paper. She wanted to please him since he seemed to be making an effort. There would be time enough for arguing later.

Julie finally folded the front cover over and stopped, stunned, staring back at the headlining news story: *Hunt for Horror Movie Killer.*

Oh, shit.

Chapter Thirteen

Keys in the door, then a turbulence of running, clothes-shedding, shoe-throwing and an out of breath Jack.

'Mum, there's a serial killer on the loose! And he killed at our cinema, where we go, like, all the time. Can we go there now? He might have left a clue or something. Do we have to wait for Tommy and William? I might walk up there with some friends now and check it out. It's going to be so cool. I've heard it's heaving over there!'

Oh my God. Slow down child. Stop talking, just stop. Think Julie, what to do? What to say? Plead ignorance? Tell him off for being such a gruesome animal?

'I wonder if I could sell something' he continued, 'like a local cinema flyer, maybe mock-up something on the computer with blood dripping down the edges and a bloody stabbing taking centre stage? I'm sure there'd be a market for it! Maybe they'll change the cinema into a tourist attraction like the Tower of London, even make it into a haunted house for

Halloween! Now, that would be awesome!' he went on until I couldn't stand it any longer.

'Jack, that sounds awful and very inappropriate, a definite No to all your suggestions,' she said, hoping he was listening and wouldn't prolong the conversation. Why was he talking about a stabbing? Could it be something else? Surely not, and why was he talking about a serial killer? As much as she wanted to shut him up, it might be better to encourage his gruesome fascination, if only to find out what stories where being passed around.

Following Jack into the kitchen, she marvelled at his grinning face, his excitement as he bounced around from cupboard to fridge to cupboard looking for snacks, his appetite far from suffering. Nothing phased him. If he'd been there by her side during that moment, how would he have reacted then? Would he have been a help or a hindrance?

'Do you think school will be closed tomorrow?' Jack shouted, not realising his mum was standing right behind him and jumping slightly on spotting her. He didn't wait for an answer, didn't really care, was just asking the question for himself breathing through the excitement of possible change. Crisps in hand, he then ran off like a tornado, flew upstairs, knocking his coat off the banister en route. Julie wasn't sure how to respond to him, she was angry, but soon realised it was more about his discarded shoes and dropped coat than his perspective on the murder. *That's my boy.*

When he was gone, she sat down heavily at the dining table, regretting not spending the time to read the newspaper before she'd disposed of it. It's not like she could just grab it from the bin, having put it through its own vigorous punishment. She had chosen to shred and soak, to blur the wording – a massive waste of time. *Like most of my life until now.*

'Hi, Mum! Have you heard – ?' William started, opening the door with a grin.

Julie couldn't bear another child revelling in the 'untimely death of an innocent' (that's what Jack had called her, likely quoting something on social media.)

'Yes, I've heard,' she quickly interrupted. 'Your brother's just told me all about it, so there's no need to go through all the gory details again. Just, please, don't mention it in front of Tommy when he gets home. I don't want him having nightmares. And take that stupid grin off your face. Somebody has died.' *Somebody has died.* She replayed the words over and over in her head, but still it didn't seem real, just a story about someone else.

William was sulking, disappointed he hadn't been the one to break the news. *It's not your news to share, it's mine!* She watched him as he sulked off, making his way upstairs away from her, slamming his bedroom door on cue as per usual. Relief. Nothing has changed, the boys are their usual selves. Whether that's necessarily a good thing is another matter.

Julie could hear William chatting away excitedly – phoning his friends perhaps, or talking through his headset while booting up his PlayStation. She was alone once more, this would have been the perfect opportunity, but she was wary of searching for more information on her phone, realised that if she were to become a suspect, the police would likely be searching her phone, amongst other things. She wished she'd taken the time to read through the article in the paper. Curious as she was, she had panicked and quickly got rid of it to keep the news from her family. She should have known the kids would be updated at school.

Her phone beeped with a message: *Please be informed, there are reports of a commotion at the local cinema, so children are advised to stay vigilant and go straight home after school. If you can collect your children from the school gates, that is advised. If not, please encourage them to walk home in pairs.*

Julie shook her head. W*ell, that's great advice. A bit of a commotion? Really? And what help is walking home in pairs unless they live together? One of them will be left on their own regardless.* She sighed. *Why am I worried? It's not like there really is a killer on the loose!* She would tell William to wait for his younger brother before school tomorrow, so they could go together. Must keep up appearances, or it would look suspect.

'Bye, boys! I'm off to get Tommy. Back soon!' she shouted up the stairs to no response.

She wondered if her boys were a bit psycho – maybe she'd passed on a faulty gene. They'd been... excited, thrilled even? She wondered what the cinema had reported but didn't have time right now to find out.

At the school gate, there was a small gathering of mums. Usually, everyone stood in a queue, on their phones, not making conversation. *The news has made its way over here too then.* She wondered how the parents would tackle the issue with their younger children, or whether they would totally avoid it. Would it be better to hear a dumbed-down version from a parent, or a distorted version in Chinese whispers from another seven-year-old at school?

'Well, I heard it's the same killer who murdered that man up in Yorkshire last year!'

'Who, the Yorkshire Ripper?'

'No, don't be ridiculous. That was years ago.'

'Was it a man or a woman that died?'

'They don't know because the killer took the skin clean off their face!'

'Seriously?'

'No! Don't be so ridiculous! As if! Look at me, I'm covering my face – am I a man or a woman?'

Laughter, gates opening up and a hushed quiet; back to selective mutism for the perfect pick-up; then the bombardment of questions:

'Hi, darling, good day?'
'So, what did you eat for lunch?'
'What did you do at school today?'
'What was your favourite time of day?'

All the usual questions, parents being parents, back to the mundane realities of their parenting lives. Kids whining, refusing to speak, asking for ice-cream from the overpriced van parked conveniently opposite the gates so there was no escaping it. Today, Julie would give in. She did it too often, and she knew it.

Hugging Tommy a bit too tightly, she felt relief. He squirmed but allowed her because he could see the ice-cream van over her shoulder, knowing that cuddly mummy meant easy to manipulate. She knew it, he knew it. They held hands and crossed over.

'One of those ninety-nine cones, please,' Tommy piped up, confidently pointing to the biggest ice-cream on the picture board.

'Here you are, young man,' the seller replied, almost instantaneously creating an obscene offering and handing it across

Tommy. The small boy took a huge lick to prevent the precariously placed ice-cream swirl from toppling off its cone and onto the floor, either for that reason or because he wanted to mark his territory.

'That will be two pounds ninety-nine please, ma'am.'

How did that make sense in any way, shape or form? Was the flake two pounds? And more to the point, what was with the 'ma'am' again? Julie had half a mind to return the now empty cone, but thought better of it. She wanted to keep Tommy calm, not start unnecessary arguments. She noted that the queue for ice-creams was much reduced today. Were other parents wondering if the seller was a danger, somehow linked to the cinema killing? She hoped so. He'd get his comeuppance for ageing her prematurely, she wasn't ready to be a ma'am.

As she strolled along with Tommy, Julie wondered who else would be affected by the incident. She knew most of the other parents didn't go *out-out* after school – not for themselves, anyway. Most, she knew, went straight home, fed their nagging kids, then made their way with them to some club or other: swimming, jujitsu, tennis, piano lessons... It was a never-ending list of middle-class necessity to extend the school day. Oh, and of course, compulsory tutors to push them through their exams and into grammar schools that would mean an extra four-hour commute each day if they passed. *Yay!*

Would the tutors come under suspicion? The teachers? All the lone strangers out walking in the area? Would mothers refuse to have them in their houses? Would their children's education fall behind because of it, their life paths changing forever? How far would the knock-on effect reach?

If, God forbid, you were murdered, the killer was most

likely to be someone you knew, according to crime statistics. Julie wanted to shout out, 'I've messed up your statistics!' But she figured it wasn't a planned murder, so they would likely dismiss her claim. *Damn*. She wondered if the victim's family were questioning each other, searching for clues as to which uncle, brother, or son had overstepped the boundaries. She smiled, feeling safe. Feeling powerful. She was in control. Julie had influenced so many people's lives in just one moment of madness.

Madness? Imagine what she could do if she actually planned a murder! The chaos and anarchy she would create. She could pick someone out whose life she wanted to mess with and fuck them up. She didn't even have to kill them. She could kill someone they loved and watch their house of cards come crashing down around them. *Oh, the beautiful simplicity!*

The taste of control was invigorating. Julie had always thought murderers must be terrible people, angry people, with revenge and hate in their blood, but it seemed the opposite. It was more a culling of the not-so innocent as a way of bleeding yourself; self-harm without the pain. She thought of the Horrible Histories series Tommy was always watching, of leeches being used to suck away an illness in early medical journals. She pictured herself as the leech, preying on the sick, in her mind, cleansing the world and making it pure.

Since the cinema incident, Julie had been thinking more clearly. She was more patient, better able and willing to show kindness to those who were deserving – the chosen few. *The friends you choose, rather than the family that is thrust upon you.* Maybe that was why a murderer was likely to be someone you knew, a family member who just couldn't cope with the stupidity of having to keep up relations when all they really felt was hatred? She wondered who she would kill first in an ideal world. Her mother? Her husband? Her sister? Her children? What would the fallout be? She wished her father hadn't died already or he would have been the first on her list, that would have been an easy decision.

She pondered over whose absence would have the most beneficial impact on her dysfunctional world, then laughed at the ridiculousness of her thoughts. *Get back to the kitchen, Julie, Dan's going to be home soon wondering where dinner is.* Maybe Dan should move up the list? *Oh, the liberty!*

She smiled opening the fridge and pulled out four steaks, resisting the urge to prod the fleshy pulp behind its vacuum-packed wrapper, the bloody lumps conjuring up images, re-minding her. What would *she* look like now? Would *her* body be served up on a slab, waiting for family members to identify her? She squeezed a piece of steak, willing it to pop through the packaging but without success. Damn. How is it some things are so difficult, when others just come so easily?

Slowly peeling it back, she breathed in the stale aroma, searching her mind for familiarity, but found nothing. She grabbed hold of one of the soft clumps of aged, dark meat, passing it from hand to hand, watching the blood seep into the creases of her palms. *Just one lick,* she couldn't resist. She would serve them up extra-rare tonight, blood dripping into a gravy on each of their plates. A smile spread across her face as she looked forward to seeing if the kids had the stomach for it, or if they were all talk.

How disappointing.

Dan wolfed down his food without a thought, and she doubted he'd even noticed the puddle of blood on his plate.

He'd picked up the Evening Standard on his way home from work, which he sat reading at the table, oblivious to the kids chatting excitedly around him while texting on their phones. She hadn't bothered with Tommy, he wouldn't have eaten it raw, cooked or cremated so she didn't include him in the meal, decided it wasn't worth wasting a decent bit of flesh. Nobody else commented on the blood, but maybe that was the point she was trying to prove: they didn't care, didn't associate. The older boys scoffed their food and ran off, leaving their plates on the table and going straight back to their gaming, shouting loudly with the usual inappropriate language.

To them, the murder was something far-removed from their personal lives despite it being practically on their doorstep. It didn't directly affect them. It was just a story, a movie trailer they could dip in and out of without it disturbing their equilibrium.

Pick your battles, Julie. Life was just too short to care about every little thing, especially when there was fun to be had!

Dan eventually looked up from the paper. What was his take on it? She waited to see if he could read her thoughts; if he instinctively knew what she had done.

'I don't want you going out, Julie. You're my wife, and I am responsible for your protection. It's too dangerous out there at the moment, and with it getting dark so early, you never know where people will be hiding out, waiting to take advantage. And don't be going anywhere near that cinema!'

Julie stared back, unsure of how to respond. What was he

expecting? She went with argumentative. He would relate to that.

'I think you're being a bit ridiculous! I mean, what's actually happened? What do we know? Somebody died in a cinema. What else does the paper say?'

She was desperate to hear and pleased Dan was willing to oblige, to fuel his argument.

'Three teenagers have been arrested after missing mother of four, Amrita Devi, was found beaten to death in the toilets at a London cinema,' he read. 'The three suspects are due to appear at the Uxbridge Magistrates Court on Friday. The charges bring the total number of suspects in the case to five. PC Tailor said, 'May I remind all concerned that these defendants are now actively awaiting trial, so if anybody has any further information, please come forward to your local police station to report it. Do not share it with the public, especially not on social media, as this could harm the case. Let's not allow the perpetrators of this heinous crime to go unpunished because of a glitch in the legal system.' Dan put the paper down.

'Wow, that was quick! We're in a modern age now, Julie – CCTV everywhere. I'm betting that's how they caught them. Five though! Jesus Christ, that woman wouldn't have had a chance.'

Julie cringed. *CCTV?* Not inside the toilets, she hoped. If they had seen footage from the day, wouldn't they have come for her already? Five suspects, and she wasn't on the list. *Thank Christ.* Surely, it couldn't be that easy?

She headed out of the room, left Dan looking smug and satisfied as he took her departure to mean her accepted subordination, that she would give in to his authority.

Upstairs, Julie locked the bathroom door behind her, then reached for the bath taps and let the water gush full-throttle as she slumped to the floor. She wanted to know what was going on and suspected her mobile would be plastered with more insightful stories than the paper could offer. *Have I waited long enough? Would it be more suspicious if I didn't check out the stories on my phone?*

She opened up her Facebook page and was greeted by a picture of the inside of the toilets, blood everywhere, hands smearing it down the cubicle walls. This wasn't the image she remembered; the romanticised release. Her body spasmed and began to retch as she closed her eyes tight, tried to block out the conflicting images – but the reported scene remained imprinted on her mind. Had something happened after she left? It was all so clean in her memory. Clinically precise, contained.

What was the reality? She needed to find out more. She focused on the noise of the water as the bath continued to fill, breathed through the horror to regain her control and looked at the articles once again. What had those kids done to put them under suspicion? Or was it just because they were teenagers, in the wrong place at the wrong time? Were they known offenders? Had they gone in after her and finished the job? But they couldn't have, could they? A million questions rushed around her head as she sat next to the cascading water and read through a Huffington Post report.

'On Monday, Police were called to a brutal murder scene at a London Hillingdon cinema, where a woman was beaten to death in what is suspected to be a hate crime. There have been five arrests so far, two males and three females, all teenagers who cannot be named. We believe this to be gang-related retaliation, and the victim's family has been taken to a safe place. If anybody has any further information, please come forward.'

What was going to happen to those teenagers? How old were they? Did Jack know them? Were they dangerous? Her mind was a blur of possibilities. Why had they been arrested? Did they do it?

She dropped the phone on the floor, cracked the screen cover. *Fucking typical.* Julie dragged herself up, leaving it to one side, and reached for the bubble bath, pouring a generous glug under the taps and using her hand to further splash it around so it didn't just sit there, a stagnant blue lump at the bottom of the tub. She stripped off and tentatively lowered one foot into the bath. Red-hot pain; pleasure. She slowly braved it, enjoying the sting as she lowered herself in, skin prickling and shivering against the scalding, searing heat, which subsided as soon as her body acclimatised.

Julie smiled as she submerged her head under the water, relaxing in the womblike tranquillity. Of course the teens hadn't done it, but they must have done something awful to be arrested. Had she done the world a favour by ridding the streets of such delinquent kids? There was a lot to be said about this murder business. But why had the police decided boys were involved when it had taken place in the women's toilets? Maybe the girls pulled them in for other reasons, a fumble that would cost them more than their virginity? She thought about the victim. *Her* victim. *Four children!* Perhaps it was for the best if her children were mixed up in a gang. No mother needs to witness that.

If Julie had the choice, she wondered, would she give her own life for her children? If it meant changing their futures, keeping them on the path to success rather than ruin? The ultimate sacrifice; that's what her victim had bequeathed her children, whether it was intended or not.

The woman's husband, if she had one, would now be realising her worth, missing her and the role she played in their world. She wondered what Dan would think if she was the one lying there cold on the slab. Would he even know how to put the dishwasher on? How would he keep up with the washing – the mountains of endless washing?

Julie enjoyed the warm water caressing her skin as she relaxed in the bath, blocking out her family's noise; the arguing, the shouting. All of it became white noise in a distant world. She felt good. The water refreshed her like a baptism, marked the beginning of her new life. *So many possibilities. So much excitement. So much fun to be had.* Why, oh why had she waited forty years to start enjoying herself? Julie felt like a woman in a nineteenth-century novel, burning her bra for women's rights before anybody had even thought to ask for equality; before bras even existed. She would be a trailblazer, it was simply a matter of planning. *Take your time and think things through. Enjoy every moment as if it's your last – because if you're caught, it will be.* But oh, what a ride would come first!

That night, Julie slept soundly, her body not responding when Tommy came in at six a.m. to give his usual rude awakening. Maybe he'd slept in for once? She couldn't remember him waking her and doubted Dan would have stirred from his slumber.

Her alarm blasted at seven-thirty a.m., and she jumped out of bed, rearing to go. The sun streaked through the blinds and made beautiful patterns on the wardrobe door. Julie opened it and grabbed her comfy vest top and dark-grey cotton jumper, threadbare but well-loved. It had sat at the bottom of the wardrobe for an age too long. Dragging a brush through her hair, she thought better of it and pulled it up into a rough topknot. Wispy bits of baby-hair framed her face and fell romantically around her neck, natural and windswept. She had fallen asleep the night before with still-wet hair and had woken up with a controlled surfer-girl look, a stark contrast to her usual frizz. She smiled at her reflection. A quick line of eyeliner, and she was done. No need for blush – her face looked flushed and glowing.

Holding Tommy's hand on the way to school, Julie had a skip in her step, her good mood inadvertently rubbing off on her son too. He smiled and chattered happily, asked if his friends could come over for a play date.

'Yes, why not?' Julie sang, waving him off happily. As she turned, she saw a couple of parents chatting by the front gate. 'Anybody fancy joining me for coffee?' she called over confidently, and both mothers nodded in agreement. *Well, that was easy!*

Julie listened to their chatter as they walked up to Starbucks, waiting for them to bring up the topic of the cinema. And there it was. *Let them lead.* What did they think? She was fascinated and enjoyed peppering the odd word in to keep involved while she listened to what they thought of the situation.

'I'm not sure I want my older kids going out anymore,' Angry Angie said.

Stumbling Suzy piped up, 'I know! It's like we're constantly told to get the kids off their electronics, get them out playing in the fresh air, give them independence, old-school entertainment, let them climb trees, ride their bikes – but it's all so dangerous! I'd much rather they stay home so I know where they are, safe. It's not like they're not socialising! All their friends are chatting away to them, even playing the same games with them over the internet, just not in person. I mean, they're together all day at school, so what's the harm in having them stay home in the evenings? It's supposed to be home-time!'

Okay, Suzy, time to rethink your nickname if you're not going to let anyone get a word in edgeways.

Suzy finally snorted and took a breath, letting Angie creep back into the conversation.

'Yes, I'm with you, especially on these cold, dark winter nights. Who wants to be going out doing drop-offs and lifts all the time? That can wait until they're seventeen and able to drive themselves. Mind you, then we'll be worrying about them driving and having accidents because they're blaring their music or getting distracted by friends.'

'Or using their mobile phones while driving!'

Angie raised her eyebrows. 'If you ask me, those teenagers did us a favour killing off that poor old dear. It means we don't have to make up stories to keep them home.'

'I know what you mean,' Julie said, feeling it was about time she contributed to their debate. 'In my house, my husband has really put his foot down. He doesn't even want *me* going out alone, never mind the kids!'

Silence. Were they judging her? She felt the need to justify Dan's controlling behaviour.

'I guess it was a woman our age who was murdered after all…because her teenagers were a part of that gang. If the kids had been around, would the killers have targeted them instead?'

They all looked at each other, taking a moment to sip their decaf caramel soya-milk lattes. Suzy was the first to comment, 'Have you seen how many calories are in the new Gingerbread and Cream Frappuccino? Nearly six hundred! I'm going to try and get through Dry October without one, save myself for the Christmas Black Forest Frostino, or the Billionaire Frostino... Oh, my God, they are just to die for!'

Sadist Suzy. That was how Julie would remember her name. How on earth had she taken the conversation from murder to fucking Frappuccinos, or whatever the latest made-up coffee concoction would be? Julie looked at Angie, willed her to reprimand Suzy's inappropriate, tactless disregard for the important news of the day.

'Just make sure you ask them to hold the whipped cream, limit the drizzle, or go for a sugar-free syrup. Then, you can keep the calories down to a breakfast and lunch combo and still hold something back for dinner.'

Unbelievable. *Priorities, darlings.* Clearly, these women were more concerned about what went into their stomachs and keeping themselves thin than worrying about a murderer on the loose. But, as far as they were concerned, the killers had been detained.

Oh, how she'd love to wipe the smiles off their smug, self-interested faces and put them straight. Perhaps they would one day make her short-list?

Chapter Fourteen

That night, Dan freaked out. 'It's in all the newspapers! It's headline news, for Christ's sake! I can't believe you went out with your friends for coffee like nothing's going on. I thought better of you, Julie. I must insist you and the boys stay home until they catch the killer! Just because they've made arrests, doesn't mean it's safe out there! Innocent until proven guilty, remember?'

Good God, man! There's nothing to worry about. You must "insist", must you? What gives you the right? You're not the boss of me! If you think you are you've got another thing coming! Just chill a bit, I've got this. You're safe, the kids are safe, and I am definitely not going to be attacking myself anytime soon, so it's all "good".

Had she said that out loud? He stared back at her, open-mouthed. *Oh dear.*

'Julie, for Pete's sake, speak! Have an opinion! Fight your fucking corner! Or are you just going to stand there looking gormless?'

Thank Christ for that. She tried to control her facial expression to not look too pleased since his words warranted a more sombre response.

'I was only out for coffee with a couple of the mums from school. I'll be more careful, but I really don't think I need to be under house arrest.' *Under arrest? Quite possibly.* 'And as for the kids, well, they'll be more than happy to stay home playing on their consoles all day and night if we let them.'

He nodded back, satisfied, and turned towards the wardrobe to hang up his suit trousers. Julie would wait until he left and then rearrange them to ensure the pleat was perfectly aligned on both sides, otherwise it would somehow be her fault later.

'I want you to be really vigilant, Julie, especially when I'm away next weekend.'

She was pleased but surprised he hadn't thought to cancel the trip away and wondered when he would break the news to her about the surprise. She would have preferred him to be open with her at this stage, so they could build the excitement together and make some plans, maybe even buy a new outfit for the spa.

'Work's been so full-on lately – I really need some downtime with the lads. Watch a few games of football, have a few beers and just forget about all the crazy goings-on.' He smiled at her apologetically as he left the room.

Still keeping up with the pretence then.

'I'm just popping out Julie, won't be long.'

'Okay. Bye!' was her automatic response to his door-slamming. She hadn't thought to ask where he was going.

Hold on, why is there one rule for him, and another for me? How come he was able to leave the house while she was stuck at home? Prising open the blinds, Julie watched Dan through the window as he walked up the road, phone at his ear, happy, content, youthful. Like when they'd first met some twenty years before, he seemed both carefree and impetuously agitated – like he was looking for adventure. Who was he speaking to now? Was it the lads he was meeting at the weekend? She grinned at her own confusion. She would make the weekend one to remember, remind him why they were together and the reason they chose each other all those years ago. Free from the role of wife or mother for once, she would simply be a devoted lover rekindling their old flame.

His trousers! The wardrobe door stuck as she tried to slide it over, forcing her to lift it clear off the brackets and move it back and forth until it found its runner. Why and how it happened to her every time, she would never know. There was nothing stuck – she had been careful – but careful wasn't proving to be the best policy. *Finally!* She managed to close it, exposing her side: the main shelf of creased staple items, and a second go-to selection of clothes she wore daily, whatever the weather.

Julie didn't understand why she kept so many clothes as she rarely strayed from a select few. Everything she wore was crumpled, like her life. In a rare emergency, she would reach for the hair straighteners and quickly run them over collars or cuffs, a stray hem that needed a quick fix. She had successfully steered herself away from any form of sewing too, rebelling against the supermums at school. Her trusty marker-pen was always on hand to write directly onto clothes that needed tagging; material glue at the ready to stick on replacement buttons or any other stitching needs. Julie prided herself on quick-fix parenting, enjoying as many shortcuts as possible to make life that bit easier. She thought of the arguments she'd had with an eco-mum at school about her overuse of the tumble dryer, but oh, how wonderful it was.

Tumble dryers. Ah, the romance! If she'd had to pick between a father figure and a tumble dryer, she'd pick the dryer every time as the more practical and beneficial influence on the children's lives. It was a life-saver, giving her flexibility to decide when to tackle the fearful job of washing. The freedom of not having to rely on the weather or blast the radiators through the height of a boiling but rainy British summer. And, God love them, the kids were not particularly forward-planning when it came to their clothes. Everything was an emergency: *I need it now! Mum, where's my blue top with the Lego on it? I need it now!*

It's most probably under your bed in a heap of filth where you left it, she always wanted to respond. *If, however, you had walked the few steps and placed it in the dirty washing basket instead of leaving it rotting at the bottom of a bag, you might find it magically appear again, folded and clean in your wardrobe.*

Julie reached into her own wardrobe to touch the rows of beautiful dresses hanging crisp and perfect on the other side, untouched; unspoiled. They had been ironed and hung up in her happier years – years of dancing and freedom and being spontaneous without fear of child retribution the morning after. The book club was her only escape now, and she couldn't even rally motivation for that. None of these dresses fitted her now anyway. She heaped them out into a pile on the floor and stuffed them into recycling bags. *No point keeping a stuffed wardrobe of wannabes.* She was left with a few frumpy-looking mum dresses, appropriate Christening and funeral attire, sacks that swamped her and provided some level of decency. She wasn't looking forward to wearing swimwear in public, all that extra weight she'd been carrying like baggage from motherhood.

Oh, dear God, grooming! She looked at her swimming costume and realised a quick leg-shave would not be sufficient for the amount of flesh that would be exposed. Could she squeeze her mum-bod into the costume that promised to have an in-built control panel? She suspected she would only spill out around the edges, but it was too late to worry about that now.

'Mum! What's for dinner?' Tommy called up the stairs.

Her life really was a constant cycle. *That time already?* Kicking the clothes back into the wardrobe, she pulled the door shut. It could wait, she couldn't cope with it all now.

'Coming, darling! Pasta tonight.'

Groans came from the other boys' rooms. 'I don't want anything,' William called. Only minutes before, he'd said how starving he was.

If you were really starving, darling, you would be grateful for anything you were given. You don't know you're born. Her grandma's phrase rang in her ears as she thought about old-school parenting and how much better it would be. *Don't offer variety. Don't ask, simply provide. Make them cook everything for themselves and do all the prep and cleaning up – that way, they will learn to show appreciation for what they receive.*

It was easier said than done. Julie felt like a slave but knew full well she was the perpetrator of her own demise. She would make the pasta, put it on the dining table and hope one out of three would eat it. If it was up to her, she would make a lovely salad with smoked salmon, pine nut kernels and a beetroot vinaigrette, maybe even put pretty purple swirls around the plate to make the creation *pop*, all accompanied by fresh, homemade seeded rolls, warm with melted butter – served on a side plate with a proper butter knife, of course. *Oh, the extravagance!*

She thought of their family prayer: *Thank you for the bless-ings of the food we eat, make us forever grateful, and thanks for our home, family and friends.'*

The kids had recited those words on many occasions, yet clearly, the meaning was lost on them. *Kids, going through the motions, getting by doing the bare minimum of everything, coast-ing through their lives... Well, life is short kids, so wake up and grow up!* She'd never understood why people said childhood was the best time of your life. Childhood was a minefield of agony: no freedom, no choices, no life experience to put things into perspective – all of it thrown in with a whole lot of mis-takes that ended in agonising mixed emotions.

Julie still felt like a child. She'd never broken free, and when it came to cooking for the kids, food had long-since lost its ap-peal. She was never hungry for her family-friendly creations yet continued to pile on the weight. Parenting had filled out her weekly meal planner with simple, basic food as her boys were just so fussy. As a result, she constantly craved something dif-ferent, so she had become a snacker, always searching for some-thing else.

She thought of Vanessa at school – her kids ate anything. Off to school with a sushi packed lunch one day, homemade sa-voury lunch muffins the next. They were the exception, surely? Or was that what she wanted to believe so she didn't feel like such a failure? Julie was jealous. *Maybe I should kill her off next*, she mused. *That would wipe the smile off her face. Or kill off the kids? Bit harsh maybe.* Who would benefit more from the purge – the children, or the mother? She figured getting rid of the kids would be the humane thing to do. She and the other mums wouldn't have to hear about Venessa's parenting perfection anymore, and the children wouldn't have to sit next to the fishy kids in the school dinner hall.

Julie walked into the kitchen to put the pasta on, realising she would have to tackle the dirty dishes first so she could drain the pasta. They were piled high in the sink, as usual. She couldn't remember ever seeing an empty sink for more than two minutes. Today, it was a cesspit of rotten food floating in leftover coffee remnants. When she'd left the oven trays soaking overnight, it was a very civilised affair – but that was no longer the case, thanks to everyone piling plates on top without even scraping the food off first.

The dishwasher must be clean. She opened it, but, surprise surprise, it hadn't been turned on, was abandoned like everything, left to her, full of dirty dishes. *For fuck's sake, she felt an uncontrollable rage as she bit her tongue, holding back the scream she longed to set free.*

She couldn't face making the dinner with the stinking mess but didn't want to wash up by hand either. *Argh! So annoying!* First world problems, she knew, but she was seething with anger regardless.

Just chill out. Or smash a few... Now, there's a thought.

She picked up a filthy, food-stained dish and dropped it on the floor. It cracked slightly. She grabbed another and smashed it full-pelt on top of the first. This time, a rewarding crash as shards of porcelain and stray peas went flying across the room.

Julie felt calm, enjoying the satisfaction of clearing the dishes. What would happen if she simply left, abandoned everything – the hungry kids, the filthy mess, the broken fragments of her life? Adrenaline raced through her as she thought of how wonderful it would be to walk out and escape, leave Dan to clean up all the wreckage. How would he cope? How would any man cope if their household help went on strike? That's how she thought of herself – not as a wife, a friend or a mother, only the home help: unappreciated, neglected, forgotten… invisible. How would Dan manage his work? She wished she didn't care enough to even question it.

She knew other single mums who struggled but managed. They enjoyed the freedom of being the sole decision-maker in the house; their word was final. One of her friends, Mary, boasted that her life had dramatically improved since she kicked her partner out. He wasn't abusive, he hadn't had an affair or been a shouter – he'd just really annoyed her. Julie remembered the moment Mary told everyone – and the hushed, shocked responses. The jealousy she had felt listening to *her* story, that Mary was brave enough, valued herself highly enough to say no to the mundane lifestyle that was boring her to death.

Julie reached for the broom and started to sweep up. She wasn't quite at that stage yet and wasn't ready to face the consequences. She looked around the kitchen. It was old and tired, and she felt an immediate affinity. She thought back to the woman whose life had ended; whose life she had taken away. *Amrita*, that was her name. Had she dreamed of escaping? Had she quietly embraced the release of death – waited, hoped, intentionally provoked Julie to attack? She had escaped the conveyor belt of domestic boredom. Julie longed to switch places.

As she gave in to her Cinderella role, she couldn't brush the thought from her head. *Just leave, Julie. Don't say goodbye.*

Escape. Nobody is stopping you, only yourself. She could treat it like a social experiment, teach her family to manage without her – but what if they could? What if she wasn't missed? What if their lives continued on without her, or worse still, if life was improved by her absence? How could she return? What would her purpose be, if not to care for her kids and her husband?

She couldn't do it. Didn't want to leave, only wanted to feel appreciated.

After the weekend with Dan, that's when I'll make a decision. See how things go.

It just wasn't the done thing, walking out on your family, but how much of a relief it would be if it was suddenly made acceptable, mainstream even. A mass walk-out of women all over the country! Equality of the sexes had not really benefitted women, only berated those who continued to carry out domestic housewife roles. The book club girls, even Rachel, made that clear enough with their constant nagging for Julie to prove her worth through something more: a job. Now, thanks to Kate, a career-driven, independent, baggage-free woman, Julie had also felt the need to shift, to move closer to the expected norm.

A woman's work is never done. Never, ever.

Dan walked in with three boxes in his hands. 'Panic alarms for the kids,' he explained. 'You won't be needing one in the house, but they have to go out to school, so they need to stay vigilant.'

'I really don't think that's necessary, Dan.'

'How can you be so calm? You're always so anxious and stressed about the stupidest things, yet now there's a killer on the loose, you don't even care about your kids' safety, never mind your own!'

She switched off from his rant, watching him as he stomped around the room like an angry kid trying to gain control of his emotions, trying to make some kind of sense of what was going on; but that's just the point, nothing made sense or would ever again.

As he babbled on and on about installing CCTV doorbells to keep an eye on comings and goings into the house, she felt like a prisoner. She couldn't explain the truth, tell him they were safe, that the enemy was already inside and that they weren't her target.

'Well, I'm not having it. Wake up, Julie, it could be literally anyone! Just because those kids have been arrested doesn't mean they've caught everyone involved and even if they have, there could be retaliation killings to come!'

She watched him all red in the face, pumping himself up, goading her, wanting her to react, but she wouldn't give him the satisfaction. 'Okay, Dan. Whatever you say.'

'What?' he stammered, caught off-guard. 'Next, you'll be telling me how you've got too much on, blah, blah, blah, but what have you got on? There's no reason why you should leave the house. Your only job is to look after us, and I don't see much of that going on at the moment.' He glanced around at the kitchen she'd just cleaned up, frowning at the pasta boiling away. 'I'm out tonight for Curry Club,' he said. 'Make sure you clean this shit up. It's filthy in here!'

With that, he walked out of the house again, leaving Julie staring after him.

He was such a hypocrite. How could he just leave? She felt tears of anger and frustration fill her eyes. *Don't give in. Use it, channel it, find an outlet and enjoy the release. Who would you like to kill next? Can I? Yes! Should I? Yes, just do it. Life is short, so live without regret.*

She started a mental list of potential customers. Maybe one of those teenagers if they got let off the murder; a retaliation on behalf of the victim's children. They obviously deserved punishment if they'd been hauled into the police station. Julie didn't care what happened to her – she had nothing to lose. But she would need a plan.

But first, their weekend away. A final chance at following the right path, the family path, Dan didn't know how much was riding on it. At the end of the weekend it would be a case of all in, one way or the other. Family life rejuvenated verses a rampage of vengeance against the deserving; proper old-school punishment.

Chapter Fifteen

Julie: *Rachel, can you keep a secret?*
Rachel: *You're pregnant????*

Julie rolled her eyes at her phone as she read her friend's instant reply.

Julie: *Fck no!!!! I was going to ask abt a bikini wax!*

A moment later Rachel sent back a disappointed emoji face along with a telephone number and a kiss.

The week had passed by so quickly, Wednesday arriving before Monday even registered, and Julie knew time was running out and she still needed to prepare for the weekend. She clicked on the number Rachel had sent her. *Okay, bite the bullet.* She pressed 'Call' and waited for the dial tone.

'Hi, yes, I'd like to book in for a bikini wax... A Hollywood? What's that?' She listened to the description grimacing in mild horror but tried to be brave. 'Okay...I'll give it a go.'

Julie hung up and went back to her wardrobe. Everything was so dowdy now she'd thrown the little black numbers out.

She stashed a few of her better trousers, vests and cardigans to one side. They would have to do.

Friday morning, Dan left for work, trying to sneak off without a goodbye. Maybe he couldn't keep the secret if they made eye contact? She no longer cared, the day had come at last and Julie was thrilled.

'I'll see you Monday evening then,' Dan said, leaned forward and kissed her on the head. He was enthusiastic and flushed, clearly struggling to keep up the pretence. He called up to the kids, 'have a lovely weekend guys! Look after your mum for me!'

I hope all this painful itchiness will be worth the sacrifice, Julie thought as she watched him. *Goodbye body hair, hello prepubescent smoothie.* She had quite literally bared all and now felt liberated, having survived the total humiliation. *Legs up, buttocks spread.* Oh, dear God, that beautician had gone to places even her gynaecologist hadn't visited after the damage of childbirth! But now she was a new woman. If she could brave that, she was capable of anything.

Tommy came running downstairs into his dad's hug, while William shouted, 'Bye, Dad!' and continued playing his game. Jack didn't even acknowledge Dan leaving, probably still in the shower. What was it with teenagers and hour-long showers? What were they doing in there? She shuddered at the thought.

William shouted again, some lame comment about Dan being too old for a lads' weekend. Dan smirked but didn't reply. He wasn't giving anything away, still keeping up the pretence as he walked out of the door.

'Have a good weekend. See you Monday!' Julie shouted with a wink as she watched him walk down the driveway.

He put his luggage in the car boot without a backward glance. So, how long would it be until she got the call to leave? Had he arranged to pick her up after work, to send one of the drivers maybe? She smiled as she helped Tommy put on his shoes for school. Seven years old, forever her baby.

Julie leaned forward and hollered up the stairs, 'Boys! You're going to be late for school!' Whose idea had it been to allow them computer games in the morning? She reached for the Wi-Fi mains to turn it off but thought twice about the potential fallout, so instead, she flicked the power off.

William shouted, 'Mum! There's been a power cut! The lights have gone out!'

Yes, son, they have. Perfect timing for the school-run. She smiled as William came jumping down the stairs two at a time and went straight out the door. No comment. No further complaint. No goodbye. *I suppose they don't know I'm going away for the weekend. Shame. It would have been nice to have a hug.*

There was still no sign of Jack so Julie went upstairs to check on him. The bathroom was empty, so she knocked on his door.

'Jack, you're going to be late for school!'

No response. She opened the door slowly, giving him time to cover himself if he wasn't dressed. But he wasn't in there either.

Fine, fine, fine. I can ignore you just the same.

'Tommy! We're going now.'

Julie returned to a peaceful house after dropping Tommy off. She couldn't help but hum away to herself as she caught her reflection in the bedroom mirror. This trip could change every-thing, renew her and Dan's bond, help the family stay together. She opened the wardrobe door and hunted for a bag for her holiday clothes, marvelling at the sliding door hinges that kept hold for a change. A good omen?

It was such a long time since she'd last been away, and Julie had no idea where the small holdalls were kept. Dan frequently travelled for work and had taken his usual bag that morning. She walked over to his wardrobe and started rummaging around in the back. So many self-help books, yet she'd never seen him read one. There were framed pictures stacked on the floor at the back, family pictures they used to display in their old house. Julie thought back to the traumatic move – not only the stress of *will-we-won't-we* when it came to the house sale, but the ac-tual moving day and all the months and years of unpacking that followed. She couldn't catch up. All the pretty things in life had been pushed to one side, stacked at the backs of wardrobes, waiting for a better day. Waiting for time to return.

Julie spotted Dan's gym bag at the top of the wardrobe. That would have to do. She jumped up and grabbed for the handle, bashing her arm on the shelves when she missed and knocking his aftershave bottles over. He had so many! She'd never noticed before. She tried again and this time caught the edge of the bag, which sent it crashing down onto her head.

For fuck's sake, ow! Why does everything happen to me?

She refused to let the minor accident affect her good mood as she unzipped the bag and tipped out its contents. His gym kit looked good as new – quite literally – tags and labels still stuck to everything, the trainers still padded with tissue inside.

Odd.

She rolled up her trousers and put them in the bag, hoping that would keep them more crease-free than if she folded them, then threw her hair straighteners in for good measure. *Just in case.* She smiled, brushing off the dust and hoping the plug hadn't fused.

Julie opened the family safe and took out the treasure – her prized necklace, sat lonely and neglected on top of a pile of important papers. It had been an anniversary present back in the early days, when weeks and months were counted as celebrations; an excuse to show each other their love and affection. A beautiful trinket from a time when their emotions ran so high they craved a way of showing each other just how much they felt. Back then, love was like a drug coursing through their veins, and the two couldn't get any closer if they tried. Julie had wanted to inject Dan into her; somehow get even closer. It wasn't possible their love could have been any more intense. If she could get only a tiny bit of it back, they would be able to make it through another twenty years of marriage.

She struggled to open the box, but when it finally clicked, it revealed the most beautiful, sparkling blue pendant sitting on top of a red velvet cushion. The necklace promised the radiance of a Swarovski crystal even though she'd received it long before she knew what Swarovski even was. It wasn't worth much, they hadn't had much money, but to her it was priceless. *Every woman needs a little sparkle in her life.* Julie smiled, reaching around her neck and pulling up her hair before tackling the clasp. It was the only piece of jewellery that her children hadn't destroyed. A tentative bind with her life before. Typically, the romance ended with the necklace slipping from her grasp and falling to the floor. 'Why?' she cursed, reaching down to feel around under the bed.

Yuck. What is that?

She couldn't bring herself to look as her fingers grabbed blindly, finally making contact with the sharp crystal edge. Julie lifted it out and attempted to rid the pretty jewel of the hair it had picked up on its travels. Now wasn't the time. She wanted to be ready. She threw the necklace in the end of the bag, hoping the gold-plated finish wouldn't tarnish as it brushed up against her toiletries. Life could never be easy, could it?

Now, it was simply a waiting game until she was summoned. Hair perfect (ish), makeup on, bag packed. It was time to chill on the sofa with a movie: Eat, Pray, Love. She'd seen it a million times before – maybe not quite – but she knew every word to every scene. There were no surprises, it was just comfortable – as was she, as she lay back on the sofa and welcomed the chance to rest. Her blinks became longer and more frequent, and she finally succumbed to sleep. A little nap would refresh her, give her more energy for the evening, and her phone was next to her, so she wouldn't miss a call.

'What's for dinner? Mum! Mum, are you home?'

The wild-child returning from school with a slam of the door threw Julie out of her relaxed slumber. She looked around, confused. Where was she? What time was it? Why was William home? So many questions spun around in her head.

A second slam of the door, then muffled chatter. 'What do you look like?' Jack's voice as he looked down at her on the sofa with a snarl. At least he was home, not lying stabbed somewhere.

Hold on a minute... Why was he home? Where was the babysitter? Why was *she* at home? She was supposed to be out, away with Dan. Maybe he was waiting until after he finished work at six? She cursed, realising she would have to get the boys' food ready – the main thing she'd been looking forward to escaping.

'Mum, where's Tommy?'

Tommy! Oh, shit!

She dragged herself off the sofa, grabbed a coat and reached for the car keys, which weren't there. Damn, Dan had taken them.

Julie ran out the door, panting as she went, trying her best to make up time and not barge too many pedestrians. Her run was a shower of 'Sorries!' mixed with bumps and bruises and dotted with expletives. She tried phoning the school office as she ran but was so out of breath the receptionist hung up, probably assuming she was a prank caller.

For fuck's sake. She felt sick. *Black mark for Julie. But it's not my fault!*

When she finally reached the school, Tommy's teacher didn't make eye contact, only looked at her watch, an invisible tut hanging heavy in the air. The door was locked noisily behind them.

'Mummy, why has your face melted?'

'What do you mean, darling?' Julie laughed, leaning in to the window to catch a glimpse. *Oh, God.* Her makeup had run down her cheeks. Smoky eyes. When would she learn, they just weren't for her? As for the lipstick...well, small mercy she was late, and the other mums hadn't seen her. Nobody welcomed a Killer Clown at school pickup!

She cuddled into Tommy, her head rubbing against him.

'Mummy, get off me!' He squirmed and pulled away, staring back with fear in his eyes.

'Don't be scared, darling. Mummy was just playing with the, er...face paints.' It had begun to rain, adding to her absurd appearance. 'Shall we run home, get out of the rain?'

Tommy sulked in response, then perked up a little. 'More time on electronics tonight?' he asked, and she nodded, then chased after him as he shot off like a bullet, grinning wide.

'Wait up!' Julie hollered up the street. 'I'm not as quick as you!'

But he was gone. He knew his way; she wasn't concerned.

Oven food. Pizza, crispy chicken and crinkle-cut chips. She repeated the mantra as she jogged home and through the door. They would like it or starve – she wasn't in the mood for a fight. She needed some time to sort her face out.

Julie opened the fridge, pulled out the vegetable drawer, then closed it again. Let the childminder worry about healthy eating for a change.

'Dinner's ready, guys!' she shouted as she left the beige, processed, stodgy mass on the oven trays, a pile of plates on the side.

Minimal effort, job done.

Why hadn't Dan called? There were no missed calls on her mobile. She tried dialling, and it went straight to voicemail. It didn't feel right to call his office, but it was getting dark out, and she knew the hotel was a few hours' drive away.

Julie went back online to look up the details and wondered how late check-in would be and whether he'd pre-booked a dinner table. She braved his office number and waited.

And waited.

And waited.

Nobody picked up.

She could feel her anxiety returning just when she'd managed to get it all under control again. *Breathe, just breathe.* She tried the office once more, concerned he might have been in an accident on his way home, praying her next call wouldn't be to the local hospital.

On the third ring, the call picked up. 'Hello? Mr. Summers' phone. How can I help you?'

Julie didn't recognise the voice, so she kept it professional, not wanting to ruin Dan's surprise. 'Good evening. Would it be possible to speak with Mr. Summers, please?'

'Oh, I'm terribly sorry but he left a few hours ago and won't be back in the office until Tuesday. Is there anything I can help you with?'

Making her apologies, Julie hung up and wondered what to do next. She opened Dan's laptop and clicked on the hotel booking. Maybe he'd gone straight over to set things up for her? Would she walk in to a surprise party? It wasn't her birthday... Perhaps a renewal of their wedding vows? Some of her friends had done that recently as they hit their ten-year anniversary, but she didn't think Dan would be up for that. She would have to rethink her wardrobe just in case – no good turning up wearing a travelling outfit if she would be thrown straight in among the party people!

Great. More stress, finding something to wear that's suitable. She'd never liked surprises.

She tried his mobile one last time. No answer. Finally, Julie clicked on the hotel number and waited for reception to pick up. She couldn't wait any longer. She wasn't prepared to let anxiety creep back into her life.

'Good evening, this is The Woodloch Spa Hotel. How can we help you?'

'Oh, hi,' she said nervously. 'Sorry to bother you. I just wanted to check if Mr. Summers has checked in yet, and if you could put me through to his room…'

'I'm afraid I can't put you through, madam, but I can confirm Mr. and Mrs. Summers checked in earlier today and are currently at dinner. Would you like me to pass on a message?'

There must be some mistake.

'Mr. and Mrs. Summers? Have checked in?'

'Yes, madam, I believe they are celebrating an anniversary. I shouldn't really say, but they make such a sweet couple, and…'

Julie zoned out. *They?* 'I don't understand. You're telling me Mr. *and* Mrs. Summers are already there?'

'Yes, madam. Now, if you have a message, I would be happy to pass it on.'

Julie dropped the phone even as the voice continued through the speaker.

What the fuck is going on? Her head screamed. *Celebrating their anniversary? He's there with another woman!* How stupid she'd been to believe he was planning to rekindle their neglected romance, that he was trying to fix things, when all this time he'd been off with some hussy getting his way. No wonder he was always so unresponsive when she tried to initiate intimacy.

So many questions rushed through her head. Was it someone she knew? Where had he met her? Was it someone from his office? From the gym? She thought back to his gym bag, the labels still in place, never used, and bile rose in her throat as reality dawned. How could he? How could he wreck their family for some fucking tart – and why? What had she done to deserve this?

Feeling overcome with rage, she cursed him repeatedly, her

body going through the various stages of grief. *Arsehole.* She wouldn't let him get away with this. To think he'd been going at it behind her back, celebrating their anniversary! How long had he been with this trollop? A year? *Years?* Tears pricked the backs of her eyes, pooled in the bottom lid, held in check by heavy eyeliner. She refused to let them fall. He wouldn't make a clown out of her again – not this time. His chances were all used up.

When she walked comatose downstairs, the kids were no-where to be seen. Their food remnants sat decaying on the table, abandoned. They had long since run off to their rooms, likely slamming their doors behind them. She was glad of it today, grateful they hadn't witnessed her upset, that they weren't there to question her. For once, Julie understood their anger and wished she could slam those doors right off their hinges and into Dan's fucking face.

Opening Dan's laptop again, she checked the dates on the hotel bookings site. The trip had been booked on the 7th June, four months ago. Her heart pounded with rage as she hovered the mouse over the 'History' button, watching the screen change to display lists and lists of fancy hotels, double suites booked for two people, none of it for business. Dan's profile page showed he'd signed up three years before. *Three years* of fancy hotels with her.

Don't cry. Save it. Don't cry. He's not worth it. She ran to the bathroom, covering her mouth with her hands, not quite reaching the toilet before vomit sprayed violently between her fingers and over the floor. Empty gasps of horror escaped her at the realisation she'd been lied to and deceived for what could have been years. She was a failure.

Jack's bedroom door opened. With a quick glance and a disgusted grunt – 'Urgh, Mum, that's gross!' – he scurried back into the dark of his pit, leaving her looking down at the mess.

An orange phlegm, with a scrambled egg consistency was splattered across the walls where it had sprayed through Julie's clasped hands. She feebly reached up to the cleaning cupboard for the bleach and began to spray it copiously around the room, allowing the splash-back to dribble down her arm and seep into her skin. She stood watching, willing it to burn off the top layer, to rid her of the violation of Dan's touch. It was not the night she had earlier imagined but somehow much more fitting to the life she was used to; her Cinderella existence as the neglected housekeeper.

Julie finished cleaning the vomit and left the room stinking like a swimming pool. Dropping into bed exhausted, she still couldn't shift Dan's scent off the bedding. In a rage, she summoned enough energy to rip the covers off and threw them on the floor, knocking over the table lamps and sending half-empty glasses of water crashing into the wardrobe door.

Tommy came running in. 'Mummy, what are you doing?' Then, spotting the pillows on the floor and the stripped bedding, he threw himself onto the bed, giggling, 'Pillow fight!' He grabbed a pillow and started smashing it towards her, his little face so innocent, so happy, enjoying the moment and making Julie smile despite herself as she thumped him with the pillow. It was strangely therapeutic and exhausting, ending with them both snuggled up for a much-needed sleep.

Time to forget life and switch off.

Julie hadn't made plans for the weekend, so when Tommy asked to go looking for conkers, she jumped at the chance, desperate to escape the walls of her confinement. She had slept fitfully, woken in a cold sweat and cursed herself for changing the bedding, knowing she'd have to start over again. *More washing*. She couldn't help but smirk at the absurdity of her situation. Her husband had been having an affair for three years – at least – and she was concerned about the washing.

As they walked along, the breeze was invigorating, blowing her hair out of her face and exposing her ears until they were numbed by the cold. Tommy skipped alongside Julie, his warm hand in hers, showing her the love and attention she craved. A simple touch with so much promise. She watched as he spotted a horse-chestnut tree and started scavenging for conkers among the abandoned shells.

'I found one!' He shouted over, holding up a prickly closed shell and running back to her.

They took turns stamping on it, crushing the untouched prison to release the jewel within. Julie couldn't help comparing it to herself, the irony of her life: was Dan's affair the ultimate punishment or her reward, contrived to release her from the ugliness of her existence? Was it the turning point, even more pivotal than the moment of clarity she'd felt ending Amrita's life?

She'd thought a lot about her, understandably, since the story first broke, but had felt no remorse. In the weeks since the cinema killing, despite extensive media coverage describing it as 'a brutal, senseless murder of an innocent', Julie just couldn't bring herself to agree. Perhaps more so since discovering Dan's affair, not that she'd brought it up with him, couldn't face the conflict. It had taken away her self-empowered confidence and put her back a step. *Nobody is innocent,* she thought, watching Tommy snatching up conker after conker greedily. Every action has a beneficial consequence, no matter how harsh the reality of the moment, everything was down to fate. Chance and consequence.

The more Julie read about Amrita Devi's life, the better she felt about her actions. If only she could ask the deceased what she thought, if she was grateful for Julie's actions as Julie believed she should be. Had she been given the choice, known the outcome of how her death would affect those closest to her, would she have made the leap, willingly participated in her own demise?

Over the weeks, Julie had made a conscious effort to read as much as possible surrounding the case. The husband had appeared on TV asking for Justice for Amrita, trying to shed a tear knowing all eyes were on him as the most probable killer. *He looked the type.* Julie wondered how many beatings his wife had endured.

The children weren't pictured, just shadows of figures. She couldn't help but judge them to be rough kids from their bony physiques. They might well be innocent, but in her mind, she fantasised they were neglected, malnourished, drug-dealing addicts. *Was she doing that to justify her own actions?* She shook her head. *No.* According to the papers, their family life had totally changed since their mother died. It was common knowledge they had gone into a police protection programme and would be given new identities to start over somewhere else. Apparently, the adolescents were vulnerable because of what was now being classed as a 'racist attack'. Who knew what they were into? If Mr. Devi was an abuser, he would find it more difficult to escape the consequences in the future now he was in the public eye.

It looked like they had separated him from the children. A job well done on her behalf then? It was easy to judge on appearance as that was all she had, but how many times had people said your first instinct was usually the right instinct? Those kids would have a new life, a new start. Yes, they would miss elements of their old world, but they might not have made it through their teens if everything had stayed the same. *I saved them.*

Julie questioned herself, was she just looking for a reason to argue away why she felt no guilt? Was Mrs. Devi's death a murder or manslaughter? Julie still believed it was self-defence. After all, life was about survival of the fittest, and in that moment, she had believed herself to be under attack. She hadn't planned the murder or killed by accident – she had retaliated against fear. Would they lock her in a mental asylum if they found her? How would they find her, anyway? She'd never been arrested, so her fingerprints weren't on police record, and she'd like to keep it that way. Julie would follow the trial with interest and mentally prepare her own statement, just in case. She had been in the cinema that day after all. Did they have her details? She was confused, relieved her credit card had been refused. A good omen. It was like life had ordained her destiny.

Cold raindrops stung her face as dark clouds shifted overhead, bringing her back to the moment. She looked over at Tommy, who was still running around, carrying a now overflowing bucket of conkers.

'Tommy, it's time to go now, lovely,' she called walking towards him and grabbing at his hand, the bucket swinging precariously in his other. 'Careful! You don't want them to fall out!' she reprimanded, but she was too late. The handle of the plastic bucket ripped off, working its way out of the tiny holes clearly not designed for an inquisitive child who wanted to carry home three kilos of conkers! She wondered how it would have fared as a water bucket.

'No! Mummy, my conkers!' Tommy started to cry as he dropped to his knees.

'Don't worry, darling, we'll just pick them up,' Julie said. She'd already half-filled the bucket again.

Tommy whined. 'I don't want them, they're dirty! They're all yucky now! I want to go and get some more clean ones.'

Oh, seriously, child. Stop being so fucking annoying. She wondered what he'd say if she just came out and said that. Instead, being pragmatic and wanting to keep the peace, she simply poured the entire bucket out again, watching Tommy's shocked face in amusement. He hadn't thought that through. He could have just washed them, but no. *Was he right to reject them? Those once-perfect conkers tainted by life, by the mud of the wet environment – could they ever be truly perfect again?*

The rain had started coming down in sheets, hitting her sideways, with a storm promising to batter them anytime soon. Julie enjoyed watching the dark, billowing clouds approach, black areas giving the appearance the end of the world was nigh. Well, maybe it was. Maybe Tommy would be better off without her. Maybe all children would be, untouched by parental influence.

'Okay, Tommy, time to go.'

His pockets bulged with conkers, and he surprised her by immediately standing and running over without a word. He was obviously starting to feel the rain through his lightweight jacket. He'd never been one for wrapping up warm. It was always an argument to get her kids into coats, any excuse for an argument.

Well, more fool you, she thought as she watched him run Hansel and Gretel-style towards her, leaving a trail of shining conkers in his wake. This wouldn't end well. Greedy children everywhere would be snatching that trail up and pocketing it just as Tommy had, and the childhood bliss of having a full stash of shiny conkers would never be found again.

That was life. There was no turning back, only one way forward, though we were forever searching for that shiny, clean start. The poignancy of the situation was not lost on Julie. She would abandon the path back to the 'bliss' of life as she knew it too, but she would embrace the freedom to come.

Just a few loose ends to tie up first. She wouldn't let Dan get away with hurting her. Nobody was safe from retribution, nor should they be.

That night, after bathing a shivering Tommy, Julie put him to bed, successfully got through the witching hour and manoeuvred her way through his usual last-ditch attempts at staying up.

'I'm hungry!'

'You should have eaten more dinner.'

'I'm thirsty!'

'Tommy, you can't have a drink before bed or you'll be up weeing all night!'

'Can I sleep in your bed while Daddy's away?'

No, child, you cannot. Today is a new day. If you sleep in my bed, then I won't sleep in my bed. You toss and turn all night, you wake me up frequently when you pat me to check I'm still there.

You frighten me half to death with your face in my face, and your bad breath used to be cute but now it's just rank.

Julie looked at Tommy's little face pleading with her and her resolve weakened, 'You can grab one more story, have that in my bed, then I'll say goodnight and tuck you into yours.' *Perhaps it's me. I need to be harder, I'm ready to move forward, ready to focus on myself but you're my little one. Be strong Julie. So what if he feels it more, you've already given seven years of your life to him, he should be grateful for that. It's more than her own mother had given little Rose-bud.*

Tommy smiled back, unable to hide his gloating, believing he's won. In that moment, he looked just like Dan, making Julie smile with relief. *Leaving this lot won't be as hard as I thought.* She kissed him on the head and wrapped him up in his extra blanket.

'Don't forget to kiss my teddies, Mummy!'

'Not tonight, dear. Do it yourself,' she said as she walked away. She could hear him moaning, raising his voice in a shouting tirade as he pretended to cry.

She didn't look back.

Once downstairs, Julie settled on the sofa in front of the television. It was a pleasure to have the remote all to herself. She would play a movie as loud as she liked, turning it up, down, up, down without anybody nagging her to stop. She flicked on the movie guide, glancing through her usual list of romantic comedy and period drama. They all looked familiar but not inviting. Horror movies were out of the question – or were they? There was an entire channel dedicated to horror. How had she never noticed? Julie flicked it on, but it was showing adverts, ten minutes to go until the next movie was due to start. She hadn't watched adverts in years, didn't realise they still ran.

Julie idly picked up Dan's laptop again and thought about the hotel, then logged in to online banking to see how much he was spending on his lady friend. Nothing showed up for today. She searched his statements from the last six months, transactions over three hundred pounds. Seven payments were listed to the same hotel bookings company. There were also the usual payments for the mortgage and car insurance, but nothing else she recognised as domestic bills. An individual payment to PRJ stood out at over one thousand pounds, so she typed the name into a search engine.

PRJ. Princess Regency Jewellery.

What had he bought? Had he been showering her with expensive gifts? It didn't seem his style. Julie searched the twelve-month statement for PRJ payments, and a full page of listings appeared.

Page one of three?

Where had it all gone wrong? It just wasn't fair. The amount he'd spent on jewellery was ridiculous – more like embezzlement! Maybe he was money laundering, and the trips were just a ruse for his underhand dealings?

Yeah, right. Stop thinking the best of him.

How much money did they have? She'd been so trusting, never thought to question or look, but if she was going to divorce him, she would need to know, to make sure she took half of everything. *At least.*

She clicked on their direct debits to see how much money they spent on a monthly basis, disappointed in herself for not thinking to look before. There was a list of mobile phones, all the same network. Hers was by far the cheapest since her kids had all pushed and pushed to get the latest smartphones on a ridiculous monthly contract. As a family, they'd made the decision to give the kids unlimited data so they could all link to the stalker app that tracked their location. Dan had claimed his phone wasn't app-compatible, but she'd figured he just wasn't tech-savvy.

Wait until I get my hands on it... She'd link his phone with her own so she could track him, see how often he met up with the slut.

There was a fifth phone number on the direct debit. Did Dan have a second phone to arrange his affair? Was he pimping his slut, or had he bought a phone for her, another treat? She thought about ringing it, but it was nearly ten p.m., past the ethical cut-off time for phoning outside of emergencies. The unwritten, unspoken rule everyone seemed to adhere to. What if it wasn't her? If it was something business related? Texting was another matter. Was it okay to text all through the night? Maybe not to a stranger. The number was likely unavailable anyway, but on the off chance it had been passed to a new owner, Julie didn't want to be the freaky night caller. She would decide in the morning or when she was brave enough to face the potential consequences, if that day ever came.

Chapter Sixteen

Julie wondered if there was anyone else out there feeling the pain that she was in, if anybody could understand the feeling of loss. She'd put all her energy into being a good wife, then when the kids came along, they sucked it all out of her. Every waking moment was spent trying to please, discipline or entertain them. Motherhood was the cycle of feed, clothe, wash, shout, and try your best to get them to sleep – all in the hope of raising them to be half-way decent human beings. She hoped she'd succeeded, at least where the kids were concerned, but it would depend who was doing the judging. She had so clearly failed with Dan.

Julie dreamed of a life where it was just her – the simplicity, the fulfilment of every desire on demand. No time restraints, no consequences; total freedom. How many other mothers felt the same? She imagined a world where every woman stood up for themselves and just said 'No, I'm not going to take it anymore.' That was the dream. Society would break down, family life would be chaos, children would be neglected and left to their own devices, working partners would be unable to go off to their jobs, instead thrust into the thick of parenting and domestic duties. Finally, there would be some recognition of the domestic goddess's unseen efforts! And what about single parents? Why shouldn't those women leave too, just run away and live life for themselves, let the world face the consequences? Blissful chaos!

Maybe a temporary walk-out would be enough to shock people into appreciating women like her. Enough for them to literally take a break. She wondered about the mums at the school gates – would they join in? Leave everything? Were they struggling beneath their perfect exterior? They all seemed so in-control, painted smiles on their faces, making minimal conversation as they rushed off elsewhere. What was going on behind those glass eyes? They gave nothing away.

Julie loved her kids and didn't want to put them in danger, but at the same time, why was everything down to her? All she wanted was some time off, ideally with the shock factor to make her family appreciate her more. She wanted to be missed. Julie fantasised about leaving the house on her own – just opening the door, walking out and shutting it behind her. No last-minute arguments about who hadn't tied their shoes or moaning about the necessity of wearing a coat in the rain, no vomit on her shoulder or shouts of, 'Mum, where's my...?'

I'm leaving. No more responsibilities, only wild abandonment.

Her thoughts were interrupted as the television blared, announcing the movie was starting.

The film was eerie and dark, but Julie wanted to be scared. She wanted to feel something so overwhelming that it would take her mind off the life-changing affair she had just discovered.

She embraced the emotion, no longer caring if someone broke in and attacked her.

It didn't matter that Dan was away on one of his jollies tonight. *Jollies! Ha, what a joke!* She wondered how many of his 'work trips' had been trips away with the other woman. Who was she? What was she like? Why did he need more? She wanted to be angry but mainly felt disappointment and something else, relief? She could breathe again. It was like he had given her the key, offered her a green light to go forth, and the world was out there waiting for her.

Julie couldn't concentrate, she wasn't fully engrossed in the movie, instead critiquing the vampires that weren't realistic enough. In her mind, she was writing a review for her blog, mentally dissecting every scene. It just wasn't happening. She flicked over to another channel, true crime drama. *Contains violence, gore, drug use, scenes of a sexual nature and subjects some viewers may find distressing.*

Great.

A woman had gone missing, and the hunt was on to find the kidnapper before he raped and killed her, disposing of her body in some gruesome manner reserved for television dramatizations only. The guy was a suspected serial killer, and missing Violet was not the first in a chain of disappearances in a quaint little Dorset village.

This is more like it. She turned the volume up.

Julie listened to the police investigators as they tried to work out how they would capture the killer. How did they come up with a plan? It seemed so much of their time was spent thinking and travelling to potential leads where nothing paid off – either that, or acting the stereotype tucking into doughnuts. The drama flicked to a scene of a dark room: a woman's face, dirty, with matted hair. She was sweating and shaking, whimpering, scared. How did the killer set the scene? Make it look like a dungeon? At what point had the woman become a mad-eyed, blood-streaked, dirty-faced victim? Julie noted her greasy hair and wondered if the actress found it difficult to leave it in such a state between shoots. Had the villain bundled her into a van, bag on head, so she couldn't see where he was taking her? Did he know the victim? Perhaps he'd befriended her and she'd willingly gone with him. She wanted to know more of the back story and wished she'd flicked over sooner. Why was she the chosen one? Oh, how Julie would love to throw Dan's slut to the wolves, watch them devour her in a dungeon along with the amateur actress onscreen.

She ran away with the thought, imagined Slut calling for help, bound and gagged, the panic of not knowing what was to come. That would be exhilarating. Pure terror. Make her wait. Julie felt excited planning how she would blindfold her for good measure, take away her sense of awareness. Would she give hints as to why she was being punished – for breaking the female code of allegiance by taking another woman's husband? Julie would use her own eye mask, a nice touch. Would Slut recognise her perfume? At least it would be a hint her attacker was a woman. She smiled as she imagined Slut squirming in fear.

The police assistant onscreen ran around with a clipboard and pen, incompetent, a joke, tagging along to every meeting and being sent off to buy more doughnuts. Would Julie need to worry about pen-pushers finding her and Slut? Slut plus Amrita would make two victims. Would that make her a serial killer? If she got away with it, maybe her new vocation could be taking home-wreckers and working her magic. A serial cleanser! Kidnap and torture. Could she do it? Hell yeah! She'd offer her services to other women who wanted revenge on their partners.

She got up to grab a glass of red wine, pouring the large glass a third-full, enjoying the aroma as she swirled it around and around before taking a full sniff. She would hold out for a first sip; a first taste of pleasure. The wait would be worth it.

The girl on the television pleaded for her life while the attacker watched, patiently waiting, relishing the moment, leaving the audience hungry for an evil laugh to make it feel more real.

Julie grabbed a pen and scribbled into her notebook: *Leave them hanging. Suspense is not only for TV!*

She leaned forward and smelled her blood-red wine, still not ready for that first taste. Pausing the show, she returned to her notepad.

For her title, Julie wrote 'Revenge' and then began her list of priorities. What would make Slut fear for her life? What would ruin her? Julie would show Dan what it was to feel fear. She would ruin Slut, not give her the sweet release of death. She would plan something fun, a house of horrors. She finally picked up her glass and allowed a little bit of wine into her mouth, held it still, allowed the sour taste to attack her salivary glands and send them into overdrive. She held it and waited until it was almost unbearable before swallowing. Drip by drip, it trickled down her throat.

Julie looked at the wine, the blood of her first victim, giving her strength. She drained the glass and left it in front of the TV screen, pressing play again as she made her way out of the room. The lights were already out since she had tried to build tension for the horror movie earlier, and as she left the room, the woman's scream permeated the house and followed her upstairs, filling Julie with renewed determination.

She would not be in such a hurry to give Slut freedom. It would be interesting to observe Dan's actions now she knew what he was up to. How would he deal with Slut's abduction? How long would he chase her memory, try to find her? Would he be at home more if he didn't have her arms to run into? Would he be an emotional wreck? Oh, how she hoped so. She hoped he suffered, really suffered. That he kept his confession to himself, struggling with the internal turmoil of his guilt, no outlet for sympathy or comfort. What if it went the other way and he reported her missing? Came clean, she wouldn't take him back. Not now. Not ever.

Julie was excited to have a purpose. She promised herself, Slut would be shown no mercy. Julie would never get back those years of neglect. For three years, Slut had been sleeping with her husband, so three years would be her punishment; a prison of her own making.

Now, just to work out who she was.

There was no need for lights as Julie walked into the bathroom to brush her teeth; her eyes had acclimatised to her surroundings and her altered mentality. Adrenaline rushed through her with the thought of her new focus: planning Slut's kidnap. She was glad she'd watched the horror channel at last, as it had confirmed her new realisation that there was nothing to fear.

She winced as she scraped her gum, being too aggressive with her electric toothbrush. It would result in an ulcer, no doubt. She leaned forward to look in the mirror, and as the moon shone through the window blinds, she caught a glimpse of a shadow behind her. Turning, she saw it was just a black bath towel.

Julie wiped the toothpaste from her mouth and looked at the luminescent stain left behind on the towel. She let it drop to the floor as she looked back at the mirror to admire her already throbbing ulcer. She embraced the pain, holding her gums back in a grimace – the sneer of an attacking dog ready for the hunt. As she stood staring at her own reflection, the world around her changed like a magic-eye painting, making her feel disorientated and slightly nauseous. Gradually, she noticed the shapes around her face forming into one; a figure with long, floating hair billowing out at the sides. The figure moved forward, into view, piercing dark eyes staring back at her. Julie was fixated. She had seen that face before, on the news, in the newspapers.

Amrita, back to haunt her killer.

She was beautiful, an image of perfection, with unblemished skin and the hazy glow of an angel; the innocence of a new-born child. Was this the afterlife, or was she stuck in limbo, waiting to complete a mission before she could rest in peace?

They stared at each other, and time stood still.

Julie was ready. She'd been ready all her life; had anticipated this moment and was relieved it had finally come, that there *were* ghosts waiting in the wings, glinting in the corners of her eyes, reaching to come out in the night. She wondered at the irony of all those years of fear and anxiety, and how the reality was a calming tonic in her otherwise crazy existence. Had she always known? Had she seen something in her childhood that had left a lasting mark on her subconscious mind? Or did ghosts only appear to those who were there at their moment of passing? Those who had pushed them over the bridge into eternal life – or eternal death?

Julie felt no fear. She stopped snarling, stood upright and stared back, mother-to-mother. Was Amrita waiting for an apology? Julie felt no guilt or remorse. She had freed this woman from her confinement. She smiled into the mirror, and the figure responded by lifting her head, nodding and then fading to nothing.

A brief smile had crossed between them. Only a glint, but it was there.

Was that a thank-you?

Amrita was at peace now, thanks to Julie. She walked away from the room, got into her cosy bed and closed her eyes. *There's nothing to fear except fear itself,* and she was no longer afraid.

Chapter Seventeen

The days that followed were oddly blissful. Julie enjoyed having her new focus: planning to end the life of another. She had a notebook of research, had studied serial killers and was getting stuck into a variety of detective novels and horror movies. She enjoyed the thrill of keeping it all hidden, the plans (even if they never actually happened), the fun of the chase. She had no idea who Slut was, so she would have to do some further digging. She wondered how long it would be before Dan had to 'work late again'. She tried to pick up clues in what he said – where he was going, who he talked about – but nothing seemed out of the ordinary. He'd been hiding it for years after all; lying had become second nature to him.

Dan had returned from the spa like an excitable puppy, bounding all over the house hugging the kids and leaning in to sweep her off her feet. Making her question herself, could she have got it wrong? *No, that's impossible, stand firm.*

'I'm exhausted, but I missed you lot! We literally didn't sleep,' he explained, looking from her to the family photo and back again. 'I need a holiday to get over the holiday! All that drinking, all the late nights and early mornings – I'm proper shattered.'

Julie looked at him in disgust, really seeing him for the first time, knowing full well why he'd had no sleep and the real cause of his exhaustion. Still, it had put a smile on his face, and that meant she didn't have to oblige. He'd be 'too tired' for a while now, then he'd likely have to go on a 'work trip' for his next fix. She didn't know why it had taken her so long to realise something wasn't right in their relationship.

When she was a teenager, that was all friends talked about, but somehow, once married, sex was taboo. Nobody talked about what was normal anymore, so how was she to know? *Don't share the marital bed* – the unspoken rule.

Well, fuck you, Dan, for sharing ours.

How could he keep up the pretence? Why would he? If he wanted someone else, he could have just left rather than wasting his time and hers.

Life is short, you've got to grab it with both hands! Those were her aunt's words when she'd first met Dan. Well, Slut would find out just how short life could be – she'd be begging for an end by the time Julie finished with her.

In hindsight, Julie realised her aunt had only been trying to fill her mother's shoes, jumping in with her religious opinions because she knew Julie was vulnerable. She remembered her aunt warning her to not go around 'acting like a man', 'doing like the other girls', 'spreading it around,' every time they spoke it was the same thing. Oh how she wished she hadn't followed that advice. If only she'd met a few other guys, she would have had more experience and been able to make better judgements. She should have known better, learned from her parents' mistakes, but she just hadn't been strong enough. She was broken, and Dan had offered to make her whole. Julie wondered what influence her actions would have on her own children, how they would remember her. Would they blame her for their choices?

She reached down and picked up Dan's mobile, entered the generic pin he'd never thought to change. It was the same one he used on every device in the house. Surely, if he was up to something, he would be more protective of his phone? Perhaps he'd become complacent over the years, cocky in his arrogance, enjoying the thrill of hiding in plain sight.

She clicked into the app store and pressed 'Upload' on the stalker app, sent her own phone an invitation and synced the two. *Sorted.* She hid the file inside another app folder, knowing he was too trusting to ever suspect Julie of messing with it.

'Hurry up, Dan, the kids need to brush their teeth before school!'

'Okay, I'm nearly done.'

She picked his phone up again to look through his messages, but there was nothing glaringly obvious. A few women's names: Anna, Sarah, Rachel, Abigail. They were all people she knew, friends of the family, but there was no unusual correspondence. *Very odd. Surely, they would communicate? Who goes without texting their partner nowadays?* Dan even texted her daily – usually something to do with dinner, or some excuse to say why he wouldn't be joining them.

The other mobile number! He must have two phones!

She listened at the bathroom door. The shower was still running, so she picked up her own phone and rang the number, making sure to withhold her own. It rang, but she couldn't hear it in the house, not even a vibration.

Maybe it's not his.

The answerphone clicked in: *Sorry, I can't take your call at the moment, but if you leave your name and number, I'll get back to you.* It was an automated voice, nothing to implicate Dan. She would have to do further digging.

'Dad, hurry up! We're going to be late!' William pounded on the bathroom door.

'Stop banging! Do you know how much that door costs if you break it?' Dan called.

Oh, for God's sake, here we go again. Just leave already so the kids can leave. So I can leave. Forever.

Julie fantasised again about leaving her life, about the enjoyable future looming in the distance, just beyond her reach.

First, she needed to find out more about Slut.

She picked up her phone to make an appointment with Kate. Maybe the life coach could point her in the right direction. Maybe she'd agree to meet up with her outside the office today for a coffee meeting – Starbucks at the cinema complex where *it* had happened; her guilty pleasure. There were no toilets there, so that would be Julie's excuse to head into the cinema, feel the tingle, relive the moment. She would enjoy leaning against the cool white tiles, rubbing her fingers into the cracks left behind from that fateful day, drawing slowly over the stained grouting, knowing. Would Kate find herself drawn to that cubicle too, if she knew what had happened there?

Julie set up the appointment, disappointed Kate's secretary insisted it take place at the office.

'Tommy, get down those stairs now! We're late – hurry up!'

He came running down, cursing and blaming his dad for hogging the bathroom as he pushed his feet into muddy black school shoes, not bothering to untie the laces. As they left the house, she pulled the door to, but the open back windows made for an almighty bang, surprising her, and making Tommy jump. She smiled as she thought of how Dan would be seething, blaming Tommy. If challenged, Julie would quite happily take the blame and face a confrontation. She was ready.

Fuck you, Dan. Let's slam all the doors until they come right off their hinges, and then we'll see who's really to blame for what lies between us.

Chapter Eighteen

'I want you to hypnotise me.'

Julie sat relaxed and confident on the sofa in Kate's office. She'd walked in with her list of topics she would like to discuss and how she would like to approach each one. She was no longer the wilted wall flower, lifeless and desperate for sustenance, but instead the Venus flytrap, exquisitely beautiful yet dangerously deceptive, ready to catch her prey.

'Yes, I want you to take me into a state of total relaxation, so you can delve in and pull out some specific information for me,' Julie said without waiting for a response. 'I want to know where I've seen this necklace before. I recognise it from a picture on my laptop, but it's not mine, so whose is it?'

'Have you thought of asking your husband?' Kate asked.

'No.'

'Wouldn't that be a simpler way to start? To ask if he bought it?'

Julie stood up, walked over to Kate and met her eye-to-eye as she spoke. 'He's having an affair. It's been going on for years, and he's been showering her with expensive jewellery for at least six months. I want to know who it is. I want to confront her, tell her to take him, because I don't want to be in a loveless marriage anymore.'

Kate's reply was emotionless. 'Okay, I see. I'm sorry for your loss.'

Julie laughed out loud at her response. The woman seemed devoid of empathy yet, talking about Dan as if he was dead, well, that was kind of fitting.

'Well, I have to tell you,' Kate continued, 'hypnosis doesn't really work that way in real life. I could relax you and focus your mind, but I doubt you'll remember exactly where you saw the necklace. If you already know, somewhere in your subconscious, the shock when you discovered your husband's affair would have likely been enough to make you recall it. I think we should bring the focus back to you. How have you been developing? You seem to be more confident in your decision-making, which is a tick in my box.'

'So, you're refusing to hypnotise me?' Julie finally interrupted, eyeing Kate with suspicion as she noticed for the first time she was squirming uncomfortably. 'Or is it that you don't know how?'

Kate watched in surprise as Julie opened her bag, threw down some money and reached for her coat. If the woman wouldn't hypnotise her, then she no longer needed to waste her time in this stuffy office.

She turned just before leaving and reached back for Kate's umbrella. 'I need it more than you,' she said as she slammed the door behind her.

Outside, Julie enjoyed the brisk air as snowflakes silently fell onto her nose, her cheeks, her eyelashes, tingling as they collided with her skin. She thought about putting the umbrella up but instead chose to indulge in the rarity of London snow. It felt so clean and refreshing. She didn't know why she'd snatched the umbrella – maybe just to see if she could get away with it. Every action had a reaction, but what would Kate's reaction be? Would there be consequences? Only for the person who tried to prise her new weapon from her hand. *Come on, crazies, come and get me and see where I shove it*, she thought with a grin.

It was still early in the day, so she decided to go for a stroll. As the wind blew, Julie let her coat fall open, let the icy whether chill her until her body trembled. Maybe time for a quick cinema visit, if only to use the toilet. *Focus the mind*, she thought.

Christmas came and went, leaving behind a trail of credit-card debt to match the messy mountain of unwanted gifts stacked up around the house, in the corners where they had been abandoned on Christmas Day. How long would they have to keep them before they could successfully regift without feeling guilty or being found out? Julie thought Christmas was supposed to be a time for families to bond, mainly over food, but for the housewife, it was more about bonding with the oven, the hob, the dishwasher if you were lucky enough to have one. She preferred to hand-wash the dishes when Dan's family joined them, giving her more time to herself not having to make conversation. On the plus side, with the school holidays came an obvious decline in the piles of laundry since the kids lounged around in pyjamas all day, slobbing out and refusing to dress unless visitors were due. *Sleep, play, eat, repeat* – for everyone but Julie.

She was trying hard to give Dan the benefit of the doubt, having found nothing substantial to incriminate him. In the beginning, it had been an effort to hide her emotions, a permeating sense of sadness constantly there, but the holiday season had kept her so busy she soon managed to mask it under the pretence of exhaustion. She could make him happy, be enough for him; if only so that the children wouldn't have to endure a childhood listening to arguing, separation, divorce, neglect. She knew it all too well. If they could keep civil, that would be enough. She would be enough.

Every time he 'popped out', she tracked him. Every time he 'went to work', she tracked him, but the results reaffirmed his innocence. Checking her phone again, there he was, the usual journey to work which ended in the last twenty minutes of the journey without reception – him falling off the map. Even his office had no mobile reception being down in the basement and next door to the underground station, how convenient that he forgot to sink to his Wi-Fi unless he wanted her. Frustrating.

So, if Slut did exist, maybe she was meeting him at work – or somewhere in no-mans-land where he fell off the radar. She wouldn't be surprised if he purposely turned his phone off on the train so that she couldn't interrupt them. It sickened her, and frustrated her not knowing his whereabouts. There was no way he knew about the stalker-app or he would have confronted her. Any excuse for a shouting match, for a reason to stay out for the night.

Was the affair with someone he worked with? She couldn't imagine him going for any of the women she'd met back when she was invited to the last Christmas party – but that was years ago. Back then the company was more lucrative, Dan had explained, the reason recent years they'd had to cancel their plus-ones. *Had he been lying? Was he taking her? How humiliating that would be if everyone knew, if everyone was laughing at her behind her back, watching him with a girl half his age employed to fulfil his extra needs.*

Julie felt sick.

As the days passed, she tried to block out her thoughts, told herself she was being selfish thinking about leaving, that she had to stay for the kids – but on the other hand, if she could get away, how simple her life could be. Alone. She was in constant turmoil with no one to talk to, didn't want to admit that her husband was having an affair – didn't want to voice it out loud as if somehow that would make it more real.

One moment she was ready to walk out, kidnap, murder, release her demons and escape; the next, she wished for nothing more than to settle down by the fire with a hot chocolate, get Dan's tea and tuck the kids into bed. They were so innocent in their sleep, so lovingly innocent.

Amrita's death was no longer so prominent in the papers, and Julie's life was easier now. Dan had loosened the reigns a bit and allowed her out of the house again. She continued to track the investigation, but nothing new sprung up on her daily search. It all felt like a dream. She started to question her own sanity: Was she really involved?

'Why don't you take the kids away in the New Year, stay with your mum for a bit? I've got lots of work trips coming up anyway, and it would keep you out of mischief for a while,' Dan said over Christmas dinner. 'In fact, really sorry, but after we finish eating, I'm going to have to pop out. There's a mountain of paperwork piled up at the office to be cleared by the weekend.'

Julie was gutted. Christmas Day was a time for family, not for swanning off to God knows where under the pretence of work. How could he think her so gullible?

She looked up at his pale face, watched him gormlessly stare back. He was no doubt willing her to kick off so he could storm out and blame her. That was part of Christmas too, the family argument. It was tradition. The kids couldn't care less – they barely acknowledged the conversation, lost in their thoughts of how to escape the dinner table and get back to their gaming consoles. Julie didn't even know if she cared anymore. What was the point in trying if he wasn't going to meet her halfway?

As Dan got up from the table, he scraped his chair noisily along the floor, making Julie twitch with irritation. *Tuck the fucking chair in*, she screamed silently, imagining how she'd smash the dinner plate against his skull. *He's not worth the clean-up.*

'But what about desert?' Julie pleaded in a last-ditch attempt to stop him from leaving, knowing he couldn't resist chocolate.

Dan hesitated, then shook his head as he grabbed his coat and headed for the door. 'Don't wait up!'

She stared unblinking after he closed the door silently, melting away into the winter night. She wished she was the one having an affair as her thoughts were interrupted by the scurry of feet, the kids running off to their rooms, leaving her alone; totally alone.

He must be going to her. Maybe she's prepared him another meal? I bet he won't refuse her when she offers dessert.

If this was what life was, Julie welcomed the end. She wasn't going to accept this treatment anymore. She thought about the drawer of treats under Tommy's bed, wondered when she'd next get the chance for a rest. She wanted to be happy; she deserved it, but if she couldn't be, then... The relief was palpable as she finally decided it was time to take the next step.

Chapter Nineteen

Come on, Julie! She was starting to annoy herself. New Year's Eve was a re-run of Christmas day, sat home alone, dozing by the fire while the kids ignored her and Dan snuck out. Her guess, he was out with Slut again, either that or he was just looking for an excuse to be away from his wife. It was all just too exhausting to think about, far better to sleep away the stresses of what might be happening, put away the dreams of what could have been. Sleep was the only release and it got her through the holiday season. Before she knew it, January had turned into February and the winter had started to thaw, she wasn't brave enough to take the plunge, to confront him.

The kids were ratty and Dan was absent much of the time, so there was no change there. Julie needed help. Maybe a friend, but who could she trust? She surfed through her Facebook page, willing there to be at least one person who was real, more than a smiling pout over a gourmet banquet. As she scrolled, she realised how long it had been since she'd last met up with friends. She sent a quick message to find out if there was an imminent book club meeting and went to brush her teeth. Maybe Rachel could spare her a few minutes? She wasn't the best at responding promptly – although she always seemed to have her phone in hand when they were together.

Since Dan was out, Julie thought she'd relax and have a quick bath before bed to wash the food smells from her hair. She was loathed to put her jeans in the wash after only two days as it meant adding to the stockpile of washing, but they stunk of café, having taken the brunt of the spitting hob fat from that night's dinner sausages.

She looked in the mirror and saw the Julie of old, fighting its way to the forefront through the masked front she presented to the world: mother and wife. Nothing more. There was no twinkle, no excitement, only a bland existence in a dreamless world. Gone was the vivification that had fleetingly empowered her after the cinema incident. Gone was the raging anger on discovering Dan's affair and her need for revenge. Julie had resigned herself to the daily slog of life and given up the fight.

Being undermined daily had left her with low self-esteem. There were dark circles under her eyes – so dark she could see the veins pulsing beneath them like black lines drawn onto the delicate skin beneath. Her upper lids sagged down, and as she pulled them upwards and backwards, trying to imagine herself a younger, fresher model, straining to look past her reflection for something more. A spirit? A message? An omen? A clue as to her future or past? But nothing came. She longed to see Amrita looking back at her once more, but there had been no further visits since that night. Where was she now? What had it meant? Julie no longer felt scared, only tired, and desperate for something to happen.

After she finished brushing her teeth, she put her toothbrush on charge, having noticed the battery flashing as she brushed. She wondered who would charge her kid's toothbrushes if she wasn't there. Who would even bother to pick up their toothbrush, and who would wipe the muck from the sink that dried to the bowl after each of them had been in to take their turn? *It only takes a rinse, but no, too much effort for any of them.* She had failed to raise them as decent human beings. She felt the tears trickling down her cheeks at the thought of them grown up neglected, their own wives fighting for freedom from the selfish men they had chosen in a moment of weakness.

Welcome to the real world, guys, because when people get to know you, they will likely wish they never had.

Julie climbed into bed and switched the light off. The bed was cold; it was always cold. The warmth had long since left her relationship, and bed socks were a better bet. You always knew where you were with bed socks. With Dan out working late, she could sleep facing the centre of the bed. There would be no one to snore, nobody to complain if she took up more space or too much of the covers. She spread out, daring to move her legs across to his side. She would sleep at an angle, if only to annoy him – if he even bothered to grace her with his company at some point that night. The room was still, silent, dark and relaxing, and she soon dropped off into an exhausted sleep.

'Mum, it's school time!'

'Oh, for goodness' sake, it's like fucking Groundhog Day in this house!'

Tommy gasped. 'You said a bad word! Mum said fuck! Fuck, fuck, fuck, fuck!'

'Tommy, stop that! You're right, I shouldn't have said it. I didn't know what I was saying! I was still half asleep when you woke me.'

He trailed out of the door repeating himself until his brothers joined in. *Great.* What had she started? Rolling over, Julie looked at Dan. Would he be annoyed? Nope. He was asleep. As. Per. Usual.

She reached over to her mobile and turned the alarm off. No point waiting another half hour for it to go off at the time she would have liked to get up. There was a message waiting from Rachel. Julie clicked to open it.

Rachel: *Book club in two weeks! Free today for lunch? Twelve o'clock, coffee shop in Marble Arch, near work?*

Julie smiled. She could make it there and back in the school day, and Dan wouldn't notice. She would have to keep her eyes peeled though, as his office on Oxford Street sometimes brought him over that way. Best to keep a low profile.

She replied with a smiley emoji and a thumbs-up.
Julie: *See you there!*

Chapter Twenty

'Hi, lovely lady, how are you?' Julie greeted Rachel with a hug and a kiss, marvelling at how her flawless makeup had made it through to midday and wondering if any had transferred onto her own pale face.

'All good, thanks, just a bit crazy at work, but we deffo needed a catch up. It's been ages! What have you been up to? Are the kids pulling their weight more now? They're a right needy lot! Did you get a job? I'm guessing not, or I would have heard.' Rachel didn't take a breath as she expertly beckoned for the waitress to come over and ordered a skinny caramel soya latte and a granola pot. The young girl repeated her order but didn't write it down, then looked over expectantly at Julie.

'Um, could I have a burger, chips and a Pepsi, please?' She couldn't look at her friend, knowing the judgement that would be staring back at her.

The waitress nodded, reached down to take their wine glasses and plates from the table and walked away. What was the point of it, table decoration? If she had ordered wine, would they have used that glass, topped it up or brought a fresh one out anyway? How many times had these plates sat pretty on a table, waiting, with people talking over them, spreading their germs, resting their grubby hands on top? What happened to the plates and glasses once they were back in the kitchen?

'What's the matter, Julie?'

'Sorry, I just went off into my own world. What were we talking about?'

The waitress came over with the food and drinks. Julie couldn't help but wonder how they'd managed to get the food cooked so quickly and whether the microwave had been involved. She watched Rachel as she dipped a long-handled teaspoon into the mini granola pot. It looked so dainty, covered in smooth white yoghurt, with a berry mix running in pretty rivulets over the edges of the artistic creation. Time seemed to slow down as she watched the spoon enter her friend's mouth, perfectly painted lips parting to make way for the delicate flavours.

She looked down at her own plate, lifted her burger in two hands and bit into it as delicately as possible, ending up with a mouthful of bun, greasy hands and half the filling falling back onto the plate. Why had she chosen it? To rebel against Dan when he wasn't even there? He was forever commenting on her weight and how she'd let herself go since having the kids, but she knew well enough it was nothing to do with that. It was the depression that engulfed her in every waking moment of her life, had done so since she became part of the furniture of the house; functional.

'I'm going to leave,' she blurted out.

Rachel put down her spoon and looked at her. 'You have to leave already?'

'No, not the restaurant! I'm going to leave Dan! And the kids and my life and everything. I want to run away and hide, and when I feel better, I want to start my life over again.'

Rachel laughed.

'I'm not joking. I mean it! I've had enough. You're the one who told me I should leave him. Well, I'm going to.'

'But what about the kids? Will you take them with you? Where will you go?'

'No, just me. I don't care about the consequences. Let somebody else worry and plan and sort and skivvy – and *care*.'

'Julie, I can't believe you're telling me this now, when' – she glanced at her watch – 'I have to head off in, like, five minutes! Why did you let me order food? This is massive!' She put another spoonful of granola to her lips, and it flopped over the front of her blouse.

'Wow, I've managed to flummox you!' Julie laughed, as Rachel dabbed at her top, still in shock. If she had managed to shock her friend, what would it do to Dan and the kids? She hoped it would have the desired effect: she would go, they would miss her, she would return, and they would welcome her home like the prodigal son, prodigal mother – whatever.

'Fuck, I need to clean this up. Don't move out of that chair, Mrs!' Rachel rushed off to the bathroom, napkin in hand. 'Soon-to-be Miss!' she shouted from the doorway.

Julie sat surfing Facebook, not able to just sit on her own without having something to pass the time. She heard a buzz from Rachel's bag.

Bugger, her mobile phone.

The loudest ringtone started to accompany it, making heads turn. Julie reached forwards and frantically rummaged through Rachel's bag. How the hell did such a small, compact holdall contain so much makeup?

Where the fuck is that phone?

People around the room were frowning, all eyes on her as the accompanying tuts started up. *Well, it's not my fucking phone*, she thought, brandishing her own in the air to demonstrate. *Don't shoot the messenger.* Actually, shoot the messenger; if they hadn't bloody called, the phone wouldn't be disturbing everyone.

Finally! She pulled the phone out just as the ringing stopped. *Missed call.* She rolled her eyes to the sky and was just about to return it when she noticed the number. It was Dan's. Why was he calling? Always checking up on her and tormenting her friends as well now! For Christ's sake, when would it end?

Fuck off, Dan.

'What are you doing in my bag?' Rachel shouted, snatching it, the contents falling to the floor where Julie hadn't quite finished closing the zip. 'Oh, great, thanks for that!'

'Sorry, it's just your phone rang, and people were looking, and I went to turn it off but it stopped before I reached it. It was Dan, by the way! Checking up on me. God knows how he knew I was out with you. If he rings again, do me a favour and just say you haven't seen me, please.'

Rachel nodded slowly, the smile gone from her lips. She mumbled something about having to get back to work, grabbed her coat and started to walk towards the door.

'Rachel, are we all right?' Julie asked, not wanting to end on a sour note.

'Sure, Julie, I've just got to go.'

'Okay, sorry again about your bag.'

She watched as her friend left the restaurant, reality dawning on her that if she walked away from her life, she might not ever see her again. She was sad as she got out her bank card to pay the bill, then remembered how tight Rachel was and wondered if the whole overreaction had been to get out of paying. Ridiculous but quite likely, knowing Rachel. And she did know her – they'd been best friends for nearly fifteen years.

What a sneaky trick. She threw some cash down on the table in frustration at being blanked by the waitress. It always flummoxed her. Why were they so quick to take your order but not your money? It should be the other way around.

Outside, it was cold – always cold. As she walked along, Julie hugged herself.

'Miss! Miss! Stop, Miss!'

Oh, shit. The waitress was running after her. Had it been more than that? She'd probably underestimated the cost of that granola.

'Miss, you dropped your phone!' The woman handed over a mobile.

'That's not mine but thank you anyway!'

'Maybe it's your friend's? It was on the floor, under your table.'

No. She remembered Rachel's phone from earlier, and this wasn't hers. Julie pressed the home screen button, and a photo popped up: Rachel in her work clothes at her desk, posing with a pen in hand, pouting her lips.

'Oh, yes, it is! Thanks. I must have been mistaken.'

The waitress ran off back to the warm, leaving Julie staring at the phone. It was definitely not the phone Dan had called.

Rachel had two phones? *A second phone?* For a split second, Julie wondered, *Could it be?*

Don't be silly.

Rachel was a high-flying business woman; she must have one phone for business, and another for...home? But a nagging doubt overtook her. There was Dan's number again, another missed call showing. How did he know she had two phones?

Julie reached into her own bag, withheld her number and tried to call that illusive number.

Rachel's photo lit up as the mobile started to vibrate.

Why was it ringing? *Why, Rachel? What?* Was her friend spying on her for Dan? She unlocked the phone, Rachel always so predictable with her codes. The wallpaper changed to a different photo: Rachel dressed up as a pilot.

What's going on?

It was so intrusive, but Julie couldn't help clicking into her friend's photos, feeling a guilty pleasure as she browsed through image after image of Rachel posing, pouting, thrusting her breasts at the camera, bulging them out of her negligee – unrecognisable as the Rachel she knew so well, strangely mesmerising. Julie flicked through a few more, wondering who had taken the photos, what secret life her friend had been living, fascinated by her body: pert, perfect, an obvious delight to the photographer.

Then, Dan.

Naked Dan.

Naked Dan and naked Rachel.

Naked Dan and naked Rachel having sex.

She dropped the phone to the ground, watched the screen crack, the pictures still leering back at her. It didn't make sense. How could she? How could *they*? With *each other*?

Julie heaved, a lump of burger threatening to block her airways as a further heave followed. All of the arguments over Dan, Rachel pushing Julie, making out that he was terrible, that they weren't suited. The breakdown of Rachel's own marriage a couple of years ago – had her husband known? Julie had thought Rachel the stronger woman, breaking free from an abusive relationship, but had she been lying about that too? Her thoughts were a jumbled mass of confusion. How many times had Rachel manipulated her into attending parties and then left her on her own for hours when she was running late? Had she been meeting with Dan? *Oh, my God.* Had she hidden, watched her, waited for her to leave the house so she could pounce and take over? And Dan – maybe he didn't trust Rachel to keep their secret? Had she been pushing for more? Threatening to tell Julie? That would explain why he hadn't wanted them to spend time together, always making a fuss when they arranged to meet up. Or was that all an act, all part of a long-term plan?

She reached down and retrieved the phone. It was still working, the cracked screen a perfect metaphor for her life. Julie willed herself to skim the photos, cold shivers running through her, cheeks burning up with fury and humiliation. She checked the dates the photos had been taken, looking back to find the first images. How long had they been at it behind her back? The pictures kept scrolling. Then, the two of them seated at a table, arm in arm, 'Happy Anniversary!' written across their dessert plates as they sat in white bathrobes. The spa.

Julie threw the phone into a homeless man's hat. 'Enjoy the view,' she muttered as she walked away.

Anger? Relief? She wouldn't be going home that night or anytime soon – this had made her decision concrete. Let him wonder where she was, who she was with; let him worry about her, see what life would be like when she was gone. Revenge was best served cold – wasn't that what her mother used to say? Dan had brought this upon himself.

Chapter Twenty-One

As the sun's first rays prised their way between her eyelashes, Julie welcomed the day, a new dawn at last was rising. She had never been one for getting up early, *before*, but it's surprising how welcoming the morning can be when the day is spent in self-indulgence.

Three months had passed since her discovery of Rachel and Dan's affair, and since leaving she had enjoyed the freedom more than she ever thought she could. *You only live once*, she told herself daily, revelling in every moment, no matter how trivial.

Life was a pleasure. There was nobody to nag, no more demands. She lived on minimum wage, worked in kitchens or cleaning jobs, enjoyed the variation of fruit-picking out under the hot sun when the opportunity presented itself – everybody working together, comrades in arms, appreciative. Her only stress was physical; it was exhausting work but it left her satisfied at the end of the day, gave her a sense of achievement plus a smile and a chat with those around her. As long as the body kept working, the mind was free.

Had Dan and Rachel worked out that she knew? More likely, they thought she'd had a breakdown! No doubt Rachel would have told Dan all about their meeting, the things they'd chatted about, Julie's admission she felt undervalued and was threatening to walk out. Would she have mentioned Dan's missed call, the bag dropping? Had Rachel noticed her other phone was missing, perhaps suspected Julie of taking it? She had so much time to think over every scenario and only wished she could be a fly on the wall, hacking into their conversations.

She thought about the kids but not as often as she had expected to. There was a little niggling pang of guilt over leaving Tommy to fend for himself. *It will be the making of him,* she told herself, *and the other boys.* Her absence would teach them all a bit of independence, force them to look after each other like brothers should, kill off their selfish streak. She was itching to find out but couldn't bring herself to return. Life was so short, and she was enjoying the time she had. She had played her part in procreation, used her body to supply the next generation, the continuation of humanity, but for what purpose? If she didn't enjoy her life – if humanity didn't enjoy life – why continue the human race? Since leaving, Julie had found an inner peace; a strong sense of self. She knew what she wanted from her life. She was free in body and mind and was excited to plan for the future, feeling no remorse about what would come next.

She planned to borrow a car. Her boss wouldn't miss her for a day or two – he was a free spirit too. Julie would find Rachel, and they would 'talk'.

She smiled. Tomorrow would be the start of something beautiful.

The keys had been left inside the Land Rover. It looked a bit battered and certainly wasn't a flashy number to drive down the street, but it was perfect for what Julie needed: large enough to carry a body in the boot under a well-placed tarpaulin, and not dirty enough to be pulled over as unroadworthy. The number plate was old, a jumbled mess of letters, less memorable than a newer plate. Ideal. Julie smiled at the irony of the spade and gloves in the boot. Maybe this vehicle knew its own fate, or maybe it already had stories to tell.

She looked forward to the drive; to the beginning of the end. She scrawled *'Clean Me'* on the back of the car before getting in, then smirked. She turned the keys in the ignition, attempted to tune the radio and was on her way. Julie felt like Alice in Wonderland – everything provided for her, even a full tank of diesel to get her on her way towards her adventures.

No delays, just drive.

The road ahead was clear, so she put her foot down and tried to bring the old car up to the speed limit, finding herself singing along with some Eighties tunes. They were ingrained in her being and made her feel free. She let her imagination wander to everything she had planned, what to do first. As much as she relished the thought of scraping her eyes out, burning her hair, pulling her fingernails one by one, she didn't want Rachel to pass out too quickly. She would need to make a list, order everything correctly – but how do you find out that kind of information? As she mulled over the gruesome reality, she wondered what unforetold problems might come up. *It's going to be messy, is it really worth all that cleaning or is there another way?*

Capture, incarcerate, instil fear, push for confession, question, watch her beg for forgiveness – then rev up to more extreme torture, ensuring Rachel remained conscious to endure the pain. *Note to self, save her eyes till last, make her watch.* If she passed out that would be no fun. At that point, she might as well just end the party.

Julie tapped her handbag on the seat next to her, smiling, knowing the solution at the end was inside. She'd taken some of the treasures from her bottom drawer when she'd left her family, wanted to be prepared in case she couldn't cope. She told herself that if she had a weak moment, a few pills would help it pass to help her regain her conviction, but she hadn't needed any. Now those pills would help when the end came for Rachel, perhaps she would join her in the final cocktail. She hummed along to the radio once more, smiling at the road ahead. The clear straight path ahead, trafficless, nothing standing in her way at last.

Julie had given Rachel no warning, no clue that she was coming. She thought her own disappearance might have been reported by now, *if anybody cared.* If she was down as a missing person, she wanted to stay that way.

As she glanced in the rear-view mirror, Julie marvelled at the change in her appearance. Her face somehow altered, devoid of the usual tense worry lines she'd spent the last twenty years nurturing. The outdoor lifestyle suited her. She was tanned, leaner, stronger. Living for herself was easy; an active lifestyle and time to make personal food choices had made it easy to quickly shed her excess weight, the weight that had tormented her for as long as she could remember, like a forgotten child.

She was ready. *Rachel, I'm coming for you.*

Outside the office building, the streets were crammed with people going about their daily business, unaware of what

Julie was planning, most of them staring blindly down at their phones. Nobody worried about having things stolen anymore – hundreds, even thousands of pounds held precariously in the palms of their hands.

Julie took her own phone out of her pocket and dialled Rachel's number.

'Hello?'

'Hi, Rachel, I'm outside.'

'Julie?' Rachel screeched down the phone. 'Julie, is that you?'

A heavy silence hung between them, both waiting for the other to speak. The pivotal moment, everything was about to change.

'Come now, alone, and we can talk,' Julie warned, 'Don't tell anyone or I'll go into hiding again.'

She hung off and waited, watching the back door of Rachel's work, wondering how long it would take her to come down in the lift and make her way out – and there she was. Dressed in a thin floaty material, stiletto heels finishing the look. *Tart.* She looked around frantically, then stopped still, staring as their eyes met.

'Julie! I can't believe it!' Rachel shouted across, at the same time appearing like a gust of wind had swept them together. She gripped onto Julie holding her tight at arm's length to take a proper look, then gasped, 'You look so different! Are you OK? You're so tanned! So thin! Where have you been?' She hugged her close, Julie uncomfortably accepted the embrace. *She doesn't know. She doesn't suspect anything. Have to keep it that way.*

You are not my friend. But, if you hadn't taken my husband, I'd still be stuck with him, so for that I am grateful. For that I will give you your moment.

Rachel slowly released her grasp, still clutching her friend's arm as if scared she might vanish if she relinquished. *Perfect, that makes life easier. Just come with me to my car, follow me, your future awaits,* she thought, guiding her towards her car. If only she knew the truth behind Julie's smile, that she was looking forward to unshackling herself from the constraints of humanity, torturing the beauty before her, cutting off those objects of Dan's desire so he would never be able to enjoy her again. The horror-movie scenes she had recalled often over the past months excited her. It would be a challenge whether she could cope with the reality, the blood... the horror... but she was up for it.

Julie thought back to Amrita, her death in the cinema seemed like a lifetime ago. She was a different person then, yet she could still see the bits of bone shattered around the walls, the streaks of deep beetroot blood dripping down the porcelain. The only thing she remembered was the smell, the rich iron scent of raw meat – fresh, metallic; the clean white and the dark red against it. The image in her mind conflicted with the images she had seen on the internet, she regretted looking. They didn't know the truth, shared only lies.

Her time with Rachel wouldn't be the same. This was planned. But how could she knowingly torture someone she knew. You don't know her. *The slut is not your friend. Damn right.*

Julie licked her lips. They were dry; she was thirsty. Hannibal Lecter would have drunk her blood. She blanched thinking about it, not her style. Maybe she could smear it across her face, Game of Thrones-style? *Messy.* She could cut off a finger, dip it in dripping blood, write with it on the walls of her enclosure; cut off Rachel's eyelids so she was forced to watch everything, her own torture. *Would the blood drip in her eyes so she couldn't see? Maybe it would kill her?* Julie wasn't sure, hadn't done enough research, only on the ways to cause pain, and happily, there seemed to be endless opportunities.

She looked over at her 'project', unable to refrain from grinning and was met with a squeeze and a warm smile.

'Wow, Julie, what big eyes you've got!' Rachel exclaimed, ridiculously.

'Yep, I'm the big, bad wolf!'

Why was Rachel laughing along? *Stupid girl.* She wondered if Rachel had stepped into her role back home, if the kids had welcomed her as their new mother, if she'd been over all the time under the pretence of helping with the family.

While away, Julie had dipped in and out of the stalker app, noting Dan had spent most of his time at home during her absence, didn't even seem to be going to work regularly. Had he brought in help, a nanny, perhaps? *Someone else for my revenge list? Keep focused, it's Rachel's turn.*

'We're here – climb in!' Julie shouted, reaching the Land Rover.

'Whose car is this?'

'It's mine for the day, just borrowed.'

Julie bit down on her tongue to stop from screaming, she was losing patience. *Shut up and get the fuck inside!*

'We'll just go for a ride. I want to show you where I've been living. It's nice – you'll like it.' She didn't recognise her own voice, the velvety-smooth focus in it, the confidence. She wasn't listening to Rachel's array of endless mumble, but when she tuned back in, it was still coming.

'Where have you been? Why did you go? Are you okay? Are you coming home? Dan was so worried! And the kids, they've grown so much. You must be desperate to see them again!'

'I'm sure they were fine with you there, in my place.'

'It was the least I could do for you, my friend.' Rachel smiled in response.

My friend? Who says that? Was she feeling guilty about the affair? Trying to persuade herself she was still a good friend? *What a joke.*

Julie revved up the car, cool and calm under Rachel's fixed stare. Months of alone-time had focused her body and mind. She was able to control her physical responses, knowing Rachel was likely assessing her every move, trying to work out what was going on.

'I'll explain everything when we get there,' she said.

'Where are we going?'

'Patience, patience!'

'I need to tell work I'll be out for the afternoon. I literally just ran out of the building!' Rachel said, looking around the car, then tutting when she realised she hadn't brought her bag.

'Can I borrow your phone?'

'Um, no, sorry,' Julie said, stalling. 'It's... out of battery. Don't worry, you won't be missed.'

Rachel looked confused, but leant back against the chair and relaxed, accepting that fate was out of her control.

Chapter Twenty-Two

'But this is a storage place! Surely you haven't been living here?'

Of course she hadn't been living there, had no intention of doing so, but Rachel didn't need to know that. Why did she have to interrupt with her questions, didn't she realise the dilemma Julie was going through – whether to kidnap, torture or murder? It was a tricky one, to say the least. She looked at Rachel, still so perfect, unphased, actually believing that Julie might ever choose to live in a storage unit. Ridiculous. It wasn't safe, it wasn't humane, come to think of it, why wasn't Rachel pushing her to return home instead?

Because she wanted Dan to herself. It suited her perfectly to keep Julie away.

Looking over at Rachel, she tried to work out what was going through her head. She looked innocent, made Julie pause, wonder if she could have been mistaken. If her *friend* was really guilty or if she'd somehow muddled things up.

But those phone pictures. She'd seen the evidence with her own eyes, images burnt into her memory that seemed an impossibility, yet were undeniable. Was Rachel humouring her now, biding her time until she could inform Dan, warn him perhaps? Planning how she could still keep Dan for herself and keep Julie away. She bit her tongue watching, Rachel's cool exterior giving nothing away.

'I don't live here – yet, but I'd like to,' Julie breathed the appropriate response to the questions that hung in the air, 'that's why I need your help.'

Would Rachel agree to help? Their fates entwined depended on it. Was it believable? A realistic plan?

'I'll pay them cash, so it doesn't come back on you. Don't look so worried. *This isn't going to work. Come on Rachel, stick to the plan.*

'This is stupid. You can't stay in a storage place, it's dangerous … and creepy.' Rachel shuddered but kept pace with Julie as she headed towards the office.

'Just do this one thing for me,' Julie said, 'You owe me.'

Rachel's eyes narrowed. 'What's that supposed to mean?'

Backtracking quickly so as not to ruin the surprise, Julie told herself to stay patient. *Plan Julie, slowly slowly catchy monkey.*

'Nothing, it's just I really need your help with this. It won't work without you.'

They weighed each other up as the man on the desk spoke.

'Okay, so, which of you lovely ladies is going to be signing up today?'

After a few seconds of deliberation, Rachel finally caved in, much to Julie's relief.

'Me. I'd like to set up a month, please.'

'You get the first six weeks for one pound if you sign up by direct debit on a monthly contract, but I'll need ID.'

The man looked from one to the other, his burly frame sweating around the rim of his shirt, discolouring the peach with a darker hue. His suit shimmered slightly, bulging under the effort of maintaining his bulk, reminding her of a sausage roll, the meat poking out of the pastry, trying to escape. She had imagined he'd be in a uniform, nondescript, a minion to the system, a faceless name that would carry out the transaction. 'Simon' his nametag read, 'Here to help.'

She didn't want to know his name, didn't want to humanise him, *but she had to make him feel special, use her feminine charms to get what she wanted, without making herself too memorable.*

'I'm afraid I don't have my bag on me. We'll have to come back another time,' Rachel said, interrupting the silence, making Julie flush crimson that she'd glazed over in thought. Simon smiled back, taking her blush as flirting, giving Julie the nudge she needed to work him.

'I have cash! LOTS OF CASH,' Julie butted in, repeating herself slowly and watching his wondering eyes. 'Can't you make an exception just once for us damsels in distress?' She batted her eyelids, slowly lowering her glance down his body and up again to meet his eyes. She let them fix and linger, hoping it would be enough, if Rachel's beauty hadn't already won him over.

'She's just had her bag stolen and wants a safe place to put her remaining jewellery while she sorts out her house security, surely you wouldn't see her beautiful jewellery put at risk? Just a few days, pretty please?'

Simon leered over at Rachel, eyeing up her necklace – which was obviously worth thousands – the rings on her fingers, her sparkling earrings so unique. They'd won him over.

His body responded like a cartoon character, salivating at the mouth, tongue out panting with excitement. It had been a waste of time flirting with him but when it came to greed he was much more pliable.

'I'm sorry, it's a no. No arguments – those are the rules. Now, leave before you get me into trouble.'

Damn. Really?

Julie was sure she had him, but it didn't look like today was going to be her day. What to do now, she wondered walking away with Rachel.

Was Rachel disappointed too, she wondered, secretly hoping to keep Julie away from home? *Will she try and persuade me to go home now? That's what a true friend would do, would have done already if there was nothing in it for them.*

Rachel's ice-pick heels clicked along determined heading out of the building and back to the car. Think Julie, but she couldn't, watching Rachel's curled locks bouncing as she walked was mesmerising, floating then resting, kissing, floating then resting again, kissing the pea-green silk of her blouse. *Oh, how she would love to burn them off one by one, watch her distress, relish the smell of burning.* Unconsciously reaching to flick her own matted hair, she wondered at their differences. *Another reason Dan had fallen for her?*

Rachel hadn't mothered kids, had time to exercise, dress well, create healthy meals – time for herself. Julie's family had taken that away from her long ago and why bother anyway for Dan, the lazy, selfish, egotistical adulterer.

Revenge. Julie was entitled.

They were nearly at the car when Julie realised, with heart pulsing, that she wasn't ready to let this go, had to at least question her and make her admit her guilt. Also, she wanted to know about Dan, what had been happening in her absence, had he been under suspicion from the police for her disappearance, suspected of killing her off? She hoped so, that would be fitting. Hopefully he'd been under house arrest awaiting the outcome of her disappearance. She made a mental note of what to ask her hostage. *Where are all the abandoned warehouses when you need one?*

'Ladies, hang on!' came a distant shout from Simon, the surly old letch, puffing away as he attempted to jog over to them, a heart-attack waiting to happen. There was still a chance! She grabbed roughly at Rachel's arm, pulling her to change direction. Questions coming thick and fast once more with the adrenaline of opportunity.

'Just had to get the CCTV sorted. Turns out, it's not working, so...'

'So, you'll take the cash?' Julie jumped in, confident. He didn't have the charm, and she didn't have the patience.

'There's just one thing. Obviously, without the ID, I'm not able to put you on the books, so I'm going to give you a place over on the far side. It's derelict, to be honest, and there are a few rats around, but it will do for now until you can bring back some ID.'

He stared fixated on Rachel, clocking the green emerald in the centre of her necklace, winking back at him. Would they have trusteed him in normal circumstances? Clearly not. He knew they were up to something as much as they knew he was after those jewels. It took all Julie's reserve not to yank that necklace from Rachel's dainty skin, knowing it had likely cost Dan more than Julie's yearly allowance. Life just wasn't fair. She'd make sure Simon got his hands on it. *Or maybe on Rachel?*

'No, thank you Sir, that won't be suitable,' Rachel said, at the same time, Julie handed over the cash.

'Well, little Miss, beggars can't be choosers!' he said, gleefully pocketing the payment, his bit on the side. 'I'm sure your jewellery won't mind a day in the dark. 'For five hundred, you can have it for three months. Nobody's going to go sticking their nose in your business when you're tucked over that way.'

Rachel turned to her friend, whispering, 'Julie, this is nuts, you can't live in a storage unit! What are you thinking? Come back with me, honestly, you can't do this – it's a joke, right?' She seemed genuine, *her and Dan must be estranged.*

'Just go home! Dan will be so relieved to know you're all right. He's been very worried, not sleeping at all, and the police, they've been looking for you! They need to be told you're okay. Oh, Julie, we thought you were dead!'

So she did care. But was her concern for Julie, or for Dan? Trying to clear his name then toss her aside once more? She couldn't hide her disgust, fighting the scowl on her face as she stood hesitant, trying to process her thoughts into words. *How does she know he's not been sleeping? Unless she's been there with him, at night.*

Simon and Julie shook on the deal, much to Rachel's horror, and Julie walked away with the key, following his directions.

'This is ridiculous! You can't live here. It's disgusting!'

They stood rooted to the spot, staring at the small room one of them would be staying in for the foreseeable. The stench was overwhelming – an added bonus as far as Julie was concerned.

'What is that?' Rachel squealed, walking over to the far end of the room where a pipe was protruding through the wall. 'It's leaking sewage! OH, MY GOD!' she shouted as she began to heave. 'It's a fucking dead rat. Seriously, Julie, you can't stay here! Who thought it would be a good idea to put a pipe inside a storage unit anyway? It's ridiculous!' You could catch all sorts! When that door's shut, how do you know if you'll even be able to breathe? This is a terrible idea.' She looked up at Julie's silhouette in the doorway, bringing her hand to her brow to focus better.

Julie said nothing as she reached up and hauled the old metal door downwards in one swift motion. There was a screeching noise and a firm click, the old bolt mechanism still surprisingly functional. The metal was cool against her cheek, the rusting smell strangely comforting as she patiently revelled in the moment, listening to Slut's pleading confusion quickly turning to panic.

'Julie, what are you doing?' Rachel's feet clicked across the floor, her hands pounding on the door; unaware of Julie's cheek resting on the other side.

'You can't leave me here!' she screeched.

Julie didn't respond, just smiled and listened as a piercing scream filled the air. A perfect start.

'Julie, wait! You can't leave me in here!'

Another scream.

'There's a fucking rat in here! What's that? There's something on the floor! Julie! Julie? Where are you? Open the fucking door!'

'Just giving you a little taste of your own medicine,' Julie whispered back, then, a little louder asked, 'So you can breathe in there?

Slut responded with renewed vigour. 'Yeah, yeah, very funny. You win, now let me out.'

Julie stared at the closed door, wondering whether to open it. No point getting Rachel all worked up before she even knew what she'd done wrong. She didn't want to miss out on the fun of the torture. Her thoughts were interrupted by more screams.

'Let me out! Rats! Rats! They're in here! They're scratching me! Help, Julie, open the door! Now! Please, Julie, open the door!'

Looking around outside, the cloudless sky promised a clear night ahead. Nobody was coming. If the area was monitored someone would have been there by now. They were isolated and nobody could hear her pleading.

'Julie, please, stop this! Please open the door! Please!' Whimpering, begging for release. 'Help! Somebody, help! Julie, where are you? Are you there? Come back! Where are you?'

As Julie walked away, she didn't look back. *Perhaps this is better.* She'd underestimated the fear of being locked in that room. Maybe she wouldn't have to bother with all the messy stuff, all those tools, the cleaning up. She rolled her eyes wondering how much effort it would take to cut through bone. Looking down at her nails she tried to prise one off but it held tight, pushing it back caused a reasonable amount of pain, maybe that was an alternative option or pushing things up the nail beds? That would mean less cleaning up at least.

Give her time, torture her with her own thoughts.

How long would it take Slut to realise that Julie knew?

Maybe some quiet time would focus her mind. A couple of days? She would be starving, scared to death. The total darkness, the rats, the mental anguish of not knowing how long she would be there.

Perfect.

Maybe it would be enough. Julie wouldn't need to kill her, necessarily.

Living on after the mental torture might prove worse punishment than death. The dreams, the nightmares that would haunt her forever. Julie smirked at the thought of perfect, spoiled Rachel sleeping in her own shit and piss for days. *Bliss.*

And, if she didn't repent...?

This would be a wonderful start to the torture party she deserved. Weaken her, then offer food and drink, bring her back to reality before deciding on stage two: threaten her, release her, or start chopping off limbs. It would depend on how much she was enjoying herself and how loudly Rachel pleaded, how repentant she was for her actions. Julie pictured her sobbing in the dark and smiled at how easily everything had worked out, far better than she could have hoped.

Chapter Twenty-Three

Julie could smell the remnants of Rachel's perfume in the car. It was such a distinct scent – the Coco Chanel of yesteryear that made her feel the mature sophisticate. Julie had never liked it. When Dan bought her a bottle for her birthday, she'd wondered why he hadn't gone for the light floral scent of Givenchy Code she'd favoured and hinted at repeatedly. Dan had pleaded ignorance, and she'd made the right noises to voice her gratitude while feeling quietly disappointed. She'd tried to wear it, but the scent clung to her clothes and was so strong it reminded her of her grandma, who always seemed to have doused herself in half a bottle.

Now, she realised with a sharp intake of breath, it was all part of his plan. His deceit and subterfuge; not wanting to get caught smelling of another woman after he'd been with her. This time, Rachel wouldn't come up smelling of roses. She wondered how long the scent would last with her locked in the storage unit.

Was she being overly harsh? *Yes, Damn it, but why the hell not?* Why should Rachel's life be more important, held in higher regard than her own? Julie had wanted to die when she realised the extent of Dan's affair – how he hadn't cared for her or the kids or what they'd built their life to be. She could have forgiven a one-off, *maybe*, but years of deceit and with her friend? How could he?

She turned the radio on in the car.

Ooh, I like this song. George Michael's 'Freedom' started to play on the radio – now, he was one taken too soon. Julie sang every word, nobody there to hear her let loose. *I forgive you*, she thought when Dan popped into her head. *I will not give you up. I will go back home and put on a brand-new face. The way we play the game will definitely have to change though, Dan.*

She was overcome with the urge to eat, suddenly ravenous. First, return the car to work, eat some fruit in the fields. It was one of the perks of the job and would give her time to think before returning to the crazy world that was family life – no doubt to the bombardment of questions waiting for her back home. Then, back to Rachel.

Julie smiled as she thought of the sweet, ripe strawberries waiting in the field, picturing her co-workers with pots of cream dipping and picking. They were on a basic wage for their back-breaking labour, she didn't begrudge them.

That night, she couldn't sleep, tossing and turning on the hard floor of the barn as she bedded down with the other workers who had no other accommodation. She couldn't stop thinking about Rachel, about what she had done and the fear her friend would be feeling in there, alone, overnight. How could she go back and free her, knowing she'd likely report her to the police for locking her in? But when she knew the reason, that Julie knew about the affair, maybe she would understand.

Maybe they would forgive each other and move on. Never be friends again, but at least know each other – *really* know each other, a new level of mutual respect.

As the sun began to rise, Julie flitted in and out of sleep, waking to the noise of scratching and imagining herself locked in the storage unit, with Rachel and Dan laughing outside, walking off into the sunset. She was relieved when the alarm finally rang, waking her from a night of terror. Julie was soaked with sweat, the reality of what she had done and the potential consequences for her own life gradually dawning. She wasn't a killer, not really. No matter how much she wanted to believe she could torture or end Rachel's life, she just couldn't go through with it. A calm realisation came over her as she finally had clarity – she didn't love Dan any more. Didn't care. Didn't need to punish Rachel or separate them. She didn't want him. Life would be better if they continued their affair – that would provide the freedom she craved.

Julie prayed the workday would go quickly so she could make an anonymous call, she'd do it on the way down to London, arrange for Rachel's release. *No doubt, she'll be straight over to Dan, knocking down the door, telling him everything. I have to get there first, explain everything.*

Julie hoped Rachel would be okay, wondered how the hell she'd imagined herself able to torture another human being, no matter how angry she was. Horror movies made it look so easy. *But the killers don't have a moral compass, they act on impulse – and they're just acting. It's not reality!*

After Amrita's death, Julie had managed to persuade herself she'd done a positive thing, that she'd acted in self-defence, a moment of madness that had worked out for the best. If she had reported the incident immediately, that might have been the case, but looking back now she felt sick, thinking over her gruesome fascination which followed. Had she been in shock all this time? Was she of sound mind, planning her retaliation on Rachel? Was it all too late to take back what she'd done?

'Thanks so much, Anna, you really have been a Godsend,' her boss Peter said interrupting her thoughts as he brandished an envelope in front of Julie's glazed eyes. 'Earth to Anna – hello?'

'Sorry, I was miles away.'

'Well, don't be a stranger. If you ever want to come back, my door is always open for you.' He held onto the envelope, gripping a bit too tightly.

Julie looked up into his eyes and suspected he wanted her for more than just fruit-picking. 'Thanks.' She smiled back, snatching it firmly. She owed him her gratitude, his overzealous drinking had kept him from noticing her absence the previous day along with his car's little outing. He didn't realise what a pivotal role he had played in providing her with the means and alibi for Rachel's kidnap. She knew Peter would swear 'Anna' had been on the farm the whole time, if questioned.

She wondered how Dan would react on her return. Would he be relieved, happy, excited even? Most likely, he would be angry, blame her for being selfish. *I know I have been,* she thought, *But he doesn't understand anything, he never did.* Would three months be enough to have changed him, she wondered, taking calming breaths as she walked down the dirt track and started the three-mile walk, through the countryside and towards the station. The trees were swaying in the breeze, talking to her, no human sounds interrupting the peace of nature. If only life could stay this way. Perhaps her reunion with the family would be a fleeting visit, an explanation to break ties for good. Nature was her friend and she longed for them to stay together far more than she longed to be reunited with the draining force of her family.

The train journey down to London went quickly as Julie dozed, again dreaming of Rachel. Her hair was matted, stuck to her face, chunks missing as she'd pulled them out. Her nails were chipped and jagged, blood stained and inflamed from scraping at the unmovable walls, pounding on the unrelenting steel door, attempts at prizing up the cement slab flooring. There was no way out. The days had turned into weeks and she lay crumpled on the floor a bony mess of starvation. Her eyes were wild, bulging prominently from her skull-like face, drained of colour and flesh.

"The train is approaching King's Cross, please disembark. All change here, all change."

Her eyes snapped open as the announcement pierced her fitful slumber. She looked around feeling vulnerable and exposed, self-consciously wondering if other people had been watching her sleep, if she'd mumbled anything damning.

Had any of them locked someone up and left them there? Was there a serial killer amongst them? *That's what I will be, if I kill Rachel too.*

Julie hadn't made the anonymous call during her journey, and now she was back in London, it would be too incriminating if she did it now.

But Rachel knows you did it!

The thought screamed through her head. She couldn't just release her or she'd never hear the end of it, Rachel would be straight onto the police – friend or not, unless she understood why. No, no, it wasn't worth it. She needed more time to think. Maybe leave Rachel an extra day – prolong the hunger, humiliation, the fear – then go personally to release her. Explain everything, decide then if it was necessary to end Rachel's life to save her own.

She wondered what Rachel was up to now, regretted the fact there was no camera set up inside the room to enjoy her trial. How long would she shout, cry, claw at the door, she wondered. Was it really that bad anyway? It was dry shelter after all, warm weather so not likely to be freezing inside, so she might have a stomach ache and a dry mouth. *So what!* Would one more day make a significant difference?

Only two days mind, don't spoil her for the inquisition. That would be no fun. She didn't want to traumatise Rachel so much that she wouldn't even remember the reason she was imprisoned in the first place.

Julie rose from her seat, pleased the train had cleared and she wouldn't have to grapple with the other passengers. Grabbing her jacket and small holdall, she made her way out of the station and into the fresh air. Just a quick breather before the onward journey.

She hadn't planned to hire a car, but as she passed a garage offering just that she couldn't resist the opportunities it would provide. She could go snooping back at her house, a quick trip to watch the kids on their way to school and perhaps follow Dan to work, then go to the house. She still had her house keys, so assuming the locks hadn't been changed (and she couldn't think of a reason why they would have been), she'd let herself into the house and see if she'd been missed; if anything had changed since her disappearance. She could be in and out before anyone knew about it. Following that, she would be ready to open the storage unit door – release the caged rats and tackle her rival.

'A small car will be fine. Yes, please, that Astra looks perfect.' She handed over a wad of cash and marvelled at the lack of identification or safety measures required for hire. *Simon should get a job here, he'd fit right in.* The place looked shifty and Julie hoped the car was roadworthy; that she wouldn't get pulled over by the police for that or something stupid like having stolen number plates. *That's all I need,* she thought, unwilling to identify herself yet; not ready to announce her return and face an interrogation, not until everything was in order.

Julie was on an adrenaline-fuelled high as she neared her home town, but driving around the old neighbourhood made her feel sombre. That's the park where William first sat in a swing, his giggles filled her memory; and that's where we went to Paint and Play for Jake's fifth birthday party, and that playground, where Tommy took his first steps. Everything felt sharp and raw, impossible, like a fairy tale that had gone horribly wrong. The last little piggy hadn't built his house out of bricks because he was selfishly taking a roll in the mud down the road, taking time out for himself, so his friends had nowhere to run to when the sly wolf came calling. Delicious pork steaks.

Could Julie get away with this? *Should* she? It was more fantasy than reality. She wondered what Kate would make of it, what she could pull out of Julie's psyche if she was allowed to probe. Could Dan really be held accountable for all that had happened or was her revenge plot that of a psychopath? Was she culpable or entitled?

If somebody deserves what's coming to them, who are we to decide on the punishment? Courts around the country would have you believe they held the power, that people, bystanders, those who had been wronged should not be allowed to retaliate, but surely the victim has the most right to cast judgement, decide the fairest punishment?

As she approached her road, Julie felt conspicuous. Thinking back three months felt like years as she tried to remember if Dan would have left for work by now. Perhaps things were different. She parked up behind two other cars, just a few metres from her front door, and reached into her bag for her trusty summer hat that protected her on her fruit-picking days in the hot summer sun. She waited patiently, fingering the floral-patterned swirls, tracing each slowly with her weather worn hands.

That's my front door, my house. Julie felt like she was seeing it for the first time, the boundary that stood between freedom and servitude. She still had a choice. *I could leave, vanish and nobody would know.* Her heart was pounding, reminding her of the lifestyle that was waiting for her behind that door. As she watched, it opened and Jack and William tumbled out, smiling and babbling, walking together in their school uniform. *Beautifully pressed.* Their hair was longer, floppy on top, both styled similarly with the back shaved up through the grades – not a style their traditional barber would have carried out. It wasn't right. Something so trivial yet it made her want to scream and rush out to them, take them under her maternal control once more. Force them to go back to the baby-cut-style, the simple, innocent childhood that had been left behind.

She opened the window and preened towards it, hoping to catch their voices on the wind, their words. Were they happy? Had they missed her? She slouched down into her seat, undecided as she watched them approach... then they walked on by. They were talking about their teachers from what she could fathom, 'If you get her chatting, she forgets all about classwork and doesn't shut-up! Just ask her about what she had for dinner last night, she loves talking about food...'

They were so tall, so confident, so...together.

Julie waited in a bubble of sadness, hoping a glimpse of Tommy would show him distraught, neglected, missing her. She wondered what the nanny would look like, whether Rachel had allowed him to hire a pretty young thing or whether she had sat in on the interviews and employed someone of no competition.

Note to self, Julie: Next time you make friends, make sure they're ugly.

The door opened again, and Tommy appeared, holding hands with Dan. They were early. *So he's not working,* she thought as she watched, entranced. They ambled slowly along the road away from her. She would give them a little head start before following in the rental. Dan was animated, talking with enthusiasm – about what, she had no idea, but Tommy was enraptured. He wasn't pulling away his hand. Instead, he seemed to have a skip in his step and was comfortable, content.

Had she made a mistake imagining her presence in the house had been important, that her role as mother, wife, slave wasn't really necessary? She was angry as she started the car and moved among the slow traffic. *What's the point of any of it? They don't need me. What's the point in just existing for no reward?* She thought back to Rachel, hardly the sacrificial lamb. *Everything's messed up because of her. There's nothing to lose. I'm coming to get you.*

As she neared the corner, Julie looked to the left to see how far up the road they had walked and saw Dan talking to a young woman she didn't recognise. Did Rachel have competition? *Who is that?* They were way too friendly. *How dare she put her arm around Tommy!*

She pulled forward to get a closer look, following them up the main road, eyes on the *girl* – and then, an almighty crash. Slow-motion. Tommy and Dan turning around to face her, the woman's mouth open, shocked.

A grating, scraping noise entered Julie's consciousness as she felt herself being thrust forward, realising a car had shunted her from the rear side as she turned into the road. The force made her car carousel out of control, and as she struggled to try to regain the steering, she locked eyes with Dan. Again, time seemed to stop as they both took each other in. He mouthed her name as the lamppost appeared and crushed into the front of her bonnet with enough power to release the airbags – if there had been any.

Then, silence. Darkness.

Relax, Julie.

A dim glimmer of light hovering above her as she willed her eyes to open – but nothing. Her body wouldn't respond. The light was getting brighter, and she felt the pull as she travelled towards it. She listened to the voices around her, fought the urge to relax and let go; to switch off and take a break. This was what she had dreamed of, a release from her mundane life – and now, a release from the crazy noises assaulting her ears.

'She came out of nowhere!'

'I witnessed it.'

'Why didn't she look?'

'She just pulled out!'

'She had a death wish.'

Julie lay numb, sirens breaking into her dreamlike state. Then, more voices.

'I can't find a pulse.'

'Oh, dear God, no!

'Get that kid away from her!'

'Mummy! Mummy, you came back!

'Julie, is that you? Julie? Julie?'

'Why isn't she waking up?'

Chapter Twenty-Four

DAN

As the seasons changed and the snow came in, Dan tried his utmost to plan an amazing Christmas for the boys. He had long since left his engineering job to be a full-time father when he realised the shock of their mother's absence had not really hit the boys. That was, until the accident. Now, it was all too raw, seeing her lying there, living but not living, unresponsive. He had tried to keep them positive, encouraging them to talk to her when they visited the hospital, but as the weeks and months passed, Julie was showing no sign of improvement.

After two months, scans showed her brain activity to be stable, at which point the doctors removed her feeding tubes to see if Julie could breathe on her own. Dan remembered standing in the family room hoping and praying while they explained that if she was unresponsive, the family would need to prepare for some tough decisions.

Standing at her bedside, Dan waited, feeling he deserved everything that had transpired. He had never appreciated Julie until the day she vanished, but Oh, how he'd missed her. He had imagined all kinds of horrors when the police search brought up no clues as to her whereabouts. She was a missing person but not considered a danger to herself. They'd warned him to prepare for the worst – that she'd been taken, murdered even, and he'd got through the initial shock and begun to accept the possibility.

'Was she mentally sound when she left?' they asked, as far as he knew, yes – but he realised he didn't really know her at all. Had her anxiety driven her to do something stupid?

He had hoped for her return, if only to clear his name from suspicion when she had vanished, but this situation held no answers. The police were all too happy to remind him that they wouldn't rule him out of their enquiries until they'd spoken to Julie, but she wasn't speaking to anyone. Not now, maybe not ever again. *Then what?*

As he stood by the bedside willing her to breathe, he prayed for a second chance.

'Whatever happens, us four, we need to stick together kids, all right? We have to be strong for each other.' He pulled the boys towards him squeezing them tightly, then asked them to wait outside with Grandma, just for a moment. Sandra hadn't been much help when Julie was missing, stayed out of the limelight as much as possible, but at the thought of losing her forever, she'd come bounding back onto the scene once more.

Dan stood waiting, listening to the doctors.

'Ventilator is off.'

'Starting to remove the tube.'

It was like a scene from a movie, waiting for her to take the first breath, a few seconds of nothing that went on forever. Then, the machines all buzzed at once.

'The alarms mean she's not coping on her own. We may need to ventilate her again and carry out a tracheostomy.'

'Let's give her a little longer.'

And then, there it was, the visible relief on the faces of the medical staff as they smiled and said, 'Well done, Julie, that's great.'

'She's breathing on her own.'

'Does that mean she's going to be all right?' Dan asked, reaching for the door to tell the kids. 'Is she out of the coma?'

'No, not yet I'm afraid, but she's breathing,' the nurse replied. 'Which means there is brain stem activity – a good sign, but she's not out of the woods yet. Before you tell the children, I just want you to understand it's highly unlikely Julie will ever recover fully from the coma, and even if she does, there's going to be a long road back, so try not to set your hopes too high.'

'But she has a chance now? She's breathing – she's already defied the odds. Come on, Julie!' Dan said, leaning down to kiss her. *She's just sleeping, that's all it is.* He exited the room to share the news.

'But Daddy, why has she still got her eyes shut?' Tommy asked as he reached for his mummy.

Yes, I'm with you, Tommy. Dan had expected Julie to open her eyes too; to return to them, to speak, to call out to them, to tell them how grateful she was to be alive, but nothing. She might well be breathing, but that was the only change. The doctors said it was miraculous, but to a family in need, a miracle would be to have the old Julie back – an apparently unrealistic expectation.

They said their goodbyes and headed off to the hugely overpriced multi-storey car park, where Tommy insisted he should be the one to enter the vast amount of change the machine required. He dropped every other coin and caused the three-hour visit to tick over, the machine rejecting the coins and prompting them to start again at the higher rate. Dan rolled his eyes as his phone started to buzz.

'Yes?'

'Mr. Summers? I'd like to speak to Mr. Summers, please.'

'Yes, speaking. Who's this?'

'I'm Dr. Pendez, just calling about your wife, sir. I'm afraid...'

She hadn't died, not yet. It took Dan a few minutes to work out what he was hearing, what with all the kids' noise and the queue forming behind the parking machine, Tommy entering every five pence piece he could find. Julie had struggled to breathe the moment they left and had been put back onto life support. Dan didn't even tell the kids. Why upset them when it didn't seem to make any difference whether she was breathing or not? She might as well be dead to them.

As winter approached, Dan felt a buzz in the air, people all around him preparing for the festive season. Life went on, or so it seemed, but not for him. Shortly after the accident, people had inundated him with messages, offering help and sending their sympathy, a few mothers from the school even bringing dinners over for him and the kids (Suzy's lasagne was particularly good – Julie had refused to make his favourite when she cooked for him). Friends had come out of the woodwork with their well-wishes and empty promises of help despite their awkward silences during conversations, not knowing what to say if they accidentally spoke of her – not knowing which tense to use. Normality had resumed. Dan was back on their social calendar, invited out for drinks and parties. Didn't they realise he was a single parent? How did they expect him to go out, to make it through the morning after, when he'd have a full-on day of demands from the kids, starting at six a.m. with Tommy? He still hadn't adapted to the early mornings.

At what point should he let Julie go? Could he? Was he allowed to without feeling guilty? He was responsible for making the decision to turn her life support machine off, to kill her, to all intents and purposes.

It was at times like these he really missed Rachel, wished she hadn't abandoned him when he needed her most. She should be there, at his side, supporting him through the most difficult time of his life. Was it just coincidence that she'd stopped phoning him, stopped replying to texts around the same time as Julie went to hospital? Or had she heard about the accident and felt guilty, regretted their relationship? After three years she owed him more than that. Maybe Rachel *wasn't* taking the cowards way out? Should he be grateful that she had been strong enough to break their ties after hearing about the accident? Still, an explanation would have given him closure, he deserved that at least.

At the same time, Dan was relieved she wasn't flaunting herself, making demands of him when he had to put his children first. He couldn't let them find out he had planned to divorce Julie before her disappearance, and now, there seemed no point anyway. Their affair had dwindled somewhat over the previous months, when there was no more need for sneaking about. With Julie out of the picture, it just didn't have the same appeal, coupled with the fact he was feeling more tired than he ever thought possible. Handling this parenting lark was a joke.

Now he questioned whether he even wanted Rachel anymore. If she were to phone him, would he answer? Should he? Being distanced from her now, focused on Julie lying there unresponsive in bed, he didn't know what he wanted. Was it selfish to keep Rachel waiting in the wings, just in case Julie didn't pull through? But if she was waiting and Julie returned to the family home, he'd be right back in that dilemma all over again, trying to escape marital 'bliss'. It would be easier if she just died.

Another month passed, and the routine continued, Dan speaking to Julie as if she could hear, telling her trivia about their days, their lives continuing as they watched her change visually but never return to them. Dan was angry, knowing it wasn't her fault, but she had brought it upon herself nonetheless. If anybody bothered to ask him how he felt, he wouldn't have known how to respond anyway. He was going through the various stages of grief, despite Julie still being 'alive' – more a classification than a reality. *God help our family*, he thought. Meanwhile, Tommy treated Julie like a toy doll, always upbeat, never questioning what if, but only asking when?

'Daddy, can we go Christmas shopping?'

'Really, Tommy? I thought you'd moan if I suggested it. What do you want to buy?'

'I want to get a present for William and Jack, and Mummy! We could get her a bunch of flowers, and she can put them in her room, and they will be so bright they'll wake her up, and she'll say, "Thank you, Tommy, I've missed you!" and then hug me, and we can all go home and have Christmas Day together. She's been sleeping a long time.'

Dan hooked his arm over Tommy's shoulders. He'd had to bear so much in his short life and he deserved a really special Christmas.

Oh, God, why did he have to go through all of this? He felt the guilt of his affair like a rock stuck in his throat; he was unable to swallow, not wanting to take a breath, not worthy of breathing when his wife, his poor wife, could not take a breath on her own. She had been such a good mother. He leaned down to cuddle into Tommy, who looked up and smiled, oblivious to the situation. If a shopping trip could momentarily put a smile on Tommy's face, then it's the least he could do.

They exited the building and threw themselves forwards, an offering to the biting elements of the world beyond.

'Look, Daddy! Santa! Can we, Daddy? Can we?' Tommy broke free and ran across the shopping precinct, not waiting for a response.

Dan nodded and tried hard to raise a smile for Tommy.

'Santa, I would like my mummy for Christmas!' he said, trying to climb onto Santa's knee while being ushered to the side by the elves, who were trying to keep politically correct and avoid any hint of a lawsuit.

Santa looked over at Dan. 'Where is Mummy? Off shopping, buying you lots of nice things?'

'No, she's just lying in bed,' Tommy said.

'Oh, well, Dad, maybe together we can make a special Christmas wish that Mummy gets up a bit earlier tomorrow, so she has plenty of time to get ready for Christmas?'

Dan didn't know where to look. Tommy had a big grin as he leaned over and grabbed a present from Santa's sack as instructed. 'Thank you, Santa! And thanks for bringing my mummy back!'

As they walked away, Santa moved on to the next child. What would he promise them? World peace?

The doctors had been talking about turning off Julie's life support machine. Dan had been told that if they took her off it and she went without breathing again, her brain damage would be irreversible and resuscitation was not advised. The family was offered councillors to help them through the decision-making process, to explain it wasn't something they should feel sad or guilty over because it was beyond their control. *So, why mention guilt?* Dan thought, unable to shift the feeling.

When he'd told William, he went quiet, nodded and receded back into his room. Jack, on the other hand, stamped his feet and shouted about it not being fair, and why had she come back at all if she was just going to smash her car up and put all of this on them?

'Why couldn't she have just stayed away?'

There was a lot of door-slamming that day and not a lot of communication. Dan had cried himself to sleep wondering how he could be a mother to them as well as a father. He was seething inside, in agreement with Jack. Why couldn't she have stayed away? He had posted a message on Facebook, Twitter and Instagram telling all their friends and family of the sad news, realising he'd never really got to know her friends – with the exception of Rachel.

Dan would need to announce Julie's death. Should he share

the news he was going to be turning her life support off? He couldn't find the words to convey the anguish and emotion in the huge decision of allowing somebody to move peacefully on into the next life. But he would have to tell people somehow – or should he just take the kids to say their goodbyes and then announce her death along with the funeral arrangements? He would need to choose a beautiful picture of Julie, it was expected of him. Something unrecognisable, taken in her youth, an idealistic image which bared no resemblance to reality. That was the intention. It was his job to formulate a visual memory for her fake-suffering friends so that they could leave their emoji hearts, dove images and crying faces; the generally accepted equivalent of real-life support.

Chapter Twenty-Five

DAN

'We're going to say goodbye to Mummy and let her sleep. She's very tired, with all those tubes going in and out of her, so the doctors are going to turn off the bleeping machines and take out the wires so we can say goodbye.' Dan reached over to bring Jack and William in for a squeeze while Tommy jumped about the room excitedly, too young to take in all that was happening. The older boys knew all too well.

'Goodbye, au revoir, adieus, auf Wiedersehen,' Tommy sang, prancing about the room proudly singing his school song. *Shut up, just shut up,* Dan thought angrily, frustrated that nobody in the room was reprimanding Tommy, that everything was being left up to him. *Just think about what you are saying! Have you missed the meaning of the song completely?*

They watched the doctor turn off the switch – something so simple yet it changed everything – the room instantly unnaturally quiet. *Finally.* Dan could hear his own breathing, every gulp resonating in his ears. Then, Jack and William sniffling, trying hard to keep their control as Tommy stared wide eyed at his brothers wondering why they were sad.

'I'll give you a few minutes,' the doctor said as he left the room.

Tommy immediately jumped up onto the bed, grabbing Julie in a big hug. 'Bye, Mummy! See you tomorrow!' He looked over at his dad for approval. 'Unless we can stay a bit longer today?' *He didn't get it. Of course not, how could he?*

Dan nodded back and took a seat, signalling to his other sons to follow suit and Tommy smiled back.

'I'm glad they took all those wires away mummy, so we can have a proper cuddle now. We could put your programme on, if you like? You'll be able to hear it now you don't have all that annoying noise!' Tommy snuggled up to his mother, forcing a loud intake of breath from William, who was unable to control himself any longer, letting his tears fall freely. He got up and printed a single kiss on her forehead and then turned to leave the room.

Jack went to walk out of the room behind his brother, but faltered, turning instead to ask, 'Why, Mum? Why did you have to go and do something so bloody dumb?' He sobbed and ran out of the room after William.

'Daddy, he said a rude word! Tell him off, Daddy. William, you're going to lose your electronics time!' Tommy was still upbeat, while Dan stood crying silent, dry tears.

Yes Julie, how could you do this to us?

Tommy climbed back onto the bed and snuggled up, comfortably dozing next to her like it was the most natural thing in the world. Dan knew the doctors would be back soon, but he didn't want to interrupt their last moments, sure there was no rush. After a while, he heard Tommy's breathing change as he fell into a deeper sleep, content next to his mummy. Dan sat down in the corner chair, closed his eyes and waited. He knew he should be out there comforting William and Jack, but he just couldn't bring himself to leave, hoping they would find peace with their grandma.

'Where?' a rasping voice.

'You're in the hospital. You've had an accident.'

'Am I okay?'

'Sorry, darling, but I think we have to say our goodbyes.'

There was a lot of movement in the room when Dan woke from his dream, disorientated as he looked over at the bed to find Julie's eyes open, doctors standing around her.

'Mummy! Santa said he would give you back to me for Christmas, but it's not Christmas yet. Do you want to close your eyes and have a little nap and come back in twenty-three sleeps? It's cheating, opening presents before Christmas Day!'

Julie slowly displayed more awareness of her surroundings, moving her lips at first to mouth words, unable to make herself heard.

'Waking up from a coma, the patient can be very protracted and may have setbacks. Julie may well be muddled and confused and will need a lot of support,' the doctor explained.

'Julie, it's me, Dan,' he said, holding her hand and looking into her blank eyes.

In the days and weeks that followed Julie seemed agitated and confused, irritated by the constant noise around her. So many unrecognisable doctors, nurses, carers constantly monitoring her progress, pushing her to respond. Dan could see that the effort was all too much. She wanted to close her eyes and sleep. So tired, always so tired.

She didn't remember Dan at all in the early days. Further assessments had shown Julie's motor skills to be normal, her communication slow but improving, but her cognitive and memory issues significant and 'cause for concern'. Much to Tommy's disappointment, his mum didn't return home for Christmas but instead went on to a neurological rehabilitation centre, where she stayed for a further three months until the doctors were satisfied that she was making physical and mental progress. She was still confused, paranoid and suffering from severe mood swings, but the doctors said some of this would be down to the medication they were using to build up her strength. Her movement was limited, and she had severe, possibly irreversible concussion, but they all kept hoping, knowing she'd already beat the odds once by coming back to them.

Dan continued his visits, which became more regular as winter turned to spring, and the older boys were able to make the journey independently by bus. They tried alternating so that their mother could have at least one visitor each day. Julie's friends weren't so reliable. They'd made all the right noises but when it came to putting promises into action, they didn't follow through. *They're just uncomfortable,* Dan thought. *It's understandable they don't visit, she wouldn't know them anyway.* He wished Rachel would answer his calls but her phone just went to voicemail every time, switched off. *Or blocking my calls? Come on Rachel, forget about us, step up and support your old friend.* He assumed she was holding a grudge, knowing that

Dan had abandoned her and returned to his wife. Social media messages would have been easy to find between the school mums gossiping about the accident and *'Dan's unwavering love and commitment', 'he's such a saint sticking by her,'* and the like. Yep, he'd read the messages, but he didn't feel worthy of their praise. He had a lot of making up to do.

Although awkward around the family too at first, Julie took on the role of actress, pretending to be the person they told her she was. Dan knew it, but was grateful as it made it easier on the kids. She acted the part until it all became more natural. Julie formed a new persona and eventually started to believe that was the person she was. *Let her believe, if it brings her back to us,* Dan thought.

'Mummy's body just isn't working properly yet. She's still a bit sleepy,' he explained to Tommy when they returned home, grateful that their bond made him feel safe and loved despite his mother's intermittent rejection.

Finally, one day she reached out to Tommy for a hug, initiating the embrace. He was an innocent child, so affectionate and easy to love and he'd made her more receptive. The day she hugged them back was the day of her release.

Tommy had been hit the hardest when she left, understandably, as he was the baby of the family. He'd kicked off at first but slowly transferred his affection to Dan, who had relished every moment. He couldn't help but feel a pang of jealousy that he would likely lose that affection once she returned home. *Share his love, there's room for both of you,* he told himself repeatedly, but he didn't really believe it.

When the day came, the children's excitement was infectious. He couldn't wait to reunite her with familiar surroundings, if only to put an end to clinical visiting hours and the false reserve he'd had to endure in the 'safe' environment. Often he'd struggled to hold his tongue, but when she was home, they could return to normal, *he hoped*. It would be a slow process, they were reminded, but they were all willing to put in the effort, *what other choice was there?* Dan felt he'd been given a second chance, nothing short of a miracle and whether he loved her or not, he needed to make things work, he owed it to her.

Chapter Twenty-Six

As the car slowed to a stop, Julie looked out of the window, her world a blank. She saw the familiar faces of Jack and William, already out of the house, running down the driveway towards her, Tommy squeezing her hand in the car seat next to her.

'It's so exciting!' he squealed.

Is it? So, apparently, I'm a city girl?

She looked up at the cream pebbledash semi-detached house, it didn't scream character or neglect, or most notably, welcome. The path was uneven, tree roots from the overgrown magnolia had twisted their way free of their flowerbed and caused root heave and damage into the pavement beyond. It was their responsibility to trim it back, but through their neglect it wasn't just their family that was now suffering but those around them. She looked past the tree to the front door, the porch cracks patched up with filler, nobody had cared to use a matching colour or even a similar tone to the original workmanship, causing the appearance to look shoddy, decayed. There was nothing welcoming, nothing familiar that said 'home'. She thought she would have some memory on arrival, but was disappointed.

Dan had walked around to open her car door but as he stood arm outstretched, she froze, unable to walk, unwilling to believe this was her life. The moment passed unnoticed. It was easy to blame hesitation on her body, *it's still not functioning properly*. She grabbed onto Dan's arm and let him support her as she hobbled up the path, stopping midway to provide the expected hug for Jack and William en route. She could feel the love and warmth of their arms as they closed around her, their smell so familiar, aiding her memory and triggering the emotion that had led her back to them. She hadn't felt the same way towards Dan, yet, but supposed that too would come back in time.

Julie spent the first few days looking back through photo albums on Jack's computer, grateful he was so addicted to snapping every moment on his mobile phone. She'd seen little videos of herself and the rest of the family. It was like watching a movie about somebody else, mostly, but some things triggered feelings and she was ready to immerse herself in all they could show her. They'd had a happy life by all accounts; a lot of laughter, *a lot of eating by the size of her – or had her body just wasted away due to the coma?*

She was home at last, feeling better day by day, week by week, physically and mentally able to confront the days, but more than anything she wished for a little time to herself. Privacy. She'd had none in the hospital, or the rehabilitation centre with constant intrusions, but now, in her own home it was what she wanted more than anything. Time to focus, to grieve for the woman she had once been and move on, *if she couldn't bring her memories back.*

Dan was wonderful, encouraging, caring and so supportive. As the weeks passed, she grew fond of him and finally, bravely, gave herself to him. She was shy at first, imagining her wedding night would have been similar; she kept her clothes on to cover her scars. Their bodies knew what to do; they remembered each other and responded with muscle memory rather than love. He was quiet, timid, reserved, perhaps fearful that he would hurt her after all the trauma she had been through. *It's OK, I want this. I'm not going to break.* She tried to reassure him that she remembered their love and wanted to rekindle all that they had lost, but it took him a long time to relax.

'Julie, I've been thinking it might be a good time for me to return to work now you're back on your feet?' Dan said, interrupting the silence as they lay clammy on the scrunched-up bedding. She looked at him, trying to read more into it. How had their lovemaking led to this? *Was he leaving her?*

'Only if you're OK with it,' he added, sensing her disappointment while reaching for the duvet to cover her now shivering body. He seemed to be avoiding her gaze.

'We could really do with the extra money,' he went on, knowing she'd been worrying about the financial burden the hospital "incident" had placed on her family. 'What do you think?'

Julie reached over and draped her arms around his neck, pulling him back to bed, kissing him, trapping him, refusing to let him go. 'Do you have to? I feel like we've just got back from our honeymoon! I'll miss you so much! What am I supposed to do all day while you're at work?'

He smiled back as he pushed the hair out of her face, enjoying her scent as he leaned down to kiss her neck. 'I love you, Mrs. Summers,' he said, knowing he'd won.

'Hmm, do you think I'm such a pushover?'

He flipped her over, onto her front, and proceeded to massage her shoulders, back, lower and lower, making her squirm.

'Okay, fine. Go on then, back to work, but don't go working every hour God sends, or you'll miss out on all of this!' She kicked the duvet to the floor and watched his amused face. Despite her scarring from the accident, her body was taut, tanned and very much the tantalising teaser she knew he couldn't resist. She'd spent much of her recovery time outside, welcoming the sun on her skin as the seasons changed, feeling an affinity with nature and enjoying helping out in the garden. Then, when she had properly reunited with Dan, they had been like newlyweds, rediscovering each other after what he told her had been over twenty years of marriage. Julie was content, so pleased the life she had come back to was a paradise in comparison with how it could have been. That was most of the time, except, now and then, she felt a shudder of unease. She wasn't whole without her memories, her new self a fake creation based on video moments and social media's smiling pictures. Where was the depth? Without a best friend to share things with, who had she talked to? Dan said she had been all about family and she couldn't help but find this disappointing, that Dan was her only biased confidante.

On returning from the hospital a mere forty-five kilograms, she had been unable to fit into her old clothes, instead borrowing some of William's trousers and wearing her own tops that hung on her like pillowcases. But as she spent more time outside taking spring walks, gardening, running after Tommy, slowly, her body shape changed, and she became stronger, more confident.

'Will they give you your old job back? Are you sure that's what you want to do?' She'd asked him, unable to imagine Dan travelling to London every day to do an office job – so boring when he could be out in the fields tending to crops in the country. That would be her dream, one day.

'I think so,' he replied. 'When you had "time out", Reese and Sons were really supportive, let me have time off to look after the kids. They're very family-oriented, and I think I'm officially still on sabbatical, so...'

She'd switched off. That phrase, "time out", it made her shudder. She wouldn't just up and leave, would she? Though Dan said it had come totally out of the blue, without warning she couldn't help but wonder if he was hiding something, protecting her from reality. She'd been enjoying life, *he told her,* starting out on new adventures, even begun to write something or other – he wasn't very clear on the details – and then, suddenly, she just vanished. Julie couldn't help but wonder if her amnesia had begun before the accident and was the cause of her disappearance. Maybe her brain had momentarily shut down, early onset Alzheimer's or something similar. The doctors had said no, but they didn't have all the answers. Perhaps that was also the cause of her accident. On paper, she'd never had any driving issues before that fateful day, so why had it happened? Maybe it was because she was driving a hire car – the reason why was a mystery to them all, along with the fact no car company came knocking on their door to reclaim the write-off fees.

Nobody had the answers; they were locked inside her head.

'Well, no time like the present! I'm going off to London, see them face-to-face, better chance of appealing to their compassionate side.' He blew her a kiss and grabbed for his suit jacket, taking his briefcase just in case. He wouldn't need a coat – the weather was warming nicely – and he had a spring in his step.

'Bye, Mum! By, Dad!' Jack shouted up the stairs.

'Have a lovely day,' William added.

She enjoyed the daily routine, the older boys leaving together for school. They seemed to get on so well. Had they always been like that? She couldn't remember any teenage tantrums. *That's a relief.*

Tommy was as loving as ever, enjoying taking on a nurturing role-reversal as he nursed Julie, his "wounded soldier" back to health. He was ready early for the walk to school, bringing her stick for Julie to lean on and hook her arm through his. The mums at the school gate seemed friendly, '*Good morning, Julie!*' flying about from every direction. She wondered if she had been good friends with any of them before. If she was in a cynical mood, she might have thought they were looking at her as the news story she was.

On returning home, the house was too quiet. Julie's ears were ringing with the silence until she put the radio on, white noise to drown out the thoughts buzzing around senselessly in her head. She opened her wardrobe and started to pull out dresses, tops, trousers – so many things that clearly wouldn't fit. How long had she had them? She noticed in pictures from years before that she had lost a fair bit of weight while in the hospital, not altogether a bad thing by all accounts. Her body had quite literally laid there comatose, wasting away. What if she hadn't woken up? What if she'd just stayed there indefinitely, a human skeleton, decrepit. How long until Dan and the boys lost interest, stopped caring, wished for her to give up so they could move on with their lives; it made her shudder to think. How lucky she had been to make it through, she'd obviously done something right in a previous life.

Looking down at the heap of crumpled grey clothes she had accumulated on the floor, Julie felt sad. Is this what her life had been? Nothing extraordinary there, just blending into the background. Well, things need to change. It was high time she injected some colour into her life, out with the old and all that. With renewed vigour she grabbed hanger after hanger, ripping the fabric and throwing it with renewed gusto, tearing buttons from shirts, enjoying their fight-back as they tried to cling on, knowing this was their last chance to avoid the inferno that was threatening. The mountain just needed one little match and it would be gone. Wiped from existence.

Drifting into her quiet place, she thought about the match, an extra-long match, its furry end itching to be rubbed along its home. Safe within, yet once outside its world, one tiny scratch and the power of fire. Julie wondered, one tiny spark and say goodbye to that life, *the beautiful mesmerising fire.* Flames of passion, heat, warning, and on the flip-side release, freedom, escape. She wondered a moment too long... *say goodbye to this life,* she thought calmly, her breathing shallow with possibility. Why does everything have to be so hard?

A new song playing on the radio brought her back to the present, her eyes focusing once more on the giant mess-mountain of polyester that needed to be disposed of. What a waste, that was her life. Empty. Gone. Sliding the door closed, she felt it pull off its hinges, nipping her finger and making her curse, at the same time exposing Dan's side of the wardrobe. She propped the door back on with a struggle and looked through his clothes, leaning in to smell the fabric, reminding her of fast food, BBQs and stale sweat. His suits filthy, shirts creased but in surprising variety. At first glance she would have said he was a party goer – so many floral patterns, paint swirls, even skulls and crossbows. Why was his wardrobe trendy while hers was so dowdy? Was he required to dress up for work? *Who was the real Dan,* she wondered.

Then, right in the corner, *what is that?* A long, bright, floaty dress? She felt for the label and realised the dress size wasn't the same as her others, had he bought it for her recovery? Was she going to give it to her? It was so pretty, she felt the burning rush of shame thinking of that match once more. How could she have considered finding a way out when Dan was working so hard to keep them together. She owed it to him to try. Pulling at the dress she uncovered three other dresses, a couple of tops and a pair of black trousers. All in the smaller size, they would fit perfectly.

She put on the slinky black and green dress, just above the knee with an asymmetrical cut. It had giant daisies all over and felt as beautiful as it looked. It was gorgeous. He'd taken the labels out and sprayed them with her perfume. At that moment she wanted to cradle his head in her arms, comfort him, tell him it would all be OK. She would try harder. She would be a good wife, make him glad he had waited for her. She put the dress carefully back into the wardrobe and slipped on an oversized vest top, some joggers and a grey hoodie. She wouldn't ruin his surprise. She reached for her pumps and headed out the door, determined to enjoy the present and dream of a future that had been so close to being ripped away. She left her walking stick behind, no longer needed the prop there to support her.

Chapter Twenty-Seven

Dan got straight back into his job, embracing the nine-to-five hours and then home like clockwork by six every night – much to the bemusement of his colleagues, who were used to the stay-late attitude of before.

Julie felt a little redundant in the evenings as Jack insisted he continue to cook. She started keeping a diary, spent her time writing as much as possible, documenting any memories that came to mind; niggling triggers that felt familiar – places, people, smells. It all helped with the slow progress towards normality, whatever that was. She tucked herself up in her room, sat on the curved window seat that still pleased her every time she looked at its perfect, snuggly fit, decorative curtains billowing either side. Her daily routine complemented the children's gaming time; while they played, she listened to music and retreated into a world of calm, the whole family content in their little bubbles waiting for Dan's return.

On hearing the doorbell ring, Julie knew it was him back from work, but on the odd occasion she didn't rush straight down to greet him. Sometimes, she stayed locked away listening to the music as it worked its magic, pushing her towards an almost hypnotic state, where her thoughts were almost tactile, *almost*. If only she could pluck a few from her uncooperative memory. Dan knew not to disturb her, not to interrupt the flow. She listened vaguely as his keys jingled on the hook, his heavy footsteps making their way into the living room and beyond, greeting Jack in the kitchen. Normally, it put her mind at ease – she could relax and continue, knowing it wasn't an intruder – but tonight, something was different. She felt strangely irritated, annoyed as she listened to the usual routine, it grated on her, irrationally frustrating.

A memory sprang to mind – *shouting at the kids*. She could visualise them: moody, arguing, could hear her own voice screeching. She closed her eyes to focus, could hear the bell ringing, her voice bellowing again, they hadn't taken their keys out of their schoolbags. *Petty. Was that it?* She could hear their stomping shoes in the hallway, walking dirt through the house unnecessarily, an empty shoe rack waiting lonely in the porch. *Why had those things wound her up so much?*

Her breath came in short gasps, cheeks hot with anger, so much hatred raging through her body that it shocked her. She snapped her eyes open feeling uncomfortable with the way her body had responded towards such innocence – a hatred so familiar it sickened her. It was an unpleasant sensation but still, one step closer to remembering. Perhaps she had suffered a nervous breakdown? That would explain everything away, if she'd gone out of her mind she might well have up and left the family – or perhaps Dan had kicked her out when she lost control?

He was vague when she tried to broach the subject, still treating her like a fragile coma victim just released, but she'd changed. She was ready to hear his secrets and take responsibility for her actions. *How can I put things right if he continues to protect me?* Her reflection in the mirror was so drab, defeatist and she was no longer willing to put up with it.

Things need to change.

She slid open Dan's wardrobe and reached inside.

'Urgh, Dad, have you seen this? It's sick!'

Dan looked over to see William, head in the newspaper, devouring an article. *Well, if it gets him reading,* he thought, surprised to see him off the PlayStation.

'I'm hoping you have some engrossing story to tell me that doesn't involve my fantasy football team suffering,' he joked, jovially. 'Another player having a horrific limb break or some crisis or other would ruin me... William, are you listening to me?'

'Sorry Dad,' he responded. 'I was miles away! This is disgusting, you should see this! It's proper horrific. There's a woman in the paper who's had her face eaten off by giant rats! There's a picture and everything!'

'Don't talk such rubbish!' Dan reprimanded as he walked over, relived Adama Traoré was still in the game. 'That's not a rat, unless it's been photoshopped. It looks more like a mole or some weird hybrid otter thing!'

'Honestly, Dad, it's a rat. Check out this story!'

He started to read it aloud...

"GIANT KILLER RATS: Woman found EATEN ALIVE by monster rats who chewed off her face as she slept. It looks like she died a painful death after becoming trapped in a storage unit she rented earlier this year. Excavators of the derelict site found the remains of the woman on a blood-stained floor. Reportedly, her tongue, eyes and fingers had all been devoured. The empty storage unit had no supplies for the woman, who is thought to have starved to the point of paralysis before the hungry animals made their attack.

'When asked to comment on the incident, site manager Mr. Steven Morgan said: "Please be assured, there is no risk to local people as the rat infestation has been contained within the cordoned-off area, ready for demolition. Historically there have been lots of rats in the area as the storage site was built on top of an old council dump, but we are knowingly vigilant in protecting the operational units from unwanted vermin. Unfortunately, the area where the body was found was closed to public use some years ago and hence somewhat overlooked and neglected while waiting for demolition. Investigations are ongoing to work out how the deceased gained access to the unit. Safe Storage will remain open to its loyal customers. Stay safe with Safe Storage!"

William snorted with laughter, then he repeated in a high-pitched ridiculous impersonation – 'Stay safe with Safe Storage, stay safe with Safe Storage. How can he say that? Listen to this Dad, the police aren't bothering investigating! Shame, that would have been juicy.'

He read on, ignoring his dad's silence.

'The police are not treating this incident as suspicious. DC Gwyther commented: "So far, we have been unable to identify the deceased, and enquiries are ongoing. We were able to retrieve some items of jewellery. If you recognise them, please come forward."

'If you have any information on this tragic accident that might help to identify the deceased, please contact DC Gwyther on 0208 287 4647.'

Dan stood dry-mouthed. 'This can't be real. Seriously, what paper is this? How can they make up stories like that? It's like April Fools, but it's only March. Disgusting. The press should be made to answer for their actions – scaremongering, sensationalism...'

'Can we go down there and check it out?' Jack blurted out, having miraculously appeared from the kitchen, where he'd been listening in on the horror story.

'No, you bloody well can't! You are sick in the head, Jack. If that is real, then think of the poor woman's family. What's the point of putting pictures of jewellery in the papers as if someone would recognise that lot?' He glanced over and stood motionless, staring, feet rooted to the spot. 'What the...?'

'What's up, Dad? Rat got your tongue?'

'William, that is just so bad,' Jack chuckled, giving his brother a shove.

Dan's face turned to ash as he stared at the jade pendant. He turned the page to look at the other items of jewellery but remained silent.

'Oh, now you're interested, Dad! Proper getting into the story, are you? Well, don't throw it out when you're done – I want to keep it. I'm thinking it would make for a good school project. Modern Day Plague or something along those lines. It's just a shame it didn't happen on the school grounds. I mean, can you imagine? They would have to close the school! Throw a few teachers in to feed the rats too – it's a win-win. Some of them would benefit from having their faces rearranged!'

'Shut up, just shut up!' Dan broke the silence, glaring at William, his face like thunder as he closed the paper.

'Okay, chill, Dad, they're not coming here!'

'I don't want that article on your wall or anywhere your mother might see it. Don't you think she's been through enough without seeing this horror?'

'Fine, fine, fine,' William said, stomping off upstairs, bedroom door slamming to mark his departure. Jack, sensing the animosity, had slinked off, back to the kitchen, to continue with his culinary delights – a role he had embraced since his mother's abandonment. He peered back at his dad, doubled over the closed newspaper, slumped in the dining chair, a shell of his former domineering self.

DAN

Dan was alone. Detached, unable to process what might be. Icicles prickled his skin as he opened the newspaper once more and looked at the article, unwilling to entertain the notion of that jade necklace... He bit on his lip to contain the scream that threatened to escape his body. The boys were gone – they'd left him at the table at some point. When, he couldn't recall, but he presumed it was after his outburst, them misunderstanding his response. He focused on the images as he turned the pages:

the jewellery, the daisy diamond earrings – so expensive, so intricate, so unique – an amber centre to each, with a swirl of red running through the leaf that clasped the sparkling jewels in their diamond daisy petals.

'The yellow represents our sunrise, the dawn of our love; the white, the purity of our love; and the green…' He'd been lost for words. What could the green be? 'The green leaf, the beginning of our lives together, a plant ready to grow and be nurtured. You are the oxygen I breathe.'

He could hear himself speaking the words, and her joking reply, so full of love. 'Oh, Dan, that is truly horrific! You are so corny!'

His Rachel.

She'd put her arms around him and hugged him close as they both laughed at his attempt at romance. If he wasn't married already, that would have been the moment he proposed. He'd been trying to declare his love to her, had spent over a year designing those earrings on a crazy-expensive jewellery site, and her response: she'd teased him – but in a good way, and they'd been her favourite ever since. She never took those earrings out.

He looked back at the printed pictures. There was no question in his mind as he ran to the bathroom and retched into the toilet bowl, cramps shuddering through his stomach, his chest tightening as he gripped the porcelain, struggling to breathe. It couldn't be her. He leaned his elbows on the urine-stained toilet, head in hands, blinking through tears as they burnt his eyes.

Chapter Twenty-Eight

JULIE

Julie's mood picked up as she flicked the radio over to some Eighties classics. She assumed they were her favourites as she found herself singing along, unfamiliar with the lyrics yet somehow conjuring them up from the depths of her memory. As the song finished, she was surprised to hear the hourly news being introduced. *It's really late, must get a move on.* She couldn't resist picking up her mobile for a quick surf while the news headlines continued.

God, this rat story is everywhere. She wondered if it was real or more likely a dramatization created to go viral on social media. *Clear up your rubbish, or you encourage vermin. Remember to always recycle, recycle, recycle.* Her Facebook immediately picked up on her browser history and started to share adverts for pest control, cleaning companies and her favourite: a photograph of a grinning man holding up a giant rat by its tail nearly the same size as him. *Nice.*

Apparently, jewellery was the only thing on the scene to

identify the body. Julie couldn't help but wonder if there was ever a body there to start with, and most importantly, why the people who'd found the jewellery hadn't just kept it for themselves? It was reportedly quite valuable, and if it hadn't been, why would it be in a safe storage unit in the first place? *Oh, yes, the woman was wearing it. So, what was she doing there? Why wasn't it considered suspicious?* She was getting confused trying to make sense of it all.

'Dinner's ready!' Jack hollered up the stairs. 'Mum! William! Tommy! I'm dishing up now!'

Damn, she mumbled, cursing her mobile for once again dragging her into the time-warp abyss that was social media. She opened Dan's wardrobe and grabbed the beautiful green dress, burying her head into its soft material and breathing in the lingering perfume that clung to the fabric. The scent – not altogether unpleasant but not something she found herself warming to – yet the perfume sat on her dressing table.

She had visions of a fancy, chandelier-clad house, floor-to-ceiling old-style, stained-glass windows; exquisitely beautiful, a stately home? A flash-back. She carefully lowered the dress over her head, let it fall onto her naked flesh, the silk and luxurious fabric hanging fragile upon her slender frame. Something, she couldn't quite grasp it, a memory teetered on the edge, hanging at the peripheries of her vision like the magic-eye paintings that baffled her so much; just out of reach. It wouldn't be long before she remembered, she thought, walking down the stairs to dinner.

'Wow, Mum, you look gorgeous!' Jack said, carrying through a glass casserole dish containing layers of yellow, orange and beige.

'Thanks, darling.' She blushed, enjoying the compliment, unaware of the rarity of the occasion.

William looked up from the table, gaping. 'Where did you get that from? It looks designer. Michael Kors? Not like your usual stuff.'

Julie smiled back. Was it healthy for a sixteen-year-old boy to know so much about women's clothing? Had she missed something?

'The girls at school have Michael Kors bags. And Gucci, Bottega, Stella McCartney...'

'That's crazy! They're so expensive! For school? They must be fakes.'

'They're real, Mum, I'm telling you. It's like, the boys spend out on trainers, and the girls on bags.'

'Madness. Well, they're very lucky.' *And stupid*, she thought, wondering at the absurdity of kids, the status symbols they aspired to. *So shallow. How can something designer, a mere label, make them feel better about themselves?* But as she walked, the swish of the material, the compliments she'd received, she understood. Teenagers, desperate for the approval of their friends, saving all their money for that one item – that one special something. Was that why Dan had bought her the dress, because he wanted her to feel special? Because he thought she was special? It was so different to the rest of her wardrobe though, perhaps he was trying to change her? Make her into a different person? Julie felt uncomfortable – was he controlling her? *But he hadn't actually given her the dress. She had taken it. Taken control.* She shrugged off the negative warnings.

Her thoughts were interrupted as Dan entered from the bathroom, silent and pale. She beamed at him, hoping he wasn't coming down with something. As Dan raised his head, his body crumpled and his legs gave way.

'Rachel?' he mouthed ambiguously.

'What?'

He stood staring, ashen, a ghost of the man he portrayed himself to be. He was silent, confused. She stared back, unsure what to do next, the kids being in the same room making her more anxious to get it right. Had Dan taken on too much with the new job? That on top of the months and months of worry, her disappearance, the accident, the kids, her slow recovery – everything had finally caught up with him, and he was falling apart.

'Dad, what's wrong? Are you ill, or are you just trying to get out of eating my cooking?' Jack wasn't having any of it. He walked over and grabbed Dan roughly by the arm, led him to his seat at the table.

'Dan, are you okay?' Julie stood over him, her words breaking his trance as he began to cry, tears streaming down his cheeks, dotting dark marks over the pale blue of his shirt. 'Dan, what's the matter?'

She was concerned now. He was unresponsive, irrational, bordering on hysterical. She didn't remember seeing him cry before, but her memory wasn't reliable. *Was this normal for him?* She prayed he wasn't having a breakdown. How would she look after the kids? She didn't know if she was ready, but if she had to, maybe this would be the push she needed. She owed him after all his patience and support. *Did I do this to him?*

DAN

He looked up at Julie, her blissful ignorance, wishing it was he who had concussion, that he didn't have to live with knowing. He couldn't explain, couldn't find the words.

'Dan! Answer me! You're scaring me. What's wrong?'

He had to bear the loss alone, couldn't let her find out what Rachel meant to him. *Had* meant to him.

Eventually, his mouth let out a whispered sob. 'Nothing.' He paused again. 'It's just...so good to have you home.' He hugged her to him and continued to cry into her dress, breathing in Rachel's scent, remembering. That dress, the last time she'd slept over, hiding in the wardrobe when Tommy bounded in, laughing as they behaved like teenage lovers trying to keep their secret despite their longing for each other. The freedom when Julie left, the promise of a new life ahead – for them, together, guiltily embracing every opportunity.

It had all started so well, so full of hope, Rachel gradually leaving a few of her bits behind each time she popped over. That dress. Their anniversary meal. He wondered what else she had left in the house for Julie to claim as her own, wondered if the children would say anything; if they would work it out; if Julie would remember. He looked up at her as she comforted him, silently stroking his head, marvelling at how beautiful she looked wearing it. The irony of her choosing that day, that exact moment, to wear that dress felt like a message from beyond the grave. But what?

'My love', he breathed, pulling her close as he rubbed his eyes dry against the silk. He lifted his head slowly to see her smiling back at him, his family around the table waiting for the episode to pass, Jack visibly cringing at his dad's display of affection.

He gulped, composing himself, slowly standing, holding onto Julie's hand for support, and addressed Jack. 'So, what marvellous medicine have you created for us tonight?'

'About time, Dad. What was that all about? No need to answer – it was a rhetorical question. Just hurry up and eat, or it's going to get cold,' Jack said, then whispered to William, 'Tuck in, no grace tonight.'

Jack winked and then made his way to the hallway to shout for his little brother.

'Tommy! Your food is getting cold. Tommy! Come down now!'

No response.

'He's probably got headphones on,' Jack mumbled, annoyed that his dinner was getting cold and bounding up the stairs.

'I'm just finishing!' came the heated response.

'You have to come now!'

'I'm in the middle of a game!'

'I'm going to count to three, then I'm going to turn the electric off! One, two—'

'You're not the boss of me!'

The lights went out momentarily and doors were heard banging upstairs. Moments later Jack returned to the table, a sulky Tommy in tow.

So that's how it's done, Julie noted.

JULIE

Julie looked over at Dan, avoiding eye contact, wondering again whether this was normal behaviour; if he'd had episodes before. As they tucked into the stodgy mass on their plates, nobody speaking, all in their own worlds, she was grateful for small mercies – at least she didn't have picky eaters.

She fought the urge to shout at the children, annoyance suddenly cursing through her veins with a string of expletives threatening to follow. She needed to keep control, couldn't let things spiral with Dan in such a fragile state. Looking around the table, everyone was peaceful, *so why was she panting with anxiety?* As she sat willing the situation to sort itself out, she questioned herself and all those unfamiliar emotions rushing through her, making her into a person she didn't want to be. *Was that the person she used to be?*

Chapter Twenty-Nine

When Julie's alarm sounded at seven a.m., Dan had already left for work. She couldn't remember him getting up or leaving the house or even coming to bed the night before. She went through the now familiar routine – sorted the kids out, dropped Tommy off at school, came back to the house to clean up.

So tedious, she thought, staring at the filthy mess.

Bright rays of sunshine peeked through the bedroom shutters, a fresh breeze fighting its way into the stagnant air, attempting to lift her spirits. A trapped feeling hit her like a brick, her knees buckling under the claustrophobic tension of the room – the *house* – the need for freedom palpitating her chest.

Julie gasped for air as she struggled to reach the shutters, fling them open and breathe. *Just breathe.* She could hear herself repeatedly chanting something all too familiar. Déjà vu, the soul mate of concussion; the confusion over whether it was a memory or just a feeling, with nobody to ask, nobody to answer, only the scared little girl hiding inside herself.

And then, it was gone, as suddenly as it had come on.

Was that a panic attack? She needed to put less pressure on herself but was finding it hard to accept such a transient way of living. Not having memories made her question the person she was – her likes, dislikes, what formed her. She closed the window and walked down the stairs, automatically reaching for her jacket as she exited the house blindly.

Shit, no keys. Did that door always lock itself on closing? She wondered if any friends held a key for her house – but if she couldn't remember the friends, how could she even ask? Her head was a jumble of disorientated confusion as she walked along, grateful she'd at least brought her jacket since the sun wasn't up to expectations. *No keys, no phone, no wallet.* She would just walk, relax and hopefully not get too lost.

It was a beautiful day. A ridiculous number of tiny green birds were chirping their lungs out in the trees above as she squinted up to take a look. They looked like tiny parakeets, strangely out of place for such a suburban area. She plucked a memory from the peripheries of her mind: an image of a van in an accident, the birds escaping their confinement, released into the hostile environment of London, instead of making their way to the zoo that had been their intended destination. Was it a news report? She was happy for them. They had embraced their new climate and transformed from an endangered species into a frantically breeding population; ruralising their landscape.

Let the caged birds sing.

As Julie walked, she wondered if the story was true, hoping it was and making a mental note to Google it when she got back, thankful the digital age held answers within easy reach.

How long until it could also take control of the human mind? If only she could have backed up her own memories to the Cloud. It was all very well looking at photos and videos, but they didn't bring familiarity back; the depth that made her who she was; a compilation of her responses and exposure. She was but a caricature of herself. Shakespeare had it right, her life was indeed "a walking shadow, a poor player, that struts and frets his hour upon the stage, and then is heard no more."

Must stop acting and find reality, she thought, continuing on, enjoying the fresh breeze but still nervous to hold her head too high in case she made eye-contact with another person. *What if they knew her but she didn't respond? What if she pre-empted the relationship and smiled only to be ignored?* She had no confidence, wasn't ready. The fresh air helped but nature could only fix part of her healing while nurture was required for the rest.

Looking down at the ground had its upside, she thought, sidestepping dog muck that had been squashed and re-trod up the path. Was it that people didn't care or were they just looking in the wrong direction? Had the owner known the repercussions of not picking up the mess, would they have acted differently if they had? She didn't have a dog but couldn't help but wonder, *what would Julie do?* Was she the offender or the offended, more importantly, was there anyone out there who could help her to work out the answer? Somebody before her had been brave enough to raise their head, look forwards, onwards and upwards, and that was their reward. She wondered if it was considered lucky in the same way as bird droppings when they fell on your head.

A group of mothers with empty pushchairs, redundant bikes and well-worn scooters stood chatting at the end of the road. She glanced up nervously, wanting to be brave. Should she greet them and if so, how? It was impossible to believe she had ever been a fearless warrior, able to approach people without hesitation and the more she thought about it the more her anxiety seemed too real to be just a by-product of her amnesia. Surprisingly, since Julie's accident, the more time that passed, the less confident she had become. *Think it through, work at it*, she told herself, determined.

By greeting people with a simple, 'Hi,' as she passed, she hoped their response would indicate if they were friends. Worst-case, she could put it down to mistaken identity. If they were local, they probably knew of Julie's story anyway, and she could always fall back on the excuse of having had a brain injury. She'd worked out a smile in response was a likely no. Even a wave was reactive. But a, 'Hi,' returned with a, 'How are you?' was someone who knew her – in which case, how should she reply? What did they expect? Should she give a simple, 'Good, you?' while walking past, not waiting for an answer – or should she stop, explain to them she had no idea who they were, that her mind was a mess, that her family were only barely keeping her sane, that her husband, she suspected, was bordering on a nervous breakdown? Social interaction was a minefield.

As she approached, Julie felt her chest pounding again, sweat forming clammy patches under her arms. Biting her lip, she put her head down and increased her pace. Today wasn't the day for facing her demons. She carried on walking, and walking, towards the night until she stopped, that house in front of her. Her *home?*

Ringing the doorbell, she stood nervously waiting for it to be answered, waiting to be scolded like a prodigal child returning before the parents had been given enough time to for-give – and Dan didn't disappoint. She had been on such a high, exuberant that she'd managed to find her way back home. The children should have been there to let her in. *Oh, the children! Tommy!* She'd forgotten it was her job to collect him, *but he was home now, thankfully*. She breathed a sigh of relief, then looking at Dan's face, fuming, realised he must have been called home from work.

'I didn't know where you were! Anything could have hap-pened to you,' Dan shouted furiously. 'You shouldn't go out on your own, and certainly not without your phone!'

This felt all too familiar. Hearing him shouting those words, stopping her, controlling her. It should have made her upset but was strangely calming, tantalisingly ordinary, oh how she longed to remember. Her body propelled her onwards, her mind letting it take control. She tried to explain how she'd for-gotten the keys, locked herself out, needed to escape the house but he wasn't ready to listen so changing tack she apologised and shuffled up the stairs to their bedroom. She turned round to find him right behind her, closing the door and the windows and then standing in front of her, encroaching on her domain.

He was so angry. She tried to leave the room but he lifted his arm, blocking her exit. For the first time, she felt scared, wondered if he would lash out, if this had happened before, desperately yearning for her lost memories. Was this the kind of man he was? His fists were large, his arms strong and thick, his body motionless. She dare not look at his face, afraid to see the real him, to finally know him. Her knees were trembling as she finally looked up into his eyes, her own letting out silent tears against her will.

Had she left him before, because of this?

She wouldn't let herself believe it, told herself he was just being protective, was just acting in fear rather than malice. Only time would reveal the truth but for now, she was vulnerable.

'Sorry, Dan, it won't happen again.' She opted for the contrite response, outwardly subservient while seething inside at the physical and mental prison Dan was creating. She didn't recognise him – not from memory nor from the man he had pretended to be since her return home. *Was he hiding something from her?*

At her apology, Dan let his arm drop, helping to slow her pounding heart. 'I just want to protect you,' he said, squeezing her tight.

She so wanted to believe him.

He bent his face towards her and laid a kiss on her forehead, then turned and walked away. She felt the damp residue that he left behind and wondered whether he'd been crying too.

Chapter Thirty

The days passed slowly, but with each one Julie ticked off, she marvelled at the little things that were gradually coming back to her. Tidying the house and organising things helped enormously, clearing out the junk and finding a proper place for everything. She'd buried herself in books, embracing The Life-Changing Magic of Tidying Up. Decluttering, organising, prioritising, scheduling – it was all pushing her in the right direction.

But, where Dan was concerned, there had been little progress other than regression. He had distanced himself from her since that night, or perhaps she had been more reserved? She played over the scene at the dinner table, over and over, convincing herself he must have suffered an emotional breakdown. They didn't talk about it. She was still too vulnerable, and he was coping by being away more – throwing himself into his work.

Julie whistled as she walked around the house, a quick dust here, a heavy polish there; it was easy when the children were out – except for Jack's room – she didn't know where to start. So much of his schoolwork consisted of single pieces of paper put away into drawers, scrunched in so it was starting to disintegrate. *What's the point in keeping that?* she wanted to shout at him but thought it better simply to tackle his room during the school day. She had more time today, knowing she wouldn't have to collect Tommy as he was playing over at a friend's house.

One down, two to go, she thought as she turned the radio on, music blaring while she worked her way through the junk. She suspected a normal teenager would prefer not to have their room ransacked, but in Jack's case, he was happy for her to get on with it as long as he didn't have to help.

'Ow, fuck,' she cursed loudly as she spotted the tiny Lego pieces wedged between her toes. *How could something so tiny cause so much agony?* She tried to balance to pick them off but lost her footing and fell to the ground, laughing at the absurdity of it all. She could just imagine the news headlines: *Mother suffers tragic death in bedroom after failing to successfully manoeuvre around floor toys and sharp edges.*

From her position on the floor, Julie could see under Jack's bed: crisp packets, mouldy tangerine peel, chocolate wrappers and dirty cutlery. She crawled on all fours, rubbing her head where she'd bumped it on the side cabinet, and gradually pulled herself up again. Moving the bed would make more sense – she'd be able to give it a proper clear-out, but shifting it over wasn't proving easy.

Julie dropped back down and reached underneath, using an old pole feather-duster to help pull the debris towards her. Broken remote-controlled toys and piles of picture books long since abandoned were amongst the junk that came away first. She put one ear to the floor, one eye now in position to take a better look at what was left. *A folder?* She couldn't quite reach, so tried swatting at it with the pole once more, shifting it just an inch closer to within her grasp. She dreaded to think what was hidden inside. Magazines, she suspected, but she was surprised to find newspaper articles.

As she flicked through, some of the words jumped out at her, images making her skin chill more with each new headline. And then –

That face.

That woman.

Dead.

Killed?

She felt an emotional wrench, an affinity with the poor woman, as she began to read.

'Amrita Devi, mother of four, left for dead at London cinema. Thought to have been an unprovoked attack, although linked to gang warfare...'

A photograph: security tape cordoning off the cinema toilets, blood stains on the floor, piles of sand to soak up the residue. Julie looked closer, her heart pounding; palpitations as the world around her backtracked, silently coming into focus. Why did he have these articles? Why did she feel such a strong connection? Julie *recognised* the deceased. *Had they been friends?*

She continued to sift through the articles. It was a local story – perhaps Jack knew the people involved too, or, God forbid, was he involved? That might explain why he'd kept so many details on just one story. *But she couldn't just ask him.* She was too scared, sensing that she already knew the answer and that it would be best to hide behind her concussion.

Hold on, this is different.

Julie found another story towards the bottom of the pile, the rat story she'd heard about more recently. She felt a sense of relief. Perhaps he was just overly curious, into sensationalist horror perhaps? She flicked through the new articles, surprised there were no photographs of the deceased, that meant the police hadn't made any breakthroughs to identify her or Jack would have included those stories. She shuffled the papers and found a photo of the storage unit, the site of her massacre, and more images of the woman's jewellery. She paused, wondering, *that jewellery looks so familiar.* She wracked her brain, thinking, picturing the beautiful green emerald necklace, those daisy earrings, so unique, so...so...so...

Rachel!

Julie clenched the paper in horror.

Rachel, *her friend.* Those earrings. Now the memories fell from her mind like a dark storm cloud finally relenting to release its toxins. The storage unit unfit for human habitation... unfit for storage...unfit for Rachel. She remembered being there with her, closing the door, walking away. *Why? What happened?* Damn her useless memory. The date jumped out of the paper, bold and unforgettable.

The accident!

Had it happened on the same day? *Oh, God,* if only she hadn't crashed her car, Rachel might still be alive. Her friend. Was she relying on Julie to bring her provisions? Had she gone into hiding for some reason? She whimpered as she tried to control her breathing, frantically clawing her way up, and searching the room for something, anything – a bag to control the panic attack coursing through her, wave after wave, her knees buckling as she willed her memories to recede once more. She rocked back and forth, clutching her chest as she passed out into darkness.

Chapter Thirty-One

'Mum, wake up. Wake up! Can you hear me?' Jack shook his mum, not sure what to do, remembering something about not moving a person after an accident to minimise any trauma. 'Call an ambulance, William! Mum's collapsed! She's bleeding! Looks like she's hit her head!'

'What? Don't mess about! I don't believe you.' William came running upstairs and stood fixated, staring at the body on the floor.

'Don't just stand there gawping – go and phone an ambulance!'

William rushed off, frantically fumbling about for his phone, dropping it mid-call after requesting 999 assistance and having to start over.

The delay gave Jack time. Time to watch her lying there, the cause of so many problems in his life. He started shuffling his papers back into their case and pushed them back under the bed. No doubt Dad would be on his back again for this. *Don't shock her, don't frighten her, go gently. She can't handle any shocks...'* Blah, blah, blah. She wasn't a pet; she was a grown woman! Had she really freaked out at finding his papers? Was he in trouble? She shouldn't have gone snooping through his stuff then.

He prodded her with his foot. She wasn't moving. He glanced towards the door, then reached down and slapped her hard across the face, his hand leaving an imprint almost immediately, fingers patterning in a satisfying way, coupled with the crisp, clear sound of the thwack.

'Jack, what the hell?' William stood in the doorway holding the phone, watching his brother squirm, caught in the act. 'The paramedics are asking if she's breathing.'

'I was just trying to bring her around,' Jack mumbled.

'Never mind all that now – is she breathing?'

'Yeah, she's breathing, but her head looks a bit bloody.'

Julie groaned.

'Hold on, she's waking up. Mum, are you all right?' William asked.

They both waited expectantly, the phone operator explaining that was a good sign and they should keep her awake until they arrived.

Julie stared back at them, eyes glazing over.

'Stay with me, Mum. What happened? Your head's bleeding!'

Julie looked around at William standing there, Jack crouched by her side, watching expectantly. Waiting. She reached up to her head, then to her stinging cheek.

'I'm fine. It's just a scratch. I must have fallen.' She spotted the phone in his hand. 'Who are you talking to? Is that Dad?'

'It's the ambulance, Mum. Here, you take it.'

She reluctantly took the phone, William visibly relieved he'd passed over the responsibility. He listened as his mum apologised for time-wasting, insisting she was fine and would make her own way in for a check-up if she felt any worse. She cut the call and took a few minutes to get her bearings, then tried to stand, her hand slipping as it met with paper instead of the wood floor.

William moved quickly to kick the article out of sight, helping Julie up and steering her towards the door – but it was too late. Her body stumbling along, faltered and her knees buckled, she'd seen it. He released his grip as she vomited onto the floor, sending her crashing into the doorframe, a look of disgust as he receded back into his bedroom, cursing.

'Are you okay? Can I get you anything?' William came running up, mop and bucket in hand.

'Just leave me, please. I want to be on my own.'

He hesitated, just for a second, then obliged and ran off, relinquishing the cleaning stuff for his mum to sort out her own mess. She took it unconsciously and began to clean, thoughts flowing freely with each repetitive motion.

That was when the tears started to fall – for Amrita, for Rachel, for herself. Adrenaline rushed through Julie as she felt the fog lifting, her thoughts lining up in order, making sense but no sense. Memories came crashing back: Amrita, all that anger, the release. She'd enjoyed it. *She was a monster!* She had attacked an innocent woman and left her for dead. *That poor woman.* It was all starting to make sense. This explained why she had walked out on her family, fled the punishment that was out there waiting for her.

Her thoughts shifted to Rachel, her beautiful friend. Had she tried to help her go into hiding? Had they been in contact all the time she was away? Why had she met up with her at the storage unit? All that effort to recall her memories; all those months of praying, desperate for a lucid dream, and now, there was no putting them back in the box. Poor, poor Rachel. She recalled leaving her at the unit, something about it being a hide-out but not why Rachel wanted to be there. Was Julie supposed to bring food and drink to help her? Then the crash, a tragic twist to their friendship, a life ruined through error, fate nothing but a memory time-lapse.

She wished she hadn't recognised that jewellery.

What had Rachel done to deserve such a terrifying end? Julie wracked her brain, desperately clawing for an explanation, nothing more came. She was exhausted and collapsed onto her bed a broken woman. Should she tell Dan about Rachel or go straight to the police, tell them she knew the deceased; she was her friend? Should she own up to her involvement in Amrita's death?

She waited anxiously for Dan's return, thinking about Rachel, what she'd done to her innocent friend – left her there to die. She would do anything to go back to the innocence of yesterday. If only she hadn't gone into Jack's room. What other secrets were hiding in the house waiting for her to rediscover memories? Was there even worse to come?

She was a murderer.

Did the children know? That thought was even more horrific – that she had taken her children's innocence through her insane actions. Was that why she'd left, to protect them? It was all too little, too late.

Why would Jack keep the cuttings – unless he knew?

Chapter Thirty-Two

Distant, familiar sounds: keys in a lock, footsteps in the hall, in her house. Dan shouting, running up the stairs.

'Julie! Are you okay? I came as soon as I heard!' He burst into the bedroom where she was curled up like a foetus – still, unmoving, staring with bloodshot eyes and a pale face, her hair matted with dried blood. 'Oh, Julie!'

She tried so hard but just couldn't do it, couldn't keep it from him. He was her love; he would comfort her for the loss of her friend.

'Dan, I need to tell you something.'

He looked at her expectantly, almost nervous.

'The woman in the paper...is Rachel. We were friends. I know what happened.'

She watched the blood drain from his cheeks, his smile still staining his face like a demonic painted blemish burnt onto his skin in contrast with his thoughts and words. He opened his mouth and closed it again, repeatedly scrunching his eyes tightly, straining till the veins bulged and pulsated in his forehead.

She felt sorry for him as he tried so hard to spare her feelings, to protect her. The room was silent, their eyes fixed, neither speaking. Then, finally Dan bent over, crouching.

'I'm so sorry, Julie. I should have told you before. I didn't love her like I love you. She was just sort of there, and you weren't, back then...before.'

What was he saying...? She felt her mouth open, her breath catch as she stared at him, his words making no sense, his body crumpled as he laid out the bare bones of – *an affair? His affair?* Words kept tumbling out of his mouth, not registering: 'mistake', 'love', 'Rachel'.

Her Dan...and Rachel?

How could he? With her best friend, right under her nose! His admission of guilt, the details of their relationship, how it had all been a huge mistake – the words kept coming as she tried to tune out.

It's a mistake, it's not real, you're dreaming, this isn't happening. Wake up Julie!

'I haven't seen her since your accident. Honestly, Julie, you have to believe me. That was the point I realised it was you I really loved, the thought of losing you forever...'

'You...and Rachel?' The words caught in her throat, giving him the chance to continue his excuses, his lies, it meant nothing.

'I can't believe she's dead and how she died. I just can't bear to think about it. Such a nightmare. I need to tell the police, to identify her. Nobody's come forward. I would have before, but as you didn't remember her, I didn't want to put you through finding her and then losing her all over again. It just didn't seem fair on you. But now you've remembered...

how long have you known about the affair? Did you know before the accident?'

Julie's face drained as she stood listening. She had been ready to bare her soul, explain her guilt – how she had locked her friend up and left her there, never meant for her to die. She'd wanted to share the agony of her loss, talk through her confusion, hadn't expected Dan's response. He'd been having an affair with Rachel! She'd been blindsided by the loss of her friend, had passed out before recalling rhyme or reason.

Their affair. Everything was becoming clear. Julie had left *her* there, the Slut. She remembered. If she hadn't had that accident, Rachel would have really known suffering, she would have made sure of it.

They had ruined her life, made her not want to live.

It was slowly coming back. She hadn't just left her there, locked her in by accident; she had planned Rachel's torture. Planned revenge. Contemplated murder. So, that was the kind of person she was. That was why the memory of Amrita's death had brought a smile to her lips. She was a cold-blooded killer. She flicked her tongue around her teeth, thinking about her new persona, it felt right.

Her voice altered, filled with venom as she spat out her questions with renewed vigour. She couldn't remember the specifics, wasn't listening as he pleaded forgiveness, his answers drowned out by the sound of rats scurrying, scratching...

'How long was it going on?'

'It's not important anymore. She's gone.' Dan paused, a broken man. He'd started to cry again. This was becoming a common occurrence that wouldn't be tolerated. He'd loved Rachel. *So what.*

She remembered everything. He wasn't entitled to grieve, he needed to take responsibility and pay the price. All that jewellery, the lists of receipts on their joint account, the pure front of it all!

He took her silence for probing and spoke again. 'Three years. Julie, I'm so sorry. It meant nothing. I just didn't realise how much I loved you. Life just kind of...got in the way.'

Shut up, shut up, shut up! she screamed internally, channelling the anger, feeling like a woman possessed – but he kept going.

'I was so worried, after everything you've been through. I'm so proud of how far you've come. The affair – it was all so long ago, like a different lifetime.' He pleaded with her, reached out, tried to bring her back to him, but she pulled away, turned her back on him and their life.

'Get out.' Her instruction: simple, clear, precise.

As he left the room deflated, she closed the door firmly behind him and started to think about what to do next. It might all be old news to him, but to her, it was a fresh bleed; a wound she didn't realise was there, prized wide open. She lay in bed, tossing and turning, the television blaring something, unsuccessfully trying to distract her from her thoughts.

The front door slammed, and their car started up outside.

How dare he act like the injured party. At least he had the sense to leave.

It was a long time coming, but finally, amongst the noise, intermittent screen changes and too many pillow turns, came the sweet release of sleep – but with it, the nightmares of her reality.

Chapter Thirty-Three

Julie awoke to the sound of footsteps, anger coursing through her. She refused to live in fear any longer. The door opened, and Dan climbed into bed. She was stunned he had the nerve. Those creeping hands mauling at her when they'd been all over Rachel. His touch was like a knife cutting into her skin, mumbled apologies as if words would ever be enough.

'Stop!'

She jumped out of bed and ran from the room, felt her way through the dark to the bathroom and locked the door behind her, leaning over the sink.

'Amrita, where are you now?'

She surfed her phone for Rachel, her Facebook profile – clear, beautiful images, her wallpaper changed to a dove flying away. Dan had told the police; people knew. She scrolled through Rachel's photos, pausing on that green dress. Disgust brought with it the taste of bile. He deserved everything coming to him. She unlocked the door and crept out to check on her boys, lingering long enough to kiss them goodbye.

She could never forgive Dan. He would be punished in a way she'd never been able to punish Rachel. She'd been robbed of that satisfaction. So what if the bitch was dead. Julie hadn't been able to confront her, to hear her plead, enjoy her suffering.

Lucky rats.

She went back into the bathroom, her sanctuary, she used the toilet and flushed it to see if it would wake the kids – nope, nothing would wake them up that night. She turned on the taps to wash her hands and recalled Shakespeare's scene, Lady Macbeth trying to wash away her guilt. Julie could see no spots on her own hands, but still, she continued, glancing up at the mirror once more.

Had she deserved this life? Was it the one she was supposed to live, or had she made the wrong choices? Her wild hair hung smooth at the sides of her face, but there was something more. Brunette blending with blonde, brown eyes and blue, the perfect blackberry pout combining with her own chapped lips.

Rachel...

She'd come. She wasn't smiling, only staring through hurt eyes – sad, lonely, abandoned, knowing. Julie wasn't scared. She held her phone to her lips and breathed, 'Help me,' and cut the call. She was ready.

'Dan,' she whispered, 'Please come.'

He didn't respond, so she tried a little louder, playing the vulnerable innocent, calling for him.

'Dan, I need you!'

A slight pause, then his response.

'Julie, are you OK?'

She let his words hang in the air without a response,

wondering what was going through his mind, wondering if things would work out, and eventually she heard movement.

'I'm coming,' he said, irritation in his voice.

He had no doubt been sleeping peacefully, oblivious to her suffering – *how dare he!* She heard him thud out of bed, and in the time it took for him to cross the landing, she let out a scream loud enough to wake the neighbours, at the same time smashing the mirror repeatedly with the hand soap, fracturing Rachel's image into deadly pieces.

Dan stood in the doorway horrified, staring at the crazy scene in front of him, his gasp the only noise breaking the ringing silence of the aftermath. The kids were blissfully unaware. All those nights tiptoeing over creaking floorboards, trying not to wake them... Julie stood motionless, gripping a shard of the mirror, staring wild through the dark as it cut into the warm flesh of her hand, blood drip-dripping onto the floor. She smiled manically, knowing he'd be cleaning up the mess this time. *His mess.*

'Julie! What have you done?'

She continued to stare, holding the shard in front of her, pointing it at Dan. 'You did this. You ruined us. You destroyed me.'

'People have affairs, Julie. I've told you, I'm sorry. It's over. What more can I do?'

'You killed Rachel.'

'No, Julie. I promise you, I didn't. Put that down – you're hurting yourself.'

'It's all your fault. You put her in that storage unit. You left her there to die. It's because of you she was in there.'

'Julie, it was just a terrible accident.'

'Oh, no, Dan, it was very much planned, and she deserved everything she got.' Her grip was like a vice; she could feel the power, wielded the sharp edge as the pain enlivened her senses.

'What? Julie, you're not making any sense. Please, put that down. We need to talk. You need help.'

'She's lucky the rats got to her before I had a chance to go back and finish her off.'

'Julie, what? What are you saying?'

'You're going to suffer for this.'

He stared back at her gormlessly, not a wisp of recognition, not listening to her, never really listening.

'It was an accident, nobody's fault. Julie, please, put that down,' he said, gesturing towards the shard as she brandished it in front of her, aiming it at his exposed chest.

'I killed her. I locked her up.'

'What? What do you mean?'

'I knew about you, Dan. Both of you.' She stepped forward with a jabbing action, catching Dan off-guard. He side-stepped and disarmed her, taking the sharp weapon from her hand.

She let him.

The sound of sirens filled the air. Julie reached forwards once more, clasped both her hands over his and forcefully pulled them with all her strength, letting the weapon plunged deep into her chest, ending her suffering.

Dan screamed, scrambling on top of Julie as her body slipped through his blood-stained hands. Panic, shock, fear as he grabbed for towels, the rug – anything to stem the bleeding.

Her face was pale and it shone in the dark, blood bubbling out of her lips as she tried to speak.

'I don't forgive you.'

The sirens were even louder now, and then there was banging at the front door, knocking, pounding as the door came in and the cavalry arrived.

'I warned the police,' she gasped, blood gurgling in her throat, drowning out her words. 'You did this.' She smiled, her blood-red teeth a vicious snarl.

Looking up at his reflection, Dan saw himself, a shattered image of the man he thought he was and a glimmer of something more. *Someone in a green dress.*

'Rachel?' he stammered in horrified confusion., 'Julie?'

A loud crash, and the sound of boots running, entering the house, shouts of, 'Clear!' and warnings of, 'Police! Put down your weapon!'

Dan looked down at his hands, her blood. What else would the police see? A fearful 999 call, a bloodied weapon covered in his prints, his wife in a pool of blood on the floor – and evidence of his affair with Rachel, which he'd told the authorities about only earlier that day. He had taken responsibility for his infidelity to help identify her. It hadn't entered his mind he might be linked to her death; implicated in her murder. But if he could kill his wife...

Dan was flung against the wall, pinned and cuffed, before being led with force from the room and downstairs. He could hear them discussing plans for social services to take the children into custody, to lead them out of the house without showing them the crime scene. He watched, gasping, as they were carried out, one by one, still as death.

'No! Dear God, please, no.'

What had she done?

'Suspect detained...'

'IC1... Female, around 40 years old... Looks critical...'

The officer spat in disgust as he looked over at Dan and spoke into the radio:

'Three kids unresponsive, looks like they were drugged.'

Biography
Janet Preece

Janet is bursting onto the scene with this thrilling ride of women's enlightenment. An obsessive follower of psychological thrillers and the quest for a one-sitting read, drove her to create debut novel Occupied. She has an eye for detail and knows how to spin an inescapable web of intrigue to suit her audience.

In her novels, the characters are uncomfortably real. The life of a so-called housewife is never enough for the wider community who consistently push to pigeonhole her into a traditional career pocket they can understand. Janet is fascinated by the fight that woman have to put up in order to stay home with their families, just to then defend their Cinderella lifestyle and the struggle to be appreciated.

Occupied voices the unspoken word, the struggle of mothers, wives and how they lose their sense of self to focus on their families with Janet shouting the questions that society taboos, what if women give up? What if they leave their families and refuse this treatment? What if they retaliate against the acceptable and take revenge and punishment quite literally, not caring what people think.

Living with her husband, three children and two oversized cats, Janet is most often seen dressed as a witch or a super-hero living by the mentality that life's a game and it's time to play.

With a Masters in Children's Literature and ten years' experience in journalism and PR, Janet's background includes self-published children's novel *'Blink, Super Squad'* and various specialist magazines and newspaper articles – writing about anything from trucks to cows to asbestos, you name it, she's written it.

Printed in Great Britain
by Amazon